An
ANCIENT
BOX

The Columbus Plot

An
ANCIENT
BOX

The Columbus Plot

David O. Lynch

Rutledge Books, Inc.

Danbury, CT

Rutledge Books, Inc.
107 Mill Plain Road, Danbury, CT 06811
1-800-278-8533
www.rutledgebooks.com

Manufactured in the United States of America

Cataloging in Publication Data
Lynch, David O.

   An Ancient Box: The Columbus Plot

   ISBN: 1-58244-169-3

   1.Fiction

Library of Congress Catalog Card Number: 2001096104

Dedication

To J with love

Contents

Foreward

Birth of America

Go ahead, keep children happy. Tell 'em Santa Claus and the Easter Bunny exist and that the tooth fairy will replace their extracted teeth with money. Tell 'em the moon is made of green cheese and the stork brings babies. But don't saddle 'em with the preposterous belief that Columbus *discovered* America. He never, ever set foot on our continent!

Some kids later hear that a Viking, Leif Ericson, *discovered* America in 1000. That is also ridiculous, because thousands of years ago the prehistoric ancestors of native Americans crossed to Alaska and migrated down. Ericson may have *rediscovered* America for the Vikings, but we'll never know the nonliterate barbarian who *discovered* America.

Nonetheless, celebrate Columbus for his awesome courage in sailing mile after mile across 2,600 miles of uncharted ocean water despite his crew begging he turn back. He led Europeans to the New World, eventually civilizing our continent. Columbus is America's roots!

As best we can tell, mariner Christopher Columbus kept a journal on his first voyage under the Spanish flag, but the whereabouts of this journal is unknown. It is not even known if it continues to exist.

After his return on that first voyage Columbus presented his journal to Queen Isabella. The original was never seen publicly again. Thereafter, numerous attempts have been made to reconstruct that journal, but we are left with less than the original and authentic version. Moreover, no other person who sailed with the three-ship fleet on voyage number one kept a diary, so we are left with the well-meaning speculation of family members and others who attempted to reconstruct that journal in their own languages.

While Columbus lurks in the backround, *An Ancient Box* is the tale of Don Talbot, who borrows thousands of dollars and breaks archaeologists' Rule number 1, buying an ancient box from a needy Haitian family. Talbot tries to make a name for himself in archaology. And you? Too set in your ways to change your mind?

Talbot, with the help of the university employment office, had searched long and hard for this job in his chosen field. However, keeping an eye on the men spooning dirt was the only professional employment he could find. He slapped his thigh in frustration. After taking on so much debt for his education, including his advanced degree, he wondered if this stupid, low-paying job was all that awaited him at the rainbow's end? Perhaps he was thinking like an American. Certainly these poor Haitians were thankful to earn any money at all, however tedious and repetitive their work. Haiti's unemployment continued to be high. The United States military intervention of 1994 had not changed that.

The snake shied away from the vibrations the men gave off talking and veered toward the tents that housed the permanent staff. With mouth wide open, the serpent held its short fangs poised to strike. Again and again its sensitive tongue flicked out, gauging what was near. Gliding across smooth earth, the snake warily approached the plywood floor of a tent newly erected in its path and came to a halt.

Inside the tent, Talbot sat working on his machete while awaiting Sandy. The weapon was much sharper than the pocket knife he had carried when a boy. Running a finger against the shiny blade to inspect his efforts, he worried how he would ever repay his mother and older sister for all they had sacrificed on behalf of his education.

The serpent flowed up under the flap at the rear of Talbot's tent and hesitated once more. From outside the tent its body seemed to hang down like a piece of thick

Chapter One

Haiti

Six hundred miles below America's rich Atlantic coast a hot, impoverished Haiti wallowed in the Caribbean Sea. North of the republic's capital city of Port-au-Prince, near an archaeological dig, the head of a coral snake parted the grass concealing its nest and slipped away. The serpent's head displayed protruding fangs.

3:45 P.M. Almost quitting time.

American archaeologist Don Talbot toweled off his perspiring face and neck and checked his watch. Still a bit early, he thought, but what the hell. He folded up his bleached canvas chair and waved to the two Haitian men working beneath a tarpaulin that shaded them from the blazing sun. "That's it for today, fellas. . .uh, Messieurs," he called out.

The pair of thin, black men rose and stretched muscles grown stiff squatting over the grid assigned to them. Talbot walked to his tent carting his book and chair as the workers collected their things.

The snake slithered around a boulder and slid over a rotting log, writhing along a sinuous trail of its own. In its unblinking vision were the bases of trees, tangled underbrush with motionless insects and sunlit patches in a dark and murky world. No human ear could detect the creature's approach.

rope. On the opposite side of the tent, Talbot finished polishing his machete and laid it aside on his cot.

Though blessed with the powerful shoulders and arms of a star athlete, Talbot was also born with a strawberry birthmark on the side of his face. Strangers noticing the blotch usually turned away. When a boy, he had tried to conceal the offensive mark. Before going to school he would rub cold cream over it and dust it with generous amounts of talcum powder until classmates jeered the "ghost" in their midst. Sometimes he covered the ugliness with his hand. Once, standing before a tattoo parlor, he counted out the little money he possessed, only to find he lacked the special low price posted in the store front window for services which he hoped might hide the eyesore. Now, long hair partially concealed it. He no longer felt like a sideshow freak unless some un feeling person called attention to it, bringing back the terrible hurt.

As Talbot put aside his machete, thirst prompted him to rise from his cot for a drink of water. Suddenly, with one foot on the floor and the other suspended in mid-air, he snapped fully alert.

A twisting movement softly easing its way at the edge of his sight made his skin crawl. Hackles bristled at the back of his neck and the warm blood in his veins ran cold.

Damn! Talbot mouthed the word in a silent shout.

Trying as best he could to hold his head steady, Talbot slowly moved his eyes to watch the hypnotic grace of the colorful snake slowly hunching its supple body farther into the tent. The body stretched out full length. Talbot shuddered. It seemed as though an unwanted stranger had barged in all of a sudden brandishing a loaded gun.

The snake moved to the front of the night table where lay several pieces of hard candy wrapped in wax paper. The creature paused. Talbot knew if the thing wandered back out everyone in camp would be exposed to the peril and he would have done nothing to prevent it. He had to act.

Talbot's tan face took on a pasty white color. Sweat dribbled down, the back of his shirt and seeped under the top of his pants.

The snake paused, in no apparent hurry to pry.

Talbot stared down at the reptile's mouth, looking not at death but at death's hiding place. Talbot cautioned himself to remain very still. Snakes were cold-blooded and lacked compassion. They would easily sink their fangs into possible enemies just as a matter of survival.

Talbot's suspended leg began to tire and refused to be still. He continued to eye the red, black and yellow bands ringing the reptile's body. He wished he could exhale through his ears rather than in the direction of the intruder's sensitive tongue. Additional sweat trickled down his back. Sensing it was not alone, the snake curled around its tapered tail, looking like a garden hose rolled up.

Moments later, the snake uncoiled its body with the languorous, excruciatingly slow moves of a striptease *artiste*. Its tongue began to unfurl again.

The born killer approached closer.

Talbot felt an itch he dreaded scratching. Watching the unwelcome intruder come nearer still, he prayed it would turn in another direction. He was certain it could not help but run straight into him on its present course and feared his grungy pants gave off the smell of the human body. The snake would not ignore the odor.

Seconds passed.

Talbot's adrenaline kept building. Don't panic, he warned himself:

Get ready. Focus on one spot.

His muscles grew taut. Get ready!

With a smooth motion that was speeded by fear, Talbot swept his machete up off the cot and swung the weapon down, slicing through the serpent's neck in a blur. The snake exploded in violent motion!

Its head and body convulsed separately. Each writhed as though shocked by a tremendous bolt of electricity.

Blood squirted across Talbot's shoes.

His hand gripped his machete harder, desperately ready to slash again if needed. But the thrashing parts and his own labored breathing made the only sounds in the tent.

Talbot gingerly took the headless carcass by its tail and carried the wiggling length in his finger tips to the entrance of the tent. He made a distasteful face as he hurled the bloody mass far into the brush. He heard it fall through leaves to the ground. Returning, he used the tip of his machete to flip the twitching head into an empty tin can before tossing it out.

Drenched in his own sweat, Talbot congratulated himself on being able to cope in this wild place. He had hungered to prove himself and felt he had. Talbot gulped down the water he had thirsted for earlier and poured a portion into a battered, white enamel basin to clean the blood off his shoes. No point, he thought, in upsetting Sandy with his brief adventure.

After spilling the remainder of the water over his head, he pulled his wet shirt in and out to fan his body. Grabbing a towel, he dried himself off and wiped his machete clean before putting it back into its sheath.

His agitated body trembled as he hurried over to the outdoor latrine to empty his bladder. Along the way he tripped over roots he ordinarily saw and avoided.

He returned to the tent and paced back and forth awaiting Sandy's arrival. What was keeping her, he wondered. He yearned to hear her voice and to look straight into her eyes that never turned away. Whenever he peered into her eyes, the color of coffee beans, he found they were so full of love for him he often failed to notice her pretty, turned-up nose below.

Minutes later, a breathless Sandy ducked into their tent. The young Puerto Rican woman was as slender as Talbot. She hurried to him on crippled legs hidden by a long, beige skirt, which she wore with a yellow cotton blouse, sleeveless and light. The yellow color always pleased him.

"Yellow is my favorite color," he had said when they first met in a bodega in Miami, Florida. She had moved into the neighborhood with her parents when they emigrated from Puerto Rico. "Now I know why I like that color so much. On you, yellow looks like pure gold, absolutely beautiful." He was so serious it did not sound like a line.

She smiled her thanks and in that instant transformed the ugly toad into her handsome prince.

Three months later she had moved in with Talbot while he was still a university student. The first evening she let him bathe her. They splashed so much water onto the floor, he feared for the ceiling in the apartment below. That night they learned many things about each other.

Sandy reached up and kissed Talbot, hard. "They're here," she exulted. "Mrs. Paque brought her husband. He seems like a nice man. And they've brought different pictures of the box that fascinates you. They also have copies of two of the writings inside the old box. That's all that's in it, writings of some kind in Spanish. No jewels or coins. No more guessing." She preened, appearing elated with her news.

"How do the Paques look?"

"Poor. They have too many mouths to feed. They need money. When I talked to Mrs. Paque up at the open-air market, she tried to act as though she didn't care whether we bought or not. Well, you'll see for yourself. They're desperate."

"Where'd you park them?"

"Over in the Visitors' Tent, like we agreed. Let's not rehash that. Mrs. Paque is seven months pregnant with her fifth. She's big and she's pooped. Wait 'til you hear her gulping down air. They were lucky to catch a free ride down here, only it was in a crowded, beat-up truck. No air conditioning. It's sad what a mother has to go through on this island paradise."

"Ash doesn't want outsiders coming in here, snooping."

"We've been all over that, but Mr. Ash doesn't own this camp. Southern State Museum does. Besides, you said not to mind him. Well, let's not. Don't get cold feet on me."

She gnawed on a hangnail. "The main thing is for you to focus on maybe buying the box and the papers. It could give your career a real lift. Last week when you looked at the picture Mrs. Paque let me borrow, you said it was interesting. But I could tell it was more than that. The picture turned you on. You didn't sleep much that night nor any night since."

Tears shimmered in her eyes. "That night you thought the wood box might contain important history. If we're ever going to get out of here, this is your chance. Don't tell me what Mr. Ash wants. Tell me what you want. Aren't you the least bit turned on?"

"I sure am." He believed he had already gone through enough for one day and now there was this. In any event it was dangerous to let their emotions get out of hand. What if the whole thing were a fake?

"Don," she implored, "you're on to something. These are good, honest people who simply need money. For hundreds of years no one in their tiny village read the papers inside the box mostly because, like ninety percent of Haitians, they are illiterate. They don't know what they have."

She sat down on her cot. "Mrs. Paque told me the grandfather inherited the box and kept it in the family."

Sandy pressed her fingers to her temple. "What's going on? Suddenly lost your ambition?"

"Sandy, it isn't that. We must stay calm. We don't know where this is headed. Want to bring Mrs. Paque some cool water and fruit?"

"Yes, only do something for them. The times I saw Mrs. Paque at the open-air market I built you up. They're expecting great things from you."

He wagged his finger at her. "Shameless hussy, you ought not to carry on about me that way."

"I only told her the truth. Put your glasses on, would you? Those stern, black rims make you look like a distinguished scholar."

Leaning over, Talbot gripped her face in his hands and kissed her on the lips. "I love when you're worked up like this," he grinned. "And, yes, I've got my motor running. It's been revved up so much today, it was racing a while ago." He raised his hand. "Give me a moment to change my shirt and I'll be with you."

"Could you leave your silly machete behind?"

"My intentions exactly." Slipping the sheath off his belt, he set the machete aside. He donned a clean shirt and tucked it into his dampened slacks. "Ready. Let's not dawdle. We don't want the Paques to get bored and run off on us." He took her hand and pulled her to the entrance of the tent.

"Want me to carry you?" he asked.

"No, I'm fine."

The young pair strode hand in hand past the underbrush. Sandy never noticed the remains of a once deadly snake.

They hurried across the rough wooden planks that served as a raised walkway over the marsh in front of the Visitors' Tent. There was no sound but their footsteps echoing on the planks and the music coming from a radio in a neighboring tent.

"Your hand feels sweaty," she said. "Maybe your motor is revved up."

He smiled. It would be best not to mention his fear that the whole thing was a well-crafted Haitian scam. "Let's see what they have," he said. He tried to conceal his excitement and the increased pace of his breathing.

"When I came in, you didn't look good. Are you all right?"

"Let's keep going," he said, "and don't talk like a wife."

"Is that what I sound like? When shall we get married?" she asked warily.

"Maybe soon," he said.

"Yeah, and maybe never." She shrugged.

He knew he was not ready to support a wife. For graduate studies he had gone south and studied at Miami University in Florida just to stay warm. Other students seeing the holes in the elbows of his sweaters, had cruelly sneered at the "Poh white trash."

Let them laugh, he thought. He had always been poor and for a time had no idea how he would spend his life. One summer he found some Indian arrowheads in the woods behind the apartment building where he lived. His father built a small display case and gave him an Indian head penny for his collection. From that time on he wanted to become an archaeologist.

After his father's operation and death, his mother often fell asleep while eating at a card table, the only table in the small living room. One evening he and his sister slipped the table away and folded it up as their mother slept and snored like a kitten purring. When the woman awoke, she gasped at the table's disappearance. Her children giggled. They didn't mind being poor back then.

Talbot felt he had to succeed. It was payback time. Would the box be valuable, he wondered.

Chapter Two

An Old Box With Spanish Documents

In the Visitors' Tent, Sandy pointed to the seated woman and said in an eager voice, "Don, I want you to meet Mrs. Paque. She's the nice lady who I told you makes those wonderful straw baskets. Remember? She was good enough to help me the time my legs weren't working too well when I was up visiting the market."

Talbot smiled down at the heavy Haitian woman. "I'm very happy to meet you."

The woman tugged at her rumpled dress. Her legs were spread wide apart, stretching the fabric to its limit. On her left foot a bunion seemed cramped for space.

"You've been wonderful to Sandy. I appreciate that," Talbot said to the woman. "Thank you. If you need anything right now, let us know."

Appearing exhausted, the woman smiled shyly.

Sandy continued, pointing her hand to the man, "And this is her husband, Raphael."

Talbot turned from Mrs. Paque to the Haitian seated beside her. "Good to meet you, Raphael."

The middle-aged man beamed, showing bad teeth. "I have great honor to meet you, Monsieur."

Talbot noted that the man's thin, scarred body was not puny. Tough sinew lay beneath the skin's bruised surface.

Raphael had the bony arms and callused hands of a day-laborer or a fisherman. But taking a workday for this meeting suggested to Talbot the man had no regular job and must want to sell. "Your wife must have had a rough ride coming down here. It's a long way for her to travel in her condition."

Paque inclined his head in polite agreement. "You read a lot?" he asked changing the subject.

"Yes, I've always liked reading history."

Sandy said, "Mr. Paque, while I'm helping your wife with something to eat and drink, could you show Don what you've brought us today? He's already seen the picture your wife let me have last week."

Paque held out a plastic shopping bag.

Talbot took it and removed four photographs, each wrapped in tissue paper. The paper rustling and the heavy breathing of Mrs. Paque intruded on the expectant hush.

Without looking up, Talbot asked, "You live with the whole family in St. Pierre up on the northern coast?"

Paque said, "Grandpere, everybody together live few kilos to Cap Haitien, the capital before Port-au-Prince be capital."

Talbot raised his eyes. "You found the box and papers near where you live?"

Paque hesitated and shook his head. "May I correct Monsieur? My great, great, great grandfather did the finding. He go to Cap Haitien in 1842, the day the earth shake. It wreck so much. He lucky to live. On his way home along the beach he see'd the old box sticking out the sand. The earthquake must bring it up. He never see'd it when he go to Cap Haitien. He take the box home. Ten days later, he fall over, dead. Grandma Paque blame the old box for that. She very sad all the time 'til she die."

Talbot nodded. "Your family has kept the old box and papers ever since?" He kept his voice low, non-threatening.

Paque looked into Talbot's eyes. *Mais oui.* But, of course.

The man seems honest. If what he says is true, thought Talbot, the value of the box and papers has been climbing for a long time, but be careful. "You think the old box was buried before the quake popped it loose?" he asked.

"I think, *oui.* It had seaweed stuck to it like it was buried long time. one hundred and fifty years gone by since the box was there. It very old, *n'est pas?*" Isn't it?

Talbot shrugged, conceding nothing. He became aware of Mrs. Paque staring at his face as she sipped water. He pushed his glasses up on his nose. Examining each photo closely, he saw an old box like the one in the photo Sandy brought to him earlier, but these photographs were taken from a different angle. Was this angle purposely concealing something, he asked himself.

His tongue clucked as his eyes swept over the way metal filigree was crimped against the corners to strengthen the box and keep its weathered top shut tight without requiring a hasp or lock.

The intricate construction confirmed that very skilled artisans had fabricated the box. He appreciated the way a master craftsman had poured a tar-like substance over parts of the wood to preserve it. Judging by the adult hand and arm he saw in one photo, Talbot estimated the box was about three feet long and two feet deep. It looked as though new leather pieces had replaced the old hinges. Otherwise the box had the look of being in its original state.

Still, he wondered about its authenticity until, looking at the fourth photograph, he almost let out a loud whoop as though he were a university student again. In that photograph there appeared a distinctive marking he had not seen in the photograph Sandy brought him the week before. A shiver ran through him as he remembered coming across the very same detail in his university studies. What do we have here, he asked himself, trying to recall the exact circumstances under which he had seen the unusual design before. It was more than mere decoration. It identified the owner. Who could that be, he pondered. He shut his eyes tight searching his memory, but recalling nothing. The design excited him far more than he expected. He must see the actual box. Touch it. Turn it around and upside down. Examine it thoroughly. Get some sense of its present condition.

For several seconds Mrs. Paque continued to look at Talbot's face. On opening his eyes, he caught her staring at him. Must be my birthmark that mesmerizes her, he thought. "I hope my face does not upset, you, Madame."

With an embarrassed look she lowered her eyes.

"I don't think she meant any offense by that," Sandy said.

"No offense taken. At least I didn't ask her what the hell she was looking at, like I usually do when some dopey stranger stares at me."

"You saw something in the picture, Monsieur," Paque interrupted.

"I don't know. It has a familiar looking design."

"And you recognized it?" Paque persisted.

"You're very observant, Mr. Paque. I saw a resemblance." Talbot's face held a puzzled look. His voice was filled with confusion. "An unusual motif is carved in the box. It's an identifying mark of some kind much like the birthmark on my face that so attracts your wife. I'd swear I have seen it before, but I can't place it right this minute. Give me some time. It'll come back."

"What do you think it means?" Paque asked.

"Don't know, but I'm impressed." He looked at Mrs. Paque and laughed. "Madame, you may start to breathe again." Always, he thought, that damn birthmark seems to attract attention. He examined the photograph further. "That box is beautifully made, although not by a machine. At the moment I have only questions. Lots and lots of them." He pressed his hand to his forehead, trying to think.

Paque said with pride, "We have always keep spongy plant in the box. Sucks up wetness. The papers stay very dry inside."

Talbot acknowledged the good practice with a smile. "I hope those before you were as careful." He re-wrapped the photos in their tissue papers and reached into the bag for a photocopy of a page from the box. The document was in the form of a letter. It was handwritten in old Spanish. He knew then, even if someone in St. Pierre were able to read, that the person with his or her French-African speaking background would be unable to translate the Spanish.

He studied the letter trying to unravel what it said. The handwriting gave him trouble. The very first phrase contained a word that looked like *caballo*. As far as Talbot knew, *caballo* was the Spanish word for horse. He rubbed his eyes. It was a strange salutation with which to begin a letter. Why would anyone write to a horse? The old Spanish expressions were going to take a great deal of puzzling. But he felt the contents of the box could turn out to be as valuable as the box itself. He and Sandy were onto something. He wanted to shout to the world, "Ash be damned!"

He studied a photocopy of the second paper. It was in the form of a handwritten letter, too, and like the first it was in old Spanish. It's possible, he thought, that the box and papers go back more than two hundred years...if they are authentic. He winced. He knew it was a huge *if*, one that always haunted archaeologists. Even though these people seem nice, stay alert, he cautioned himself.

"This other paper looks like the first," he announced softly to the Haitians. "I can't tell you much about it, either, right now."

Paque looked disappointed.

"But you're right in thinking it's old. Offhand, I'd say the paper is probably centuries old." Talbot shrugged, removing his glasses to relieve the pressure on the bridge of his nose.

Mrs. Paque appeared to have difficulty following the conversation and turned to her husband. He whispered to her at length. She nodded several times.

Talbot said, "One other thing I might mention is these two pages are both in Spanish. The language itself is an important clue to their age. Not much Spanish has been spoken in Haiti ever since the 1600's when the French took over and killed every Spaniard they could find. It's possible these papers were written before; that is, *before* 1600. They could have been written in the early 1500's."

Steady, Talbot cautioned himself, don't get carried away. Why reveal all his archaeologist's knowledge? Sandy tapped her foot on the tent floor while listening to what the men were saying. She seemed unable to sit still any longer.

In an anxious voice, Paque asked, "Are these papers worth money? Would someone pay us many American dollars for them?"

Ah, Talbot thought, now we're getting to it. "Don't think me rude for not answering you right away, Mr. Paque, but why didn't you or someone in the Paque family show these things to your government? You've had plenty of time."

"We not trust government," Paque replied with a sour expression. "Nobody trusts it. It never works for people like us."

"That's a shame," Talbot said holding his excitement in check.

"Would someone pay American dollars for the pieces of paper in the box?" Paque repeated.

Scratching the side of his face, Talbot said, "I'd need a little more time to think about it. Do you have friends near here you might stay with tonight? I can drive you to them. Tomorrow I'll take you and *Madame* back up to St. Pierre. I'll give you my answer after I've examined the actual box and papers. How does that sound?"

Paque spoke quietly with his wife. She put her hand on

his arm; appearing to restrain him. Turning back to Talbot, he said, "You very kind to offer, but we take too much of your time. And maybe we not sell. Our family had the box and papers so long it would be hard to let them go. And Grandpere would not be happy to see them leave."

"Well, you've aroused my curiosity. I'd like to bring you two to St. Pierre. I'm sure you will let me look at the box and the papers. To be frank, people are always trying to sell us stuff they claim is very old but isn't. It's best to see the objects themselves and to look at where they were found. Then, if you want to talk about selling for American dollars, that's up to you."

Paque bowed his head. After a further quiet discussion with his wife, he agreed to Talbot's offer.

Sandy jumped up, startling the Haitians with her sudden movement. "I'll go with you, Don. It'll only take me a second to fetch the keys to the Jeep. I know right where they are."

"Hold it!" Talbot shook his head. "You'll be more help if you stay put."

She pouted. "Why do I always get stuck?"

Talbot ignored her and returned the plastic bag to Paque "Now, if you'll excuse us, I'll go get the keys myself. Give Sandy and me a couple minutes to talk before I come back for you with the Jeep."

Sandy and Talbot hurried away to their tent. He asked, "How are your legs holding up?"

"Just fine."

"Sure?" His eyes narrowed.

"I'm sure."

Chapter Three

Glimmerings

Back in their tent, Sandy's eyes sparkled. She snickered. "Something in those pictures caught your eye." She reached out mischievously as if to tickle the truth from him. "You're convinced the box is important, aren't you?"

Talbot dodged away, his head brushing the tent wall. "You're right. I saw that same design at Miami University. The rhythmic pattern of the chisel marks gouged into the box mean Spanish royalty."

"I knew it. You're onto something."

"And," a jubilant Talbot said, grabbing her waist, "those chisel marks don't mean any royal person. They designate the Queen of the Spains. Notice the plural, the Spains." He whirled Sandy around, causing her skirt to flare out.

"Hey, don't squeeze so hard. I'm no tube of toothpaste."

"The Spanish Queen Isabella was not only Queen of the dukedom of Castile, by birth but also Queen of the dukedom of Aragon by marriage. That marriage united two Spains."

Sandy enthused, "I love it."

"We know that Her Majesty did not leave the box over

here in Haiti, but only a person of very high rank could have possessed the box belonging to Her Highness and brought it here." His mouth broadened into a smile. "A friend who was Admiral of the Ocean Sea had the rank and might have brought it to Haiti."

"You believe the Queen gave the old box to Columbus?"

"It's quite possible. The Spaniards did make Columbus an admiral, so he did have the rank." He winked.

Sandy seemed to accept the speculation. "That's marvelous, but how did the box wind up with the Paques?"

"Columbus could have brought it over, then lost it when it was buried on the sandy beach. One of the Paques found it right after the earthquake. A huge quake *actually* happened in northern Haiti in 1842."

Sandy smiled. "Things get better and better."

"I hope." Talbot paused and looked around at their crude furnishings. A bare light bulb hung from the tent's center pole. A night table stood under it. Two folding chairs pressed against the foot of their cots. A throw rug lay between to lend a homey touch. A bureau with drawers that stuck, languished at the entrance. Pathetic. Was this all he could offer Sandy? Not if the ancient box made him famous and his career took a giant step forward. In taking his stupid job not only had he placed his own future in jeopardy, but also he had gambled away the lives of his mother and sister who had worked so hard for him. He had to do something for them.

Talbot recalled when as a boy, his grade school teachers all asserted to his mother that he must go to college. When she heard of college, she was delighted, but unable to afford higher learning for him. Nevertheless, she and his older sister worked and scrimped, managing to raise the money he needed to keep going to college.

His memories made him shiver despite the heat. He recalled the months of winter's cold and at the end of his junior year at college he went to Florida. To save money, at first he slept on the beach, wrapped in a blanket. When he first attended Miami University, he drove the car of an elderly New York woman down to Florida and ate for a long time in the university's cafeteria on what he had earned.

He studied in the school library where there was free light and cooled air. He got odd jobs and studied hard. His sneakers wore out too quickly but he kept on. Sandy visited him in his shabby one room when she could until the day she squeezed in with him and stayed.

"What was Columbus like?" Sandy asked.

Talbot considered the hours of research he had spent on Columbus as part of his graduate studies. Talbot's advisor had observed, "I like the way you piece things together, Talbot."

* * *

Talbot patted his cot, motioning Sandy to sit beside him.

"Columbus was often away from his family, and he was secretive, and although he was a commoner, he aspired to much more."

"Like you?"

Talbot nodded. "Columbus also had the gift of gab in

several languages. The kings of Portugal and Spain both granted the silver-tongued Italian an audience and listened to his pleas for support. I'd guess he spoke better than most salesmen today. However, another important Italian preceded him. The Venetian merchant Marco Polo was born long before Columbus."

She looked puzzled. "What about Polo?"

"In the thirteenth century Polo traveled eastward over land, 7,000 miles to Persia and the wondrous Orient. He crossed the mountains and deserts, following an ancient trading route. He took more than three years to reach that remote part of the world. On returning to Italy years later, his glowing tales of silk, and gold-plated temples, fired everyone's imagination. Gold did particularly. Remember the forty-niners and the California gold rush in our own country back in 1849? Gold turns people on. But afterwards, Kublai Khan and the others of the Mongol Empire, who had protected the land route to India and China in Polo's day, did so no longer. Ottoman Turks and bandits made it too dangerous to follow in Polo's footsteps across land to get to the Orient and its untold wealth."

Sandy closed her eyes as if visualizing what she had heard.

"Columbus was fiercely determined to lay his hands on those riches. In Europe a tremendous demand existed for spices both to preserve food and to flavor it. Some spices were thought to help a person's sex life, like Viagra today. Spices commanded sky-high prices and provided huge profits. Also; Columbus had gold fever. To avoid the tremendous dangers traveling over land to the Orient, Columbus figured on sailing the other way and tackling the dangers of an uncharted ocean." Talbot's features were serious.

"Come August, 1492, the forty-one year old explorer set out on his first historic voyage. Spain's weather was still very warm. He started by sailing south to the already well-known Canary Islands opposite Saharan Africa. He believed the islands were positioned on the same latitude as Japan. His tiny fleet anchored in the Canaries for over a month to make repairs and pull the new crews together. For the men it was like the roller coaster excitement of future amusement parks. The crews took their time girding themselves for the terrible plunge. The respite ended and they headed out under the watchful eye of the new admiral. They sailed and sailed. A trip of discovery for Columbus; a trip of horror for the crews.

"The three ships were very small. The longest extended no more than 85 feet. Altogether the three crews totaled only about one hundred men. They slept out on the open decks, sharing each other's snores and disease-laden lice."

Talbot leaned close. "Each day the ocean's horizon was a straight line although it drooped somewhat at the edges. Ahead the sky came right down to the horizon. The crews could have wondered if any of the tales they had heard about the flat earth were true. They would have been fearful of going near the edge and perhaps falling off. The edge looked as though it were right in front of them. All day long it looked that way. The ships hurried west on the vast, uncharted 2,600 miles of sea water, seeking a new route to the Far East. The voyage took weeks and weeks, a seemingly endless journey of thirty-three days.

"Although not up in the crow's nest, the Admiral was like an extra lookout. Can you imagine him pacing back and forth on the rolling deck of the *Santa Maria*, his muscular legs balancing him. All the while he eagerly stared out across the deck that was drenched in the morning dew. He shaded his eyes against the water's glare and would search and search for a glimpse of the Orient.

"Each night a restless Columbus adjourned to his small cabin and slept fitfully, waiting to hear the glorious words, 'Land ho!' Night after night passed silently, only the sea's salty breath on his face. That long voyage was incredible."

Talbot paused.

Opening her eyes briefly, Sandy grinned. "Of course, in 1492, Columbus sailed the ocean blue."

"He had no map to tell him where he was, but he thought he knew where he was going. He pushed on. He would look out at the ocean, but nothing loomed on the horizon except the other two ships. The earth always seemed flat. A chilling wind might roughen the blue water. Swells replace the calm. Then small waves would crash against the ship's bow, but the earth would always seem flat.

"He kept records, perhaps making sketches of all he saw, but those records were lost or destroyed. Many of the law-less crew urged Columbus to turn back, but he used his gift with words to persuade them to hold on a while longer."

A crewman looked around and shouted, "*Madre de dios.* Nothing's out there!"

Cloumbus said angrily, "Soon, rich China will be out there."

Sandy shivered.

"'Land ho!' One of the Bahama Islands was sighted. Contrary to Columbus' thinking, however, it was not the Orient that was in sight."

Sandy leaned over and put her arms around Talbot. "I love you," she whispered.

"And I love you, darling, but you're interrupting me. The island they came to was not one of the Orient's East Indies, as Columbus first thought. It was an island in the Bahamas. Had he kept on and sailed due west for only another couple days, he would have stepped onto Florida's shores. Think of how incredibly close he came to North America. But the aborigines whom he met in the Bahamas persuaded him to angle off to the southwest where he would find lots of gold. He had the crew break out the trading goods and reward those friendly people with shiny hawks' bells, strings of colored glass beads and other cheap trinkets. The surprise gifts delighted the islanders. They laughed at the hawks' bells and listened to them tinkle. They held the colored glass beads up to their throats and pranced around as though they were models. The people loved all that junk. Columbus turned and sailed southwest as they had indicated and wound up in Cuba. Their information turned out to be worth about as much as his gifts to them. He found no gold to mine."

"So, on that first voyage Columbus never set foot on this continent? Then why have Columbus Day?"

"States should celebrate his terrific courage. Make no mistake; it was a prodigious accomplishment."

"Did he reach North America on any of his four voyages?"

"No, he got to South or Central America on a later trip; he never set foot on North America. Christopher Columbus no more discovered America than did the Viking, Leif Ericson, when he came over in the year 1000. There were people already living here long before the days of either man. The prehistoric ancestors of these people crossed over to Alaska and came down into our continent. We'll probably never know the name of who first discovered America. Look at it this way: Had the aborigines sailed to Spain in 1492, they would not have been credited with discovering Spain, because people were already living there. We should celebrate Columbus instead for his awesome courage in sailing mile after mile across 2,600 miles of uncharted ocean and leading the way for European emigration to the New World. Columbus is America's roots. Let us not try to cover up his close liaison with the Spanish Queen Isabella (possibly a sexual relationship) by telling little children he discovered America. We already tell kids enough like the moon is made of green cheese, that the tooth fairy exists, that there is a Santa and an Easter Bunny, and that the stork brought their little baby sister. Let's honor Columbus for being the roots of America."

"Okay. He shall be immortal."

"On his first trip under the Spanish flag, Columbus wound up in Cuba and while he cruised up and down Cuba's shores searching for the gold he never found, the greedy captain of the *Pinta* left him and sailed away to hunt for gold on his own. That mutinous defection came as no surprise. Lust for gold had spurred many of the men to sail with Columbus."

Sandy glanced up. "There would have to be lots of gold for me to be tempted to sail across a vast ocean like that part of the Atlantic Ocean."

"After a disappointed Columbus left Cuba, he headed back to Spain, and along the way he anchored off the northern coast of Haiti, near where the Paques live today. It was Christmas, 1492, and Columbus had only the *Santa Maria* and the *Niña* left of his small fleet. The sailors of those ships had a festive time trading and partying with the *Indios*, whom we call Indians. The unfamiliar ships so piqued the curiosity of the naked and near-naked *Indios*, they couldn't resist climbing all over the vessels. Of course, the startling sight of so much exposed female flesh took the men's breath away and stirred their loins."

"I can well imagine." Sandy clapped her hands while laughing.

"By late that holiday night everyone aboard the *Santa Maria* was thoroughly exhausted, including the helmsman who was out on his feet. The ocean was dead calm. 'Like soup in a bowl,' is the way history books later quoted the helmsman."

Talbot's voice grew somber. "No wind. Cloudless sky; a gorgeous-night. What could possibly go wrong?"

Sandy stopped laughing. "But something did?"

"Against strict, standing orders, the helmsman turned the steering over to a ship's boy and fell sound asleep. Realize that the steering was done from below the top deck so as to be closer to the rudder. It required less linkage than trying to control the rudder from up top, and it sheltered the helmsman from the elements. Of course the helmsman couldn't see the water from in there, but he had a compass in front of him so he wasn't steering blind. The assignment was new to the ship's boy. Before that, all he had ever done was turn the half-hour glass over whenever the grains of sand finished pouring from the top."

Sandy anticipated, "It was a tragic mistake?"

"Yes. At that point off Haiti, the coast is ringed with treacherous barrier reefs. A strong ocean current or maybe the tide running in, swirled around the *Santa Maria*, pushing and tugging her. The ship's boy was dreaming of becoming a great helmsman and was unaware the ship's anchors were not holding. The ship was dragged across a sharp coral reef that chewed up the bottom like a hungry band saw. The ship's boy paid no attention to the squealing of the ship's wooden bottom being scraped raw by coral. Afterwards, when the tide flowed out, the *Santa Maria*, her bottom gutted, was left to founder on the reef. Her seams, stuffed with hemp rope, opened up, letting sea water pour in.

"Can't you just hear the yells of those frantic seamen? The few night lamps gave off very little light. The men crashed into unseen objects and tripped over those others who were just waking up."

"Horrible. Makes me shudder."

"I can imagine what they went through. It must have been a terrible experience. Strangers in a strange land."

She nodded.

"I read that on the small *Santa Maria* the men slept, fully clothed. Maybe they loosened their belts around their bellies and took off their shoes, keeping them near their heads with a blanket roll to use against the morning chill. For them to wake up in the semi-dark was like being underwater. The emergency shouted at them to get a move on. The officers were no help. When Columbus emerged from his cabin shouting for everyone to stay calm and help save the ship, the crew must have thought he had lost his mind.

"They wanted to leave; dash to the lifeboat. Otherwise they'd drown. To hell with Columbus calling them cowards. They didn't feel like heroes. It was every man for himself. Get the hell out...leave on bare feet, splinters jabbing them. The men were not merely afraid. They were terrified. Some sailors couldn't swim. They could drown in the expanse of inky, black water. They continued to ignore the foreigner's urgent commands to save the *Santa Maria* by towing it off the reef before further damage occurred. Instead, the seamen rowed over to the *Niña*."

"I can sympathize with how they must have felt."

"When the crew was returned to the *Santa Maria* in the morning, the ship was too far gone. The men went through the motions, but the helmsman's heinous dereliction of duty cost Columbus his flagship and the crew its transportation to Spain, because with the *Pinta* away on its villainous own, the only ship left was the little *Niña*. That ship had no room to squeeze in a whole extra crew to take home."

"What happened to the *Santa Maria* and everything on board it?"

"The Indians were very kind. They hauled the wrecked ship's stores to the beach in their canoes and brought its beams ashore for later use by the sailors to build a fort to start a settlement. The Indians also transferred the Admiral's effects to the *Niña*. As a gesture of gratitude, the remainder of the simple trading goods was given those Indians.

"But imagine how Columbus must have grieved when he had to abandon his flagship. All at once after his tremendous success finding what he thought was the East Indies, things were falling apart. His weathered face livid with rage and his beard flying, the Admiral would have stormed up and down the beach, ranting and raving in his native Genoese Italian, 'Goddamnit to hell!'"

Talbot shook his head, "It must have been a crushing blow to the pride of the former Italian commoner. If on top of that, Columbus found out he had lost the wooden box, which must have come ashore in the confusion, you can picture the despairing Admiral, mad as hell, roaring at and cursing the dirty scoundrel who had made off with this emblem of his authority and his new station in life.

"When it came time to leave for Spain, the equivalent of one whole crew stayed behind to begin a settlement and to keep on searching for gold. That group never made it back to Spain. Columbus found them all dead when he returned for them on his second voyage in 1493. The ones who did not kill off each other fighting over the naked Indian women were murdered by the Indian men on account of the Spaniards' disgraceful treatment of the Indian women."

Talbot grimaced. "The box must have been buried in the sand when the *Santa Maria* was dismantled. That's why the box wasn't found until after Haiti's awful earthquake in 1842 uncovered it."

Talbot and Sandy exchanged glances. She stifled a laugh. "At least you no longer have any doubts the box is very interesting."

"You like to see me squirm. Question: Why did Columbus have the box take up valuable space on the *Santa Maria*? History leaves these gaping holes in our knowledge of the past. That's why I'm in archaeology. To use the clues that remain to fill in some of history's blank spots, some of its mysteries."

Sandy said, "That box reminds me of our senior class play back in San Juan. I curtsied and presented a similar box to a man wearing purple velvet and a pendant that hung from a heavy gold chain around his neck. At the time the 'man' was the tallest boy in my graduating class. It was a very nervous José Rodrigez, wearing the costume of King Arthur."

"But why would Queen Isabella give Columbus the box, conferring such great authority on him?" Talbot asked. "Spain had no shortage of competent sea captains aching for the chance to hunt for the Orient and precious spices. The sea captains were so good that later they placed the Spanish Armada in history books. The monarchs could have commissioned one of their own countrymen to do the exploring. They didn't need to send out an ambitious foreigner to cover himself in glory."

"Maybe Columbus was the first person to think of going to the Orient by sailing west? Would that be why the monarchs felt obliged to stick with him?"

"Ha," Talbot snorted. "Don't you believe it. That idea had been kicked around for centuries, ever since the days of Aristotle about 350 B.C."

"Yet the King and Queen authorized Columbus to go exploring for Spain."

"They not only authorized him, they backed him for one trip. But why did they keep on supporting him through three more voyages? They put up the money for ships, for extra sails, spare parts, food and other supplies. Lastly, they paid the crews' wages when the men returned to Spain.

"I can't explain why after the first trip, the monarchy ignored the fact Columbus never kept his grandiose promises to bring the King and Queen lots of gold and piles of silks and spices from the East, nor why the monarchs overlooked his huge mistakes. He told them he discovered a new route to Asia. It soon became clear he did no such thing. Another mistake was the destruction of the *Santa Maria* before he completed the first voyage. That happened because he could not maintain discipline among the crew of that ship. To get away with those horrendous errors and more, he must have had some kind of leverage." Talbot looked bewildered. "History leaves so many provocative blank spaces."

"Sometimes archaeologists fill them in."

"The packet of letters in the box could hold the answer to whatever compelled the monarchs to keep on financing his voyages. More than his badge of authority, the box and its contents could have been his round trip ticket to the New World four times over."

"Do you think the papers in the box were so inflammatory Columbus had to keep the box with him?"

"Wish I knew. That one paper I glanced at a minute ago

in the Visitors' Tent contained the Spanish word for horse. It wasn't much help. Makes it sound more like a manifest of some kind. Probably it's a list of provisions. Maybe it confirms they had horse meat with them. Yet I have a feeling Columbus held something powerful over the Spanish monarchs. Whether or not it was connected to the old box, I don't know." Talbot shrugged.

"You know, I'm beginning to wonder if the Paques will actually sell us the box and the papers. What do you think?" Sandy asked.

"You mentioned they live crowded in a one-roam shack. I expect that Grandfather Paque lives there with them, so they need every inch of space they can lay their hands on including the space the ancient wooden box takes up with its papers. Plus they have four kids, soon to be five. That's a lot of mouths to feed when they are so poor. I'm confident they'll sell for green, American dollars if they get the chance."

"I heard Mr. Paque say they might not sell. His father doesn't want the box or the letters to leave the village."

"We shall see when the time comes. They didn't travel down here in the broiling sun for the fun of it. Mrs. Paque may be your friend, but not that good a friend."

"Will you be driven like Columbus? Take a huge gamble based on your convictions? You'll be famous if it works out."

"Don't quite know. Judging by what I saw in those pictures, I'll be sorely tempted. My father used to say you gotta take chances once in a while, though after his car accident he took a chance and had the operation from which he never recovered. Sometimes you pay a high price to lose when you take a chance. In this case I don't know how big my risk is. If this is what I hope, it will give my career one helluva boost and give Ash a swift kick in the ass."

"Serve the bastard right!"

The vehemence of her remark caused Talbot to blink. He stared at her. "Hey, what's that all about?"

"Nothing. I don't like your boss."

"When I get up to St. Pierre tomorrow, I'll carefully examine and re-examine everything. I want to see what condition the old box is in. I'll do what I can which won't be nearly enough. Besides, I'd only offer the Paques the fairest price I can manage." His lips pursed. "Sandy, I could use some help. I'm broke. I keep thinking that if I'm right, the value of the old box and the packet of papers has been climbing for hundreds of years."

Here he was, he thought, talking about spending Sandy's modest savings, making her as poor as the Haitians he pitied. He reminded himself, most of the $2,100 in her bank account she had saved for an operation on her legs.

Talbot reached out to Sandy. "I have a strong feeling the box is my big chance. Would you loan me most of the money that's in your bank account?"

"We're not even married and I'm to be your banker with no security? But okay, you're the expert."

"No hesitation? It'll be very risky. I'll only be 60% certain. That's better than 50% but it's no lock."

"Take me along tomorrow. I know Spanish, right?"

"*Si*, Señorita, but your Puerto Rican Spanish isn't the same as the archaic Spanish on those papers."

"I could try."

"There won't be time."

"Will you bring along equipment to determine how old the papers and wood are?"

"The only outfit around that has the things I'd need is right here in camp. Using such equipment would alert too many of my colleagues. Besides, if I used the museum's carbon-dating equipment, it might give the museum and Ash claims they don't deserve. When I make an offer to the Paques, it will have to be based on what I see and know. Mostly it'll depend on my gut feeling and my beginner's luck. I could be a brash, young upstart making a fool of himself or a bright, new archaeologist with the magic touch. We may be talking priceless and vital documents and a valuable old box or...stuff that's worthless. It's a tremendous risk. Anyway, I've got to see and touch the wooden box and see what shape it's now in." Risk or not, his flesh tingled.

"Don, I must go with you."

He smiled. "'Fraid of the crawly things creeping around here?"

"Not especially. I'd just feel more involved."

He knew she was having a tough time adjusting to the camp. Some nights he had heard her crying herself to sleep. "I wish I could take you, but you should stay. Now I better pick up the Paques before they walk out on us." He strapped on the sheath for his machete before scooping up the keys.

Sandy looked at it and raised her eyebrows.

"It's a good thing to keep handy," he said patting the machete handle.

Walking over to the motor pool, Talbot encountered Jay Reynolds, the camp manager. The little dumpling of a man wore baggy shorts and leather sandals. Sweat streamed down his bare, fleshy chest. Grabbing Talbot by the arm, he said, "Give me a minute, young man. Did I hear your visitors say they had things for you to look at? Some old things?"

"It doesn't concern you, but no, they didn't bring me any artifacts to examine."

"Mr. Ash called. He said he wants to see you tomorrow morning at his office down in Port-au-Prince. 9:30 sharp. I have business in the city myself, so I'll go with you. Mind driving us?"

"It's all right with me. Ash say what the meeting's about?"

"Not a word."

"Did you mention my visitors?"

"Why, of course not."

"Then I'll see you in the morning." Talbot jerked his arm away.

Reynolds looked stunned by the abrupt dismissal. He blustered, "Got news for you, Talbot. Mr. Ash has repeatedly issued memos stating he doesn't want strangers invading this camp. That Haitian couple in the Visitors' Tent could get you fired. Better think about it."

Talbot looked back over his shoulder. "The people you're talking about are not strangers, nor invaders. I invited them here. They're my guests. Nice people! They won't steal anything, if that's what worries you. Besides, why should the Visitors' Tent always stand empty?"

Talbot walked away faster, brooding. The Paques would be leaving camp in minutes from now. He wondered if the repercussions from their visit would affect his first job as an archaeologist. What would Ash or the museum do about what had already taken place? The pictures he had seen could be of a box that was a fabulous link to the historic past. If so, he could buy and re-sell the box and do something nice for Sandy and for his mother and sister for all their kindnesses.

Talbot clenched his fists. He would not let anything stand in the way of his becoming a famous archaeologist. And perhaps he could figure out why the monarchy financed the foreigner, Columbus, on so many voyages.

Chapter Four

A Voodoo Warning

Early the next morning, the sun shining in a cloudless sky, a gaunt Haitian woman stood in the middle of the dirt road that led out of the Southern State archaeological camp. Her dark, spindly legs straddled the pair of ruts that stretched a quarter mile behind her to Route 100.

Wearing a shapeless gray garment that hung on her bony frame, the woman ignored the blaring horn and refused to get out of the way of the mud-splattered Jeep approaching her. She lifted a thin, imperious arm directing the vehicle over onto the shoulder of the worn road.

"Brazen witch. What do you think?" Talbot asked as he pulled off. "Could be trouble?"

"Dunno." Reynolds shrugged. "I don't trust her."

Talbot drew up behind another Jeep already parked in the deep shade. A trailing cloud of dust settled behind him.

Talbot sat with his hands on the steering wheel and his seat pushed back to give his tanned legs the room they required. Sunglasses dangled from his neck. A machete rested in a sheath clipped to his belt. Perspiration saturated his short-sleeved shirt.

He switched off the motor. "That was quick. The woman's disappeared already. Pretty spooky magic. Now what?"

Reynolds, who was also perspiring freely, shook his head. "Don't ask me." He nodded at the empty Jeep in front of them and looked around. "Where's Security? Some guard that Frank is. He and the other man are supposed to escort us."

"That woman probably waved them over to the side, same as she did us." Talbot heard a loud, buzzing noise. "Try over where that grisly sound is coming from." He pointed across the tall, sweet-smelling stalks of sugarcane that rimmed the whole area. "C'mon. Let's go." He leaped from the Jeep.

Reynolds rolled out after him.

Single file, they crashed through the thin planting of sugarcane, pushing aside stalks standing in their way and. swatting bugs that flew into them. Peering ahead, Talbot saw Frank's back and from its excited movements it looked as though Frank was agitated by whatever he had found. A putrid smell hung in the air.

When Talbot came abreast of the guards, he found them looking at the bloody, severed head of a monkey suspended from a vine woven into the animal's hair. The mutilated shape dangled from the solitary tree in the clearing. Black gnats and flies swarmed over the exposed, putrefying flesh. A soft breeze rotated the head, causing an occasional drop of blood to fall off as the dead eyes swung around to Talbot. He stared at the gargoyle mouth straining to open wider. What ungodly curse would it scream at him, if alive, he wondered.

Above, a vulture circled in the heated thermals. Momentarily it drifted from sight, then reappeared floating far above the clearing like an ominous cloud. The ravenous bird flew down in a smooth glide, alighting on a high, thin branch. With beady eyes the bird strutted back and forth along the branch, intent on the men who had interrupted its dining pleasure. It obviously awaited the unholy feast.

Seeing one guard unpin a paper attached to the tongue of the dismembered head, Talbot stepped closer. Reynolds sounded winded as he joined the others. "Who could have done this stupid stuff? Was it that woman I saw on the road?"

Frank said, "Could be. It's typical voodoo crap. Son of a bitch, I hate the slaying of poor, dumb animals. How can religious people act like such heathens?"

The other guard shook his head in disgust. "I guess it's the way their leaders grab power. Create mystery and fear. Have drums beaten under a watchful moon for some ritual of theirs. The leader sways and falls into a trance, claiming the spirits possessed him and everyone must do what he says. Creepy, huh? Between voodooism and the guys who were mustered out of the Haitian army, this island scares the beejesus out of me."

"That's why we have you to guard us," Reynolds said, moving closer. "What's on that paper?"

Frank raised a questioning eyebrow. "You might recognize it? The woman drew a picture of an old box." He handed the paper to the others.

"A cult is telling us something," Talbot said examining the paper. "Damn woman."

"For the cult to kill this harmless animal sends a helluva sick message," the guard added.

"It also says the cult is dead serious," Talbot said.

The guard scratched his head and turned to Talbot and Reynolds. "But why this drawing? I don't get it. Far as I know, it's nothing we've dug up so far at the site. This make sense to either of you?"

Both men took another look at the drawing. Reynolds shook his head. "Not to me. Kinda weird."

Talbot cut in, "Sorry, we are running out of time. I've got a meeting with Mr. Ash at 9:30 sharp. Didn't Ash say that, Jay?"

"That's what the man said."

"So we've got to get going," Talbot insisted.

"Go on ahead," Frank said. "Soon as we cut this gruesome thing down and stuff it into a plastic garbage bag, we'll catch up with you out on Route 100."

With heart pounding, Talbot hurried back to the Jeep. The monkey head held a sick warning for him to stay away from the box. He had not realized the worshippers up in St. Pierre could reach down all this way for help to discourage his interest.

Climbing into the Jeep, he seized the history book he kept on the back seat and put on his reading glasses. From between the book's pages he slipped out a photograph of the box and studied it. The photo was the one Sandy had brought to him a week ago from Mrs. Paque. Looking at the photo, the resemblance to the box pictured in the drawing taken off the dead monkey was unmistakable. He resolved no voodoo witch would scare him off. He would examine the actual box and try to sense its history and...maybe buy it.

Thinking back to last night, he remembered lying awake on his cot and hearing Sandy's troubled voice asking, "How much will the box cost?"

"I hope not too much," he had answered. "I'm sure I can work something out. The Paques want to sell."

Reynolds appeared on the other side of the Jeep and stopped. Then he moved closer and snatched the photo from Talbot. "What have we here?" the little man asked with a forced laugh. He held the photograph close to his eyes and scowled. "Well, I'll be damned. It's a picture of that box I saw in the monkey drawing."

Taken unawares by the other man's arrogance, Talbot sat dumbstruck for a second. Then color flooded back into his cheeks. He leaped out and sprinted around the Jeep, sliding his machete from its sheath as he ran.

When he was close enough to Reynolds, Talbot swung the machete in a high, looping arc, over and down so that he rapped his companion's wrist with the broad side of the machete blade, making a loud, slapping noise.

The photograph fluttered to the ground like a dry, fallen leaf.

"Ow!" Reynolds screamed in a high pitched voice as though he had lost his hand. "What the hell you doing?" His wrist was turning red and beginning to swell. He clutched it, climbing into his seat. "What a jerk. You could have cut off my hand."

"Don't worry." Talbot's voice was clipped, unsympathetic. "Only thieves in Arab countries have their hands cut off when they take things that don't belong to them. Next time keep your slimy hands off my possessions and stick to running the camp." Talbot bent over and picked up his photo, slipping it inside his shirt.

Reynolds gingerly rubbed his wrist. "You should see a shrink. What the hell's the matter with you?"

Talbot looked incredulous. "You grabbed my photo. Did you expect to get away with that?"

"Stuff it. I'm not forgetting this."

Talbot stiffened. "I'll tell you something: When I was growing up, poor as my family was, we always respected other people's property."

"Don't hand me that. You have a picture of the same box we saw in the drawing back in the clearing." Reynolds cocked his head A shrewd look came into his eyes. "Maybe you're getting too ambitious. Mr. Ash won't like that."

Reynolds leaned closer. "Where is that box?" With a sly look he asked, "Was it why those Haitians invaded camp yesterday? For a young guy starting out you're way over your head. That's not a good idea around Mr. Ash."

Talbot walked back and climbed in the Jeep. He replaced his reading glasses with sun glasses on his nose. It was a nose Sandy often told him looked flat, like a boxer's. She much approved of his face, saying he had great blue eyes and a nice, honest smile growing out of a strong jaw line. She never referred to his birthmark. And he never spoke of what it was like growing up, having to fight day after day because of the mark.

Talbot started the Jeep and bumped it onto the dirt road. Smoke and dust flew out from behind the spinning wheels as he accelerated. He saw no sign of the witch who had flagged them down. Minutes later he headed south on Route 100.

Running late for his appointment with Mr. Ash, Talbot sped along the paved highway, hoping to make up for some of the lost time. A crisp breeze blew through the Jeep's open sides, soothing the mosquito bites that speckled his well-muscled arms. He would have preferred to cool off the way he had seen Haitian women do as they squatted down in a shallow stream to wash their clothes. The hems of their cotton dresses were tucked behind their knees while they washed in the chilly, spring water flowing over their bare feet and around their ankles. How sad, he thought, to be so poor they had no running water to do their laundry at home or to flush their toilets.

Driving along the highway, Talbot let his mind drift back. He recalled as a boy the thrill of digging up Indian arrowheads. Back then Talbot had fantasized about becoming a famous archaeologist. His present job seemed a far cry from the excitement of reconstructing an ancient civilization from whatever clues it had left after it.

Looking in the rear view mirror, Talbot saw the Security Jeep fall in behind. Frank's fellow guard held a shotgun across his knees. Talbot knew there were extra ammunition and grenades kept close at hand but out of sight. Although Talbot appreciated the protection, he was sorry it was necessary.

Reynolds faced towards Talbot and shouted over the roar of the open Jeep, "When you see Mr. Ash, be sure to tell him about the drawing of the box they took off the monkey and your photograph."

"I've got to get there first. Did you speak to him about me doing something besides teaching Haitians how to spoon dirt?"

"Don't worry. You may not think much of your job, but it has to be done. I heard you're doing fine."

"What are you thinking? I'm a graduate archaeologist. I should be cataloguing artifacts, dusting off bone fragments and solving what life was like for the Indians living here in an earlier time. Did you speak to Ash about that?"

Reynolds waved a dismissive hand. "Not yet. A young fellow like you ought not to be in such a hurry to grab it all."

Talbot slammed the heel of his hand on the steering wheel. "Don't give me the ol' run around."

"Maybe you should take it up with Mr. Ash."

Fat chance, Talbot thought. It reminded him of the way Sandy reacted when first he mentioned he was going to meet Ash. Her face had stiffened, but when the expedition's head man beckoned, you showed up if you valued your job. They both knew that.

He drove on. Once he reached the littered streets of Port-au-Prince, he slowed down.

"Look out for that tub of lard!" Reynolds shouted.

Before them the rear end of a thin pig stuck out into the street. The pig was grunting and snorting, gobbling the smelly cabbage it found rotting in the gutter. The animal's intense gluttony sickened Talbot. He careened around the foul beast and into a pothole and out again.

He swerved again to dodge the half-naked boys who ran out into the street screaming and chasing each other. The boys edged closer, jostling one another as they vied to touch the Jeep. He slammed on the brakes. The sudden stopping almost caused the vehicle behind him to crash into him. Glancing at Reynolds, he saw the man grit his teeth.

"These dumb kids are begging to be hit." Reynolds leaned out. "Move, you dumb bastards, before we run you over."

The boys made faces at him and pressed closer.

A mulatto with dirty hair and pus-filled eyes pounded his defiance on the engine hood of the slow-moving Jeep.

"Beat it, you goddamn zombie," Reynolds yelled. A black youth with swollen ankles and festering open sores that covered both his legs urinated on the wheels on his side of the Jeep when it edged past. Other boys crowded around. With grubby hands outstretched, they jostled to get in front of one another, pushing and shoving.

"Money, money," a boy's voice whined.

A knobby-kneed youth assertively swaggered up to the vehicle. "Pay us lots of money," his angry voice demanded. "You using our street. It belong to de people, not to you. Pay us! This not your land, foreigners."

"Money, money, money," others chanted.

Talbot felt this was not the time to argue with the contemptible beggars. Like the street, the words were trash.

The false smiles changed to hostile glares. Foreign words filled the air. Talbot was glad he did not understand the vile, Creole epithets their filthy mouths spat at him. Pathetic, he thought, despite the lush island on which they lived, these kids were insolent panhandlers. His Jeep continued its slow progress through the clamor of the unwelcome welcome.

He noticed an older boy standing alone, unable to run with the others. A forlorn look sullied the crippled urchin's otherwise angelic face. Talbot stopped, then backed up around the Security Jeep. He stopped again and with a broad smile tossed the lame boy a pair of worn jeans and a left-over pastry. "Reynolds, why don't you give the kid something?"

Reynolds' eyes narrowed with disgust. "Not me. Giving these clowns anything is a ridiculous waste."

The boy clawed at the hand-outs, hugging them to his wasted chest. However, no joy ever replaced the hostile stare on his unwashed face and his lips never mouthed the words, "Thank you."

Talbot felt sorry he had made the gesture. Gritting his teeth, he drove on through the squalid streets, passing several women on their way to market. One woman with her upraised hand, gracefully balanced a tall stack of straw hats on her head. A dirty, barefoot farmer stood on a street corner bearing a few stalks of raw sugarcane that protruded from a piece of burlap on his shoulder. Waiting patiently for the Jeeps to pass, he appeared to have the time to wait and was in no hurry.

Talbot remembered hearing about all the Haitians who tried to flee to America, risking their lives in leaky boats made of discarded wood. They preferred being trapped below deck in smelly holds awash in filth to starving in their republic.

As they approached Harry Truman Boulevard overlooking the bay, Talbot saw sailboats, part of Haiti's fishing fleet relying on the vagaries of a fickle wind to propel them.

Their owners were too poor to afford the more consistent power of diesel. Poverty had a myriad of consequences.

Pulling up to a public building, Talbot dropped Reynolds off. "I'll come get you soon as Ash is through with me. I hope it won't take long."

"Don't forget I'm here," Reynolds said climbing out and tearing a seam in his pants as he did so.

"I'll try."

Talbot put the Jeep in gear and drove to a street named Rue des Vases. He parked in the rear of a run-down office building. The Security Jeep wheeled in close beside him. "I shouldn't be more than an hour, Frank. Why don't you two grab yourselves a cup of java and come back?"

He took off his machete and handed it over to the other guard. "Hold onto this for me. 'Preciate it."

Talbot walked through a garbage-littered alley to the front entrance of the building and pushed open its slatted, swinging doors that squeaked his arrival. He took care not to rub against paint that was flaking off beneath layers of dirt.

Inside the building he let his eyes adjust to the dark as he groped his way up a flight of stairs. Proceeding down the empty corridor, he smelled the fragrance of fresh coffee. He supposed a buyer's agent was roasting a sample batch of coffee beans to test a shipment. The glorious aroma concealed the dank odor of the building's decay. He hurried through the pungent cloud to Southern State's suite of offices beyond.

Entering the local headquarters that Southern State Museum leased in Port-au-Prince, he glanced around. Piles of reports bearing coffee stains lay everywhere. Parts of the room's walls were blackened where people had been careless. Taped to the wall behind the bookkeeper were a soiled calendar and a map of the city. Cobwebs clung to every object as though a community of spiders lurked close-by to trap the unwary.

Talbot waved to the bookkeeper seated in the far corner of the room and broke the quiet. "Morning, Harris. Mr. Ash said he wanted to see me."

Harris lifted his pen from the ledger that lay open on a cluttered desk and looked up through washed-out eyes. "Hello, Talbot," he drawled. "Yes, I know. Move those reports off the chair over there and sit." He motioned with his pen.

Talbot considered the man's untidy appearance. The bald head looked as though it had not been washed in a long time. Dirt stained both the collar and the front of his shirt. Perhaps Harris had been keeping the books for too long.

"Is Mr. Ash in?"

"Of course." Harris wrinkled his nose as if the answer were obvious. "You know you're late."

"Only by a few minutes."

"Late is late. Mr. Ash expected you long before this. He likes it best when people are *on time!*"

"Want to tell him I'm out here or…" Talbot motioned toward the inner office, "should I go right in?"

"All in good time. You can see he's on the phone." Harris pointed to the light on his own telephone. "He wouldn't appreciate you barging in on him."

Talbot moved a batch of reports to a vacant desk and

sat down. He looked at his watch. "Shouldn't you maybe put a note in front of Mr. Ash to let him know I'm here?"

"He'll be off the phone when he's good and ready."

"Sorry." Talbot raised his hand as if to ward off a verbal blow. "I didn't intend for him to drop everything for me."

Harris was a lot like Jay Reynolds, Talbot thought. Ash seemed to surround himself with sycophants. Talbot listened to the fan rotating overhead and checked his watch again. It was getting late.

Another five minutes passed before the light on Harris' phone winked out, signaling that Ash had finished his call.

Harris sipped a cup of coffee and kept on with his work.

Talbot shifted in his chair. He hoped this would be a short meeting so he could soon leave to collect the Paques and drive them up to St. Pierre. "Does Mr. Ash have another meeting right after mine?"

Harris shook his head. "The boss keeps his own appointment book. I wouldn't know unless he comes out here asking where his next appointment's got to. He was out here looking for you before."

Talbot sighed and rose from his chair. Ash was keeping him waiting on purpose, he thought. So, okay, he got the message and was ready to get on with the meeting.

Harris took another sip of coffee. The overhead fan continued to click away. Talbot leaned over and picked up a report that lay on top of one of the piles and began flipping through it.

"Talbot!" Harris yelled at him, "we won't have any of that."

"Beg pardon. Any of what?"

"Keep your hands off those reports. They were not addressed to you. So don't stick your nose where it doesn't belong."

"Sorry, didn't know they were confidential."

"I said they weren't addressed to you."

"I understand. Sorry." Talbot closed the report and put it back and returned to his seat. Eager to get the meeting over with, he squirmed at the further delay. He realized there was nothing he could do. Moreover, he felt this office held nothing to explain why the Spanish monarchy supported Columbus through four voyages. Only a real archaeologist would solve that question, he thought.

Chapter Five

An Argument

Silent and motionless, Buddy Ash stood in the doorway to the inner office, waiting. A cloud of cigarette smoke floated into the reception area from behind him. Talbot, having just reached out and put down the report, did not notice Ash immediately and when Talbot looked up, the unexpected appearance of his boss startled him. "Uh, good morning," he whispered, unable to find his speaking voice.

Ash loomed over six feet and continued to wait silently. The man's stomach slopped over too-tight pants. His fair skin had a puffy, unnatural look. His lips were thick and full as though afflicted by the same puffiness.

"In!" Ash finally rasped.

Talbot moved slowly.

Ash's hoarse voice repeated the command, "In!"

Harris called after them, "Want me to go next door for an extra cup of coffee, Mr. Ash?"

Ash waved him quiet. "Maybe later. Don't bother me with it right now."

Talbot took a seat and examined the smoky office. Dead flies lay on their backs on windowsills encrusted with dirt. Ash probably had the place cleaned only for important visitors from Southern State Museum, Talbot thought. A chair with one leg missing, faced the wall. The metal desk lamp was corroded at its base. How could anyone work in such a place, Talbot wondered.

Ash put a cigarette in his mouth and lit it. "Have the men at the site had you laying out any grids yet?"

"No, sir."

"Well, that'll come. Give it time. Have any trouble getting down here this morning?"

"No, sir."

Ash pointedly considered his wristwatch and asked in a cold voice. "Did you arrive by 9:30 as I specified?"

"It was maybe a few minutes after that, letting you finish your exercising." Talbot smiled to ease the tension he felt was building between them.

The office was silent except for the pencil Ash beat on his desk like an angry cat lashing its tail back and forth.

"In this heat I don't move around more than I have to." Ash's expression hardened. "So, don't talk nonsense about exercise."

"Sorry."

"You were tardy."

Talbot tried for a contrite, sheepish grin he hoped would also look repentant.

"Well, you were!"

"Only by a few minutes." He regarded Ash's growing anger.

"Don't be impertinent. You were told 9:30. Nothing complicated. If you miss a plane, it doesn't matter by how much. The plane leaves without you."

Talbot dismissed it with a shrug. He had no intention of

sucking up to Ash if that was what this tirade was all about.

"I'm not running a country club. From now on when you have an appointment with me, be here on time or the plane leaves without you. The first thing a fledgling professional should learn is punctuality. I don't know about the professional part, but you're a fledgling, so learn!"

Talbot wished Ash would remember the way it must have been when he had been a fledgling himself. Talbot heard that in only three years Ash rose to associate curator of the Arnold Memorial. A year later Ash became its curator. Ten years after that, Southern State Museum hired him away to make him its assistant director. By this time Ash must certainly feel he should be in charge of Southern State Museum and not merely manage this off-the-beaten-track archaeological expedition. Ash probably considered the present assignment to be a demotion but his early experience as a fledgling archaeologist could not have been very harsh.

Ash drew on his cigarette and set it in an ashtray full of cigarette butts. He exhaled slowly, then coughed. "I just talked to Reynolds on the telephone. He said you almost cut off his hand. What was that all about?"

Talbot stared at his superior. "Did Reynolds tell you he asked for it? He grabbed something personal of mine. Tore it right out of my hands. I only tapped him with the broad side of my machete blade. I didn't cut him or anything." Talbot could feel beads of sweat popping out on his forehead.

"That's not the way Reynolds tells it. He said you

attacked him with your machete. Even if you didn't draw blood, his wrist is all swollen. What got into you?"

Talbot scowled at his superior. There was no point in speaking out, but how could he be expected to hold his tongue when his boss took someone else's word?

"What about that drawing of an old box? Reynolds says you've stirred up Haiti's spooks."

"Not me." Talbot was conscious of the nervousness in his denial.

"Don't hand me that. Does it have anything to do with the visitors you brought into camp yesterday afternoon?"

Talbot tensed. Ash must have learned from Reynolds about the use of the Visitors' Tent. "Word sure gets around fast. I had friends in to visit me. They are a real nice Haitian couple. That's all."

"They were outsiders in my camp. I've forbidden that. Were they looking for easy money from you? That's the only reason they come to us. Did you examine things they claim are old and have great historical value?"

"No way." Talbot lowered his eyes, trying to avoid further argument.

"The hell you say. My guess is they showed you things they claim are very old. Every Haitian has stuff like that to worm money out of us. It's all phoney-baloney."

Buddy Ash picked up his cigarette and took another puff. The smoke choked him, making his eyes water. "Do these friends of yours have an old, wooden box?"

"I haven't seen the box if they have."

"Stop being so goddamn evasive. That wasn't my question. I want to know; do they have a box? The answer must be, yes. Why the hell didn't they come to my office and show it to me? That's the rule."

Ash looked ready to explode. His wheezing made him sound like a steam engine. "I go to the trouble of making myself available every Friday morning." He coughed. "People are supposed to check in here with me so I can make a determination. Your people should be doing that. Am I right?"

"Under most circumstances."

"Did you convince them to do otherwise?"

"No, sir." He feared no matter what he said Ash would let loose a blast.

"Then why aren't they coming here? That must prove something. Why did they stop off at camp?"

Talbot found he had a tight grip on his chair as the tirade continued. "For one thing they're not from around here. They came down from up north, near Cap Haitien. So the camp was a lot closer than coming all the way down to your office. For another thing, Sandy met the woman several times in the past. They're friends."

"What kind of dopey explanation is that? Where do you, a young subordinate, get the authority to take over?" Ash's cheeks were an infuriated red.

Talbot vehemently shook his head. "I'm not taking over."

Ash looked unbelieving. "But those damn Haitians are consulting you, not me," he roared, pressing down on his desk with the flat of his hands. "You'd be the one to get the credit if it turned out they really had something. You'd be the resident expert, not me."

Talbot thought Ash was exaggerating, letting anger get the better of him. Perhaps Ash was concerned with his own future. Talbot exercised all his self control to remain silent. This was the first time he had heard Ash referred to as a resident expert.

Buddy Ash pushed himself out of his chair and walked slowly around his desk until his ponderous bulk bulged over Talbot.

Looking up, Talbot did not like what he saw and wondered what kind of move the man was making. Talbot also stood. The two men were of equal height. For long moments each glared into the frigid eyes of the other.

Poking a cigarette-stained finger into Talbot's chest, Ash said, "I'm telling you right now, get those goddamn gooks in here to see me! I'll be the one to examine whatever they want looked at. And from now on, you stay out of such things. You hear me, fledgling?" Ash returned to his chair and ordered over his shoulder, "Sit down!"

Talbot remained standing.

Buddy Ash whirled around. "Do you understand me? Sit, ugly fledgling."

Talbot put his hand over his birthmark and sat down, continuing to say nothing.

"Cut out your silent Sphinx crap and tell me they'll be in here. I want to see that box. You have an obligation to the museum to show it to me."

"Like hell!" Talbot spoke out. "Neither you nor the museum had anything to do with it. Where were you when I was struggling to get an advanced degree at the university or working my butt off delivering groceries during the day and cleaning on of these take-out, fast food places at night? I've paid my dues. So have my mother and sister. They both slaved, worked fourteen hour days to help put me through school."

His head was beginning to ache from all the smoke in the hot, stuffy room. "And me? I'm just a graduate schoolboy, a nobody who owes a lot of money, a cluck teaching other clucks how to dig in dirt. Word of this box came to Sandy from outside the camp. It could help my career."

"Listen, smart ass." Ash leaned forward sticking his puffy face in front of Talbot. "Forget about helping your career. This job takes precedence. You're to turn such inquiries over to me." He covered his mouth with a handkerchief to control the coughing but it seemed to cut off his intake of air. His coughing grew worse.

"My job?" Talbot's eyes widened. "Teaching poor, uneducated Haitians how to dig in a grid is the extent of my job, and what do I get paid for it? On my salary I can't afford a family. My mother will be dead long before I can repay her for all her sacrifices. The payment book on my school loan has already followed me here. What do I pay it with? And you want me to turn over the chance-of-a-lifetime so you can capitalize on it? No way!"

All the while he spoke, Talbot was remembering his father saying, "If you've no money, you must do what it takes to hold onto your job."

"You miserable opportunist, you talk like the moonstruck fledgling you are, full of crazy, impossible dreams. Do you expect to find some rare artifact to make you rich and famous overnight? You're too young and green."

"How old do I have to be?"

"I'll ignore that. Just keep those outsiders the hell away from my camp. Don't serve them tea. Don't party with them. Keep them out."

Shaking with rage, Talbot said, "I didn't invite gangsters into camp. They're good Haitians like the ones the camp hires."

"The Haitians working for us don't enter camp. They go around when they come to work. We have too many valuable things that could disappear if we allowed them into camp."

"Our friends are not that kind. Nothing would disappear."

"No matter. Keep them out. Got it?" Ash took a deep breath, then started coughing again.

Talbot thrust out his chin. "No, I don't think I have got it. Whomever Sandy and I associate with is our own business. These are nice people. They're no threat of stealing anything."

"I've had enough of your lip." The raspy voice of Buddy Ash was rising. "We're in a foreign place and we're a team. Everyone, including you, must cooperate." Ash paused to cough. "You were out of line inviting those people to visit in camp. Bring those gooks down here to see me, or you're out of a job. Fired! Our supply ship is in port. It sails back to Miami in forty-eight hours. If I don't see those Haitians today, you and your Sandy better be on board that ship when it pulls out, 'cause that's all the ride home we shall offer you two. *Comprende?*"

"After what I've put into learning to be an archaeologist,

you fire me for having two friends visit us?"

"Don't keep it up."

"Back in the states this would be discrimination."

"This ain't the States, sonny."

"But we're Americans."

"You're raising the wrong flag, boy. They don't salute the ol' red, white and blue around this town anymore. Take the afternoon off and get your head on straight or start packing. You've had excellent schooling. You could be a pretty fair archaeologist, except you're in too much of a hurry."

Ash laughed. "You're suffering from ambition overload, lookin' to make a name for yourself. You are obsessed with over-achieving. Had a touch of your aspirations once myself." Ash paused. "I'll tell you what. Get your gooks in here and I might find a better job for you. Otherwise you're insubordinate. Gotta have discipline. Don't end your precious career before it starts. Paying jobs for archaeologists are hard to come by." Ash turned to a letter on his desk and began reading it.

The meeting was over.

Talbot realized Ash had the power of life and death over people who worked in camp. There was no appealing to the museum in Florida. Now he could see that Ash had intended to fire him right from the beginning of their meeting. The vague mention of a better job was insincere. It would never happen. He could feel the impending discharge eating away at his self-respect.

Talbot rose and left Ash's office. He ignored the offensive gesture a grinning Harris gave him as he walked past. The reception area looked grubbier than before.

Talbot's moist hand slipped while twisting the door-knob as he made his escape. He wondered what the hell made Ash think it was acceptable to treat employees like garbage. It would serve the man right if the Haitians' box turned out to be a momentous find. Talbot pounded the corridor wall. This was not the way he had envisioned growing in his career.

Of course this was not the time to lose a job, either. He was well aware that no openings existed for unemployed archaeologists, especially if they had so little experience. And there was something else. He remembered his father after the car accident and operation, sitting in a chair, incontinent, engulfed in the stench of his own urine. The elder Talbot had urged his son, "Don't mess up like I did." Yet, losing this job, Talbot knew, was messing up. He hoped the ancient box and its contents would be important enough to bolster his self esteem and offset the loss of his job.

His mother's words also came to mind. "Once you make your choice, son, stick to it. Don't give up too soon, because then you never know why something went wrong." Well, he wasn't sticking to it. He already knew what was wrong and sighed. With the few dollars left in his pocket he wouldn't be falling on his face quite yet, but it was close.

In the hallway Talbot ignored the delectable aroma of freshly brewed coffee that came from the coffee buyer's office. Descending the stairs, Talbot thought about the meeting and was determined to examine the box. His hopes kept returning to the possibility the box was something extraordinary. So far it was only a bare possibility, but how many times did opportunity knock on a person's door? As far as he knew, it did not occur very often even in a lifetime. If the box looked to be in good condition and genuine, he would make the Haitians a fair offer. After his meeting with Ash he felt he had to do it. He would not let the opportunity pass him by.

* * *

In Southern State's branch office that Talbot had just left, Harris licked his fingers and strolled back to see Ash. He laughed, "That Talbot is a real lulu. He's gonna do a deal with those Haitians. I can feel it all the way down to my toes."

Ash beamed. "Of course he will, and it will serve him right. He'll do a deal for their worthless junk and his stubbornness will cost him dearly. I'll sure as hell see to that. When the young pup discovers the thieving natives are trying to fleece him, he'll get the picture…only it'll be too late."

He chuckled. "Oh, Talbot will come slinking 'round here, sniffing for a bone. He will ask me to give him his old job back. I'll say, 'Awful sorry, lad. No can do.' The ugly duckling will be out of a job. He and his snippy woman will have to leave on the supply ship and they won't much like the accommodations. I'll see to that."

Ash smiled "What a sweet moment to see the distress on Talbot's face. I can hardly wait."

Ash leaned back in his chair. "On second thought, if that sucker gets lucky and the Haitians do have a piece of history to sell, I'll relieve him of that fast. Either way he will be one sorry pup."

Ash rummaged in the top drawer of his desk for a pack of cigarettes. Stripping off the cellophane wrapper, he ignored the doctor's impossible orders that he give up smoking. Ash shook his head. "I asked for a little help down here and the museum sends me Talbot, a college graduate, a kid still wet behind the ears. What am I supposed to do with another archaeologist? Some help he is, already trying to undermine me. Well, we shall see. I'll show Talbot that his ambition can be dangerous."

"Yes, sir."

"What puzzles can a beginning archaeologist unravel?"

Harris made no response. At last he asked, "What fake stuff do you think Talbot will buy?"

"Hah! Who knows?"

Chapter Six

The Eternal City of Rome

In the heart of Rome, Italy, a taxi slowed as it passed the nondescript building in the middle of the block, then came to a complete stop at the intersection of Via Crescenzio and Via del Luigi. Not far off, Saint Peter's famed basilica stood tall.

A distinguished, high-ranking Spanish official carrying a thin briefcase climbed out of the taxi and paid the fare. He waited for the taxi to depart before he walked back to the office building. He casually surveyed the area. The rhythm of the narrow thoroughfare was uninterrupted. No one paid any attention to his arrival. He buttoned his coat.

The bird-stained exterior of the office building gave no sign of the vast wealth its occupants controlled worldwide. Nor was there any indication the building housed some of the world's greatest financial minds. Or perhaps the modesty of its conventional exterior did, in a way, reveal the presence of those minds and that they were more concerned with creating wealth than in displaying it.

Upon entering the building, the Spanish official presented a business card identifying him as Manuel Moreno, envoy. The nun who served as receptionist rang for a priest to conduct Moreno to his appointment. The accompanying young priest did not inquire into the comfort of the flight over nor comment on the weather. Knocking discreetly on a door no different than the others lining the corridor, the priest ushered Moreno into the office of Cardinal Ceruli and left.The curate had said nothing when walking along the quiet hallways.

The cardinal rose from his large, upholstered chair and strode to greet his visitor. He carried himself in a much lighter manner than his girth would lead one to expect. "Ah, Señor Moreno, we are most pleased to see you again."

The rosy-cheeked cardinal was well-educated and able to converse in Spanish as well as the other romance languages, in addition to English and Latin. However, he chose to use the neutral English language, knowing his guest was quite comfortable in that language.

"We are truly honored you take the time to visit us." The cardinal's hearty laugh rumbling from deep within his broad chest filled the room with good humor.

"It is my pleasure." The envoy's rugged figure bent forward to kiss the cardinal's ring.

"Please, my friend, let us dispense with the formalities and make our association less rigid." The cardinal was living up to his reputation for having the common touch. "How have you been?" he inquired.

"Pretty good, thank you. But how is the Holy Father? We were wondering if He is well?"

"Ah, maybe that is what your visit is all about? Is His Holiness feeling well enough to make his scheduled visit to Madrid very soon?" The cardinal raised an inquiring eyebrow. "You've heard he has reduced his activities? Postponed the occasional public appearance?"

The envoy nodded. "Someone in the press said His Holiness came down with a severe cold. Others in the press make the 'cold' sound more ominous. They say it is the flu He has contracted and He is experiencing more than the usual difficulty in trying to throw it off."

"As wouldn't we all? The problem is the Holy Father is too loving. One of His foibles is that He sees too many visitors. What can we do? We dare not tell Him to stop. He continues to hold His weekly general audiences even during the height of the flu season. Of course, we do what we can. We see to it He gets a shot in the arm to immunize Him against the flu. But who can tell which flu bug will attack? We should mount a device like a metal detector to weed out those with easily communicable diseases."

The cardinal scowled. "We, personally, are blessed neither with the knowledge of a physician nor with the skills of a publicity officer who constructs those beautiful press releases. But we know the Holy Father intends to visit your country and its adoring parishioners in three weeks, no matter what appears meantime in the press. Those cold-like, flu-like symptoms, whichever they are, will have withdrawn by then."

"That is good news, Eminence."

"Don't fret. The efforts of your associates to dust off your beautiful Madrid will not be in vain. His Holiness will be there. But, please, we beg of you not to overdo your efforts to polish your fair city. We would not like to see the red tile roofs of Seville suddenly garnish the roofs of your Madrid as well." The cardinal smiled briefly, before all expression left his face.

Moreno nodded in agreement. "With respect to security arrangements, I hope the Vatican has found our people fully cooperative?"

"From all reports, your experts have been most helpful. The Holy Father is confident he will be safe. However, some of us fear the element of surprise where a protective step has become too well known generally and thus provides an opportunity for evil to breach the security. I worry. When can we ever do enough? When are we over-confident? It is a standing question like the Eternal Light. Not reassuring. The Holy Father is a public figure revered by all but one or two. We pray the one or two do not penetrate every layer of our security.

"Which brings us to the matter of publicity. We do not expect to see or hear unfavorable publicity during the Papal visit."

Moreno nodded. "However, I must tell you a small but troublesome cloud floats in the sky. The growing number of aliens, mostly Moroccans, who sail the ten miles across the Strait of Gibraltar to enter at Spain's southern tip, presents a problem. Some of them mail their passports ahead to relatives in France (their destination) in order that we don't confiscate them as the aliens attempt to pass through our country."

"We have heard about that. It is part of the Third World's attempt to find a better life."

"If the problem grows any worse, Spain will be forced to take stern measures to stop the migration passing through our country, unkind as the press may make us sound."

"Of course. Nonetheless, His Holiness would not like to hear of Spain doing that right before or during His visit. The press would clamor for His opinion on the matter rather than focus on His visit. Spain must be careful not to take one false step during the next three week period." The cardinal's head tilted to one side. "We hope we do not ask too much of the Spanish people for so short and sensitive a period."

"I understand fully. Be assured Spain will do everything necessary to avoid bad publicity during those few weeks. No untoward incidents involving the unruly Basques or anyone else."

The cardinal smiled. "That fine nation of yours cannot be too careful. During these days your people should do nothing other than to breathe in and out, nice and slow. Inhale and exhale. One whiff of sordid notoriety could turn the Pontiff's visit into a disaster He would not welcome."

Moreno groaned. "So be it." He knew when he returned to Madrid and passed the cardinal's teaching along, that the sound of the air his colleagues would expel in response would be rude. His office would resound with laughter as everyone demonstrated some form of oral flatulence. Breathe in and out, indeed.

However, despite the horseplay the cardinal's words might invite, Moreno would insist the staff understand that God's minions would not tolerate one public misstep if the Pope's official visit was to occur.

Moreno rose. "Your Eminence, you have been most generous with your time and I do not wish to intrude further. I am certain my countrymen will take your good comments to heart."

"It is a simple thing we require: behavior that becomes those of serious intent. Show restraint and contemplate God." The cardinal pressed the buzzer for a guide to escort his visitor out.

There was a soft knock. The same priest as before appeared in the doorway.

"Ah, here we are. Father Joseph will show you the way, Señor Moreno. Please forgive him if he seems unfriendly. His vows do not permit him to speak."

"Thank you again, Your Excellency. I appreciate your taking the time to see me and to share your thoughts."

Moreno bowed his head to the cardinal. *"Hasta la vista,* until we see each other again."

"Adios amigo mio y hasta luego, until then." The cardinal smiled goodbye.

Moreno held his crossed fingers out of sight as he left the room. "Let there be no sordid notoriety to spoil the Pope's visit," he muttered softly.

Chapter Seven

North By Northwest Out of Haiti

Following his argument with Ash that morning, Talbot returned to Harry Truman Boulevard and picked up Reynolds. Throughout their trip back to camp neither man spoke, except Talbot said, "Reynolds, you've got a big mouth."

After he dropped Reynolds off at camp, Talbot relented and asked Sandy to join him. She studied his face and said, "You look awful. Not a good meeting?"

"When you're lower than low, you try to accept what they dish out. But I won't compromise with Ash when he tries to muscle in."

Talbot drove Sandy and the Paques to St. Pierre, where the two Americans spent an exhausting afternoon studying the box and the many letters it contained. Talbot wrestled with the question of whether to buy the box and its contents. If they turned out to be the valueless fraud of a poor, desperate family, Talbot knew his father's demon, terrible embarrassment, would haunt him for the rest of his life.

In the early evening while there was still daylight, Talbot visited the beach where the box had been found protruding from the sand. He decided the discovery of the box had been possible the way Paque had said. Talbot struggled to rein in his enthusiasm.

That night, driving down to camp, Sandy and Talbot discussed what they had learned at the Paques' place. Occasionally they both spoke at the same time, but, they agreed, everything looked bona fide. Still, they reserved judgment.

Sandy said, "You look like you're ready to burst with excitement."

When they arrived back at camp late that night, Talbot found a note on his cot stating he was fired. His final paycheck was attached. The note gave him an order to pack up and leave on the supply ship. Ash had made good his threat once it became clear Talbot was not going to bring the Paques into the office.

Sandy and Talbot tried to put the discharge out of their minds as they started up their discussion again of whether to buy the box. They slept little the remainder of the night.

The following morning Reynolds met Talbot at the motor pool when Talbot was signing out a Jeep. "In case you didn't get the message, Mr. Ash said you're fired."

"I know," Talbot said climbing into a Jeep. "I wish I could thank you for all you've done." He stopped by his own tent and said to Sandy, "I need you to come along to sign for the withdrawal, and please bring your passport."

Sandy collected her things and rode up north with him. The bank at Cap Haitien helped her withdraw her savings from her bank in the States. Then Talbot drove out to St. Pierre, and after much talk bought the box and its contents from the Paques. He drove back to Cap Haitien and made photostatic copies of the papers. Then he drove down to camp with Sandy.

She observed, "Don, you've got such a desperate look."

"Can't help it. I need the box and papers to be important."

The next morning a taxi arrived at camp to take Sandy and Talbot down to the supply ship. At a slow pace the driver loaded their possessions in the trunk of the taxi. Talbot himself handled the duffel bag which contained the box, then he joined Sandy in the taxi.

Following a short interval, Talbot began to feel anxious. The driver was taking too long. Talbot jumped out and hurried to the rear of the taxi, surprising the driver who looked up and moved away from the duffel bag. The man slammed the trunk shut as Talbot drew his machete and held the weapon against the man's chest. "Keep your hands off that bag!"

When Talbot climbed back in the taxi, Sandy asked, "What's wrong?"

He whispered, "That guy was fooling with the duffel bag." Talbot motioned for her not to ask any more questions as the driver took his seat behind the wheel and drove off.

Everyone in camp was still asleep. No one waved goodbye, but then no one in camp knew what Talbot was taking away with him.

Sandy drew her legs up under her and looked tense sitting in a corner of the back seat. Having agreed earlier with Talbot it would be unwise for them to talk in front of strangers either about his discharge or about the box, she closed her eyes.

"You tired out by the past couple days?" Talbot asked.

"I suppose. I didn't get much sleep."

He fell silent and gazed out at the passing scenery. He had the uneasy feeling they were being watched, yet whenever he looked out the rear window, he saw no one following them, not even a Security Jeep. He failed to notice the driver often glancing at them through the rear view mirror, keeping them under observation.

Loss of his job preyed on Talbot's mind. The pain was severe.

When the taxi arrived at the dock, the driver unlocked the trunk. He lifted out some luggage, but made no attempt to help with the rest of their things. Talbot thought the driver must be an angry, former Haitian soldier. Talbot picked up the duffel bag by its carrying handle and set it beside the rest of their luggage on the dock. Then he unloaded his books.

As soon as the taxi left, Sandy slowly turned to face the supply ship leased by Southern State Museum. The vessel bore the name *Angora*. Sandy paled at the dismal appearance of the eighty-foot trawler flaunting its scrapes and bruises like a swaggering sailor would display his tattooed chest in a port side bar.

"Christ, what a stinking mess," Talbot moaned. "The ship is more run-down than our tent back at camp." He shook his head. Worn tools and broken equipment lay scattered on deck. The rust-streaked metal hull revealed a huge gash where the bow had been stove in and was patched over with a metal plate. Ugly gobs of grease made a feeble attempt to stem the corrosion festering everywhere. The mooring lines served more to keep the ship afloat than to secure it to the dock. Dry, dead leaves floated in the eddies.

The high pitched sound of squealing rats raced through the ship's hold. Sandy shivered in the morning heat. Her despairing figure slumped over. Trying to hold back the tear she said, "I don't know if we should go home on this pathetic tub. Will it get us there?"

Tears, ran down her cheek. She brushed it away with the back of her hand.

Talbot wondered if he had done the wrong thing in ignoring Rule # 1 of archaeologists, which prohibited paying needy Haitians for anything old. He held her tight. "What can I say?" His own dejection over their predicament was evident. "Want to give it a try? It's all we're going to get and it's all I can afford. Except for my last paycheck, I'm practically broke, but we've got to leave this island." He could feel her despair.

"I'm going to make it," she said, straightening up. She went to the gangway and boarded the ship. Walking back to the stern, her steps sounded hollow. The ship appeared deserted.

Talbot called to her, "If we weren't needing this ride so much, I'd tell Southern State to take this old cow and shove it." He felt bad. He had offered her so little: first there was the tent and now a ride on this.

"I'd be right behind you with a few choice words of my own," she hollered back in joyless agreement. "I can't get over the museum using this pitiful wreck."

Talbot caught up with Sandy. "I'd bet the museum doesn't even know we're on board. This is Ash's way of rubbing my nose in not letting him see what the Paques had to sell." Talbot ground his teeth in disgust. "It's something I have to settle with that guy if we ever meet again." Talbot felt somehow, somewhere, some day they would meet up. The discharge had been a cold-blooded, calculated act.

Talbot reflected on Ash firing him. It was clear the man didn't give a damn about anyone. Not the Haitians. Not Sandy. And not the effect the firing must have on a young person's career.

He glanced over at Sandy and felt sorry for how grim she looked. "I hate putting you through this. Wish I could do better."

"Don't worry. Some day you will, I'm sure."

"I'll certainly try."

She relaxed a little, but her face remained drawn. "Don't worry about it." She returned to the gangway with him. "Where is everybody? I don't see a soul."

"I'm sure they're around someplace." Talbot walked down to the dock and, in spite of his misgivings, began to carry their belongings onto the *Angora*.

When he had finished, a man dragging a club foot and wearing dirty coveralls, limped up to them. His sallow skin suggested he spent his shore leaves frequenting the many seedy, waterfront bars. The battered vest he wore, hung loosely over a .45 caliber pistol. He ignored Talbot to feast his eyes on Sandy. He raised a greasy hand to his dingy cap in a casual salute to her.

"Mornin'," he said. "Why the sour faces? Were you two expecting an ocean liner with a loud band to pipe you aboard? This ship not fancy enough for you? Well, the *Angora* is a good ship. The best. It goes forwards and backwards the same as any other. Better'n some."

He rubbed his chin. "She has her share of rust, of course. All ships do. It's the salt water. Only some ships hide it more than others by tarting themselves up so you don't notice it. But the rust is always there if you look hard enough."

He gave a harsh laugh. "By the way, if on the first night out to sea you want to dress for dinner, go right ahead. Even sit at the captain's table if you want. It so happens it's the only table we've got down there. You'll love it, but you'll have to clear a few things off'n it first."

Talbot tried to size up the rough-looking seaman. The man was like a sailor that had shipped out on too many rust buckets. "Who are you?"

"I'm whatcha call the first mate," the seaman replied in a husky voice. He still did not bother to look at Talbot. "My name's Barney. Good ol' Barney, folks call me."

"You're a member of the crew?" Talbot asked, his eyes angry slits.

"I am the crew. You noticed I'm carrying a gun. It's the same model as the captain carries. We're armed to repel unwelcome boarders such as drug traffickers. They're worse than pirates. They'd steal any ship that looked like it was easy pickings. But not to worry, lil' lady. Barney will see to it nothing happens to you. If you ever want anything, anything at all, you lemme know. You call Barney." He grinned at Sandy.

"You saw," Barney continued, "we've got lots of cargo

all lashed down. That means you folks will be roughing it. Won't be too bad though. A tiny bit cramped is all."

"Where do we stay?" Talbot cut in.

"Oh, you needn't worry." Barney continued to ogle Sandy. "We've made room for everybody. You unexpected passengers go below and you'll see what I mean. Be sure to take your bags and walk through the wardroom, past the tiny galley. Beyond that you'll find your stateroom. It's the cozy nook on the starboard side. That's your right side." He winked at Sandy. "Thought it best to clear up which is which, right quick like." He chortled, "Some landlubbers don't know their assholes from their starboard side."

"Where's the captain?" Talbot sounded as though he had heard enough of Barney's salty talk.

Barney faced Talbot. "Would it surprise you, mate, to learn the captain's getting our clearances from the port authorities? Takes tons of paper work and uses up a lot of hours. We'll be shoving off most any time so it's best you get your land-loving asses in gear and settle in before we head out. Tie everything down real good. Could get bumpy."

Talbot reached down and picked up the duffel bag. Barney's eyes casually inspected it. "Mighty mysterious bag you've got there. Doesn't look like clothes. Anything the Captain should know about?"

Talbot held the duffel bag tightly. "Just the usual stuff. In a lot of these boxes we have books. I do lots of reading. We'll go down to our cabin. Don't want to delay the captain when he gets back."

Barney swiveled around to stare directly at Sandy again. "Tell me, lovely lady, what do I call you?"

"You'll have no need to call me, so forget it." She inclined her head in the direction of Talbot. "He's Mr. Talbot."

"That clear enough for you?" Talbot took a step towards the first mate. "We like to be clear about things." There was an impatient undertone to his voice.

Barney threw up his hands but didn't draw back. "Okay, if that's the way you folks want to play it. Me, I'm only trying to be sociable. My offer still stands no matter what you say, lil' lady. If you ever need help, don't hesitate. Not for a minute. You call on ol' Barney."

The first mate turned on his heels and limped away without saying more.

"Ol' Barney," Talbot ridiculed in a low voice to Sandy.

"If he kept on spouting that nonsense, he could be charged with soliciting. I had an almost irresistible impulse to strangle that guy."

Talbot and Sandy made several trips, carrying their belongings below the main deck and struggling past cargo that clogged the narrow passageway to their cabin.

"They sure have us squeezed in tight," Talbot groaned. "We must have been unexpected passengers. And this place is as cozy as a small closet. I feel cramped as hell after spending less than a minute in here." He set down the last case of books and lashed it to the bunk that was anchored to the deck.

Sandy made a face. "The stink of cooking grease in here is vile. Can you give us some fresh air to breathe for a change?"

Talbot undogged the porthole permitting a cool breeze

to flow in. He inflated their air mattresses while Sandy unpacked the bed sheets and made up their bunks before she and Talbot stretched out on them. There was nothing more for them to do short of going back up on deck and risking further words with Barney, which they had no intention of doing.

"That guy is going to be a real pain in the butt," Talbot said, speaking to the ceiling. "You can tell by the way he came on ever so nice to the lil' lady."

Talbot pulled his collar open to cool off in the growing heat. "I said I'd be seventy percent certain that the wood box and papers were worth buying after I examined them at the Paques' place, but we can be more certain. To do that, I need your help, before I send any of this to New York for my buddy to check out. He took over his father's business and knows it backwards and forwards. Please, I want you to study the papers, every word. Use your Spanish, then your imagination and intuition. They could add to my seventy percent."

"You didn't think much of my Puerto Rican Spanish before."

"That was because it is so modern. Please. We have some time. Do what you can."

She smiled. "I'll do it, but don't expect miracles."

"I don't, but I need to know as soon as possible what we've bought."

Shortly after, the captain returned to the *Angora*. He was a slender, little man with deep lines across his forehead and dark rings beneath his eyes. The engines started up and the ship got underway. Hungry sea gulls hovered over the stern, pursuing the ship out into the harbor past derelict freighters, listing shipwrecks and skinny, unemployed men in threadbare clothes who loitered on the rotting docks.

Sea gulls followed the ship for a short distance before realizing no garbage would be dumped overboard any time soon. Without wasting any more effort, they wheeled and flew back to shore.

Once the ship sailed out of the sheltered harbor, it turned northwest. The ancient diesel engines propelled the *Angora* at a very slow three knots per hour.

Just before noon both engines quit for no apparent reason. The *Angora* plowed to a stop.

The silence that followed disturbed Talbot. He jumped to his feet. "What the hell happened? I was afraid of this. We are too isolated out here. I hope Ash isn't planning on getting at us on this ship. It would be so easy for him while we're stuck out here."

Sandy opened her eyes, but was silent. She had no word to comfort him.

He jerked open the door to their cabin. "We've got to get that old, wood box and those letters to the States and into the right hands. They need to be authenticated as soon as possible no matter what. Maybe they hold the answer to why the Spanish monarchy supported Columbus in not one, but four voyages."

Chapter Eight

The Box and a Death

On the same morning Sandy and Talbot boarded the *Angora* bound for Florida, Grandfather Paque lay sprawled out, sound asleep in the Village of St. Pierre in the shack he shared with his son Raphael and Raphael's growing family. The old man was toothless. His words sounded like gibberish unless he spoke slowly, which he sometimes forgot to do. He gummed everything he ate, limiting himself to soft food and fish. Even now with his mouth wide open the sound of his snoring was distinct.

The old man had been away from the shack on the afternoon Sandy and Talbot drove Raphael and his pregnant wife back to their little village. Nor did the senior Paque know that Raphael had let the Americans examine both the box and its paper contents on that day. The elder Paque had also been absent on the following day when Talbot returned with green, American dollars and bought the items from Raphael. On both occasions the elder Paque spent his time either gossiping with his cronies in the village square or preparing a purification ceremony for local voodoo followers. He would regret not knowing his son's affairs.

On this particular hot morning, as on every morning, Grandfather Paque was the last to stir. He did not have to get out of bed until long after the sun rose. It was a privilege extended him as the high priest of the voodoo cult in his village and as the oldest village resident.

Half awake, he rolled over on his wood-frame bed that had ropes laced across it to support a thin pad on which the old man slept. With his good ear he listened to the happy sounds of a new day beginning in the shack. Soon he would be delighting another grandchild by reading to it from the papers in the box.

"Grandpere," whispered a child's thin voice. The elder Paque reached out with a smile and pulled the little boy against the side of the bed, hugging him.

"*Oui?*" he drawled.

"You should get up now, Grandpere," the child said, squirming to escape the rough whiskers on the old man's face.

"*Oui, mon petit.* Yes, my little one, mind the splinters." He sat up on the edge of his bed, rubbing sleep from his eyes and waiting for the dizziness to pass. He pulled his trousers on over his undershorts and got up stiffly.

Grandfather Paque extended his hands in front of him and faced to the back of the shanty. Though his health was good for a man of his age; his eyesight was not. He walked stiff-legged out behind the shack to relieve himself in a lime-filled pit. On his return the aroma of fresh coffee filled his nostrils. Smacking his lips, he followed the delightful aroma to the table. "Raphael has a fine lady always fixin' breakfast for me. 'Preciate it."

"You be no trouble." Raphael's wife guided the old man into the table where he sat alone. The others had already eaten their first meal of the day.

The old man ate a plate of fish his son had caught. He also softened bread in his strong, black coffee and ate that as well. When Grandfather Paque finished, he remained at the table absently massaging his sore gums and listening to the children play.

As the morning passed, the old man called on whomever was nearest the dented thermometer, to report the temperature.

"Just looked. It's going up, Grandpere."

"I feels it. *Merci*." Thanks.

"Going higher, Grandpere. Gonna be powerful hot."

"*Merci*."

Though the doors and shutters of the shanty were shut tight to keep out the rising heat in the way Grandfather Paque had taught his son, the corrugated tin roof and the walls of thin wood and tarpaper were no match for the torrid Caribbean sun. Trapped indoors, the motionless air became stifling. The children grew listless and lay on the floor to doze. Grandfather Paque had received medical advice not to exert himself whenever the temperature mounted. He sat quietly back on his cot.

For lunch he went to the table and slowly ate more of the fish with the smoky flavor he loved and dunked bread into tea that was at room temperature. Afterwards, he usually took a nap. However, the heat made him restless. He shuffled over to the ancient box to while away the time by holding some of the papers in his hand and dreaming. But when he reached out, he touched no box. It was gone. He groped around in the space where it had once been kept.

In an angry voice he shouted, "What's going on? Where

is de box and de papers? Tell me, somebody quick."
Recklessly he overturned a chair and kicked the wall in
fruitless effort. Desperation crept into his voice. "Where are
the papers? Who stole dem? Tell me. Who was the one who
stole the box and the papers?"

Raphael rushed to his father's side and put his arms
around the old man's thin shoulders. "Easy, Grandpere.
I've been out of work. The children go hungry many times.
We had no money. And we needed every bit of space we
could get. You knew all that. So we sold the silly box. No
one stole anything. The box was just lying around with its
worthless papers that were only good to make the children
laugh."

"Birdshit!" The old man spat his favorite expression in
his son's face and shoved him away. "Don't go handing me
that. You're messing with the curse. I owned the box long
before you were born. I kept it safe. Somebody must've
stole it. Help me!" he cried out. His belligerence was to no
avail. The box was gone and with it, the papers.

In the past he had often run his gnarled hands across
the rough sides of his coveted box. He had caressed its
thick coating a thousand times and knew by heart its every
bump. Now those hands were empty.

He had made no secret of the box. The villagers of St.
Pierre knew his family handed it down from generation to
generation. He had offered to permit the unschooled
churchmen to examine the papers that lay inside. But they
were content to leave the unknown alone and let it remain
in the box. No living soul could say what secrets slept within the old box.

Loss of the box seemed to strike the old man as hard as the death of his beloved wife that occurred many years before. His anger made him frantic. He tripped over a stool in his wild, useless search of the corner where the box had rested. He recovered his balance and without caution charged to the other side of the room. Then, with tufts of his white hair floating behind him, he opened the door and bolted out.

Raphael hurried to the doorway and watched him go. "Oh no, *mon pere*, you mustn't. Please come back." The old man ignored his son's shouted pleas. The son dared not antagonize him further by chasing after him. Left alone, the forlorn figure stumbled into the hot, dusty lane.

The bewildered grandchildren ran to the door, alarm spread across their faces. They gawked after the receding image.

The elder's shrill, frantic screams echoed throughout St. Pierre, without rousing the little village from its afternoon torpor "Help!" In his soft, hysterical voice to friends and members of his cult, the elder appealed. "Please help me. I needs your help, badly. Somebody?" For a moment his body recoiled from the heat. He kicked up dust with his bare feet.

The senior Paque turned left and right, begging, "You must help me catch the thief. Please, someone."

But that afternoon no one appeared willing to brave the sweltering heat. No stray mongrel barked at the commotion. Except for a scrawny chicken flapping its wings and clucking its irritation as it fled out from underfoot, nothing moved. The parched community lay baking in the sun, apparently unperturbed by the loss of the Paques' ancient box. The village lay as if deserted.

Nevertheless, the sixty-nine year old kept on with his search. "Don't nobody want to help me," he sobbed. "I needs somebody...anybody...Where are my friends?" His voice lost all vigor. He seemed not to notice. Flecks of spittle began to appear around his open mouth.

Doors shut tight, mocked him to his face as he lurched past. Barely able to maintain his balance on unsteady legs, he passed the village center where the public fountain, over-grown with weeds, had not spouted water in years. No one was there.

He staggered on. All the while his head twisted left, then right, searching for help. He babbled incoherent words through the dry, white foam that spread around his open mouth. No one could understand his words, but everyone knew he sought help.

His slight frame shook uncontrollably, yet he pressed on. Reaching the far edge of the village, the feverish man could not continue. He paused for a moment's rest and bent over at the waist, supporting himself on outstretched arms, his hands resting on his sweaty knees. He was completely exhausted. His blank look stared down at bare feet, split open and bleeding, partly concealing the grime that collected at his toes. He reached out to unloosen the rope that crossed his belly and held his pants in place.

His thin chest heaved in a violent attempt to suck in the enormous amount of air his breathless, overtaxed body demanded. His lungs were unable to keep up. His ancient heart raced faster and faster, making a valiant attempt to exceed its limit.

"Help me," he sobbed in a voice grown weak. He gasped. His body shuddered. The terrible strain caused his faltering heart to skip a beat. His heated face revealed the pain. His whole body quivered.

No soft breeze passed to make the heat less oppressive. Only his labored breathing stirred.

His old body remained bent over, exhausted. His pulse faltered.

More moments elapsed.

His aged heart stopped altogether.

The old man fell over, dead. The rictus of death's garish smile stretched wide across his face, concealing the cynicism of old age.

Suffering the heat, Raphael came upon the fallen body within minutes. Shortly after, the villagers began to converge on the place of the shameful occurrence. The somber gathering disagreed as to what had caused the senior's death. Although everyone had heard the old man's outcry and knew he had been the casualty of extreme agitation, those who spoke would at first only venture to say, "God has called his priest."

However, in a community where voodooism and witchcraft were widely and openly practiced, another priest, stiff with age, offered the observation, "It was the curse."

"*Bien sûr.*" Why of course. A tremor ran through the group. Once voiced, the underlying cause seemed obvious. The curse.

One villager recalled that the discoverer of the old box had died soon after the discovery. Some speculated as to what would happen to the next person who possessed the box. No one expected the experience would be pleasant. There was a collective sigh of relief now that the accursed thing had left the village.

"The box would not have been happy to be torn from our village."

"Terrible."

"Shocking."

"Sorry," said a cousin.

Two voodoo adherents who had known before of the younger Paque's intention to sell the box to the American if he could, and had known the grandfather was so head-strong he would never approve, had decided not to tell the old man of his son's intentions. Instead, they had contacted a voodoo priestess who lived down near the archaeological site off Route 100. They requested her to dissuade the American from buying the box. It was obvious she had failed.

A villager brought out a blanket and covered the senior Paque. With tears streaming down his face, Raphael lifted his father's slight body and slung it over his shoulder. Hands reached out to assist him, but he brushed them aside and trudged back up the lane alone with his burden.

A neighbor called after him, "We're very saddened by the loss of our great spiritual leader and friend."

"We'll miss him," said another.

"We feel your emptiness, your sorrow." The words rang out in the heated air.

"A dear man. There were times when we had nothing and he shared his fish with us. God will admit him to Paradise."

Pity was in the air.

To every fine sentiment that was expressed on that afternoon, Raphael softly but clearly uttered the one word his father would have spoken had he been alive, "Birdshit!"

Raphael's tears blurred his vision as he lugged his father's fallen body home. The grandchildren remained behind the shack's screen door, waiting with frowning and unusually quiet faces. It was their first experience with death. One held open the door for their father. No word was heard, only Raphael's sobs.

Chapter Nine

The Power of Columbus

The *Angora* had returned to port in Haiti and then set out to retrace its route in the Caribbean Sea when both engines again quit. Talbot entered his tiny cabin. "There's no one on deck," he said. "This transportation stinks."

He went to the porthole and looked out as the ship bobbed in a light chop. "Damn, nothing's happening and there's nothing I can do about it." He dropped the book he had been reading. What was Ash doing, he wondered. Would this additional delay give the man an opportunity to interfere? "We could swim to Miami faster than this tub will get us there."

"Shh." Sandy waved for quiet as she studied a letter.

"Sorry. I didn't mean to bother you. You sound like you're onto something. Are you?"

"Maybe. I don't know yet. Give me a chance, will you." Sandy clamped her hands over her ears.

Agonizing over the delay, Talbot stomped from their cabin, again. Emerging into the passageway, he heard the engines start up and felt the *Angora* begin to move at the same slow speed as before. He went up to the after deck and looked out over the stern at the white foam trailing in the ship's wake. What was the museum saving by leasing this wreck, he speculated. He examined the palm of his empty hand, seeking an answer.

After a while he turned and looked up front. He saw Barney limp out onto the forward deck carrying a makeshift tool box. That was quick, Talbot thought. Barney must be confident the engines will work for a time.

The first mate dragged his lame foot along the foredeck to a rusted cleat, plunked down his tool box and wiped his hands on a greasy rag dangling from his side pocket. He seemed to choose the perfect vantage point from which to observe the rear deck though he couldn't hear whatever might be said back there. Barney's bushy eyebrows concealed his deeply recessed eyes so that Talbot could not tell whether the seaman was actually looking at him or was focusing on his own work. Talbot had the uneasy feeling Barney would spend more time watching than he would working on the cleat.

As the first mate poked around the cleat with a screwdriver, Talbot recalled Barney showing further interest in Sandy. After the *Angora* was well out to sea the grubby man took time off from sweating over the engines to limp past their open cabin door and look in on Sandy, who was alone. Later she told Talbot that Barney's voice surprised her. "Hey, lil' lady, enjoying the ride?" She had jumped. Her startled reaction caused the seaman to double over laughing.

As the *Angora* progressed slowly again, Talbot watched Sandy appear from below and step warily across the worn planking in her bare feet. "At least we're moving," she said. "Is Barney up here somewhere? I'd hate to leave your wooden box alone if he's still down with the engines."

"Come on." Talbot beckoned. "Barney's working up towards the bow. I'll keep track of him so you don't have to worry. Enjoy this cool, fresh air."

Drawing near, she shuddered. "I don't trust that creep."

Talbot nodded. "That makes two of us." Did Ash order the man to keep an eye on them, he asked himself. Was this delay all part of some scheme Ash cooked up?

"Where are we anyway?" Sandy asked.

"We're almost to the Windward Passage. Then we leave the Caribbean Sea and sail into the Atlantic Ocean."

"Is that still Haiti over there?" she asked waving her arm towards the shining sea and beyond to the green foliage that framed the shoreline on her right. From the distance it looked beautiful.

"That's Haiti's northern tip. Can you feel Cuba off our port bow?" He pointed in the opposite direction. "Towards the end of Columbus' first voyage under the Spanish flag he left Cuba and was on his way back to Spain, probably crossing right in front of where we are now. Then Columbus anchored among Haiti's coral reefs, where I told you the *Santa Maria* was gutted and the wood box with the papers must have come ashore." Talbot became silent contemplating the sea. What did those papers say, he wondered.

Gazing out at the horizon, Sandy brushed back a wisp of hair that had blown in her face. She remembered the old house in San Juan where she had lived as a little girl. In the early days she often leaned on the balcony railing and stared out at the distant horizon where the road dropped off. At that age she was afraid to stray for fear she might walk off the edge of the earth. That seemed silly now.

Talbot stirred and waved his hand in front of her unblinking eyes. "Hey, you still with me? Snap out of it, please." She snuggled up to Talbot and hugged him tight. Against his ear she said, "I've heard that superstitious sailors back in Columbus' day were scared of sea monsters and falling off the edge of the earth if they ever sailed out past the horizon."

"That's part of an old wives' tale. Some landlubbers used to think the Earth was flat. But every sailor who went out to sea and looked at the horizon saw only more salt water when he sailed beyond. No sailor ever fell into an abyss or off the earth or encountered any sea monsters. But sailors might have told the serving maids in the taverns otherwise just to prey on their gullibility and impress them."

She said, "All that salt water flowing beyond the horizon. I can't believe it just goes nowhere. Did Columbus hear those stories? Wasn't he in the least afraid of falling off the earth?"

"Not the Admiral," Talbot hooted. "He was no serving maid and he knew the earth was a sphere. So did men centuries before him. Also, he had experience. Columbus sailed up and down the west coast of Europe and Africa many times. He went beyond distant horizons every day of his seafaring life without once falling off the earth."

Talbot pointed. "Right now, looking out at our own horizon, you'd think we could fall off at that point. Scary, huh? Well, you're no old wife or serving maid so don't put any stock in that falling-off-the earth nonsense. And there are no sea monsters any more than a monster lives in Scotland's Loch Ness today."

They kissed. "You seem like your old self," he said.

"I hope I am. Getting away from that camp and all makes a big difference to me. How about you?" Frown lines creased her forehead. "Tell me the truth. Are you worried?"

"Not about falling off the earth."

"Oh, you know what I mean...sinking that money into the box right when you lost your job?"

"Sure, that has me plenty worried. We can't all be as cool as Columbus." He kissed her again and nuzzled her neck. "Before my father passed away he said to me, 'If you're gonna take chances, you better be lucky.' He knew he hadn't been lucky with the chance he took on having an operation after the accident, but I'm hoping I am lucky and that the box and its papers will make up for losing my job. I'm not forgetting you. As soon as possible, I'll repay you.

"But Columbus had those papers. They must be valuable. Don't forget that Americans have made him immortal, erecting statues in his honor and even giving his name to the district in which our nation's capital is located. And they named streets after him. They are as far apart as Columbus Circle and Columbus Avenue in New York City and Corso de Colón in San Francisco. Columbus, Ohio, among other cities, took his name as did the Knights of Columbus although he *never, ever* set foot on the continent of America.

"Nonetheless, he is entitled to our cheering. He displayed tremendous bravery, daring a charmingly impossible feat while his crew beseeched him to turn back. He introduced Europe to the New World, leading to an emigration that flooded, then settled our great continent.

"A native American he's not, but he is America's roots. No need to say he discovered America, though it be home of the brave."

"Think you're heading to fame and fortune?"

"I hope so. History sure has left some wide gaps to be filled. Meanwhile make yourself comfortable over on my air mattress."

Sandy flopped down on the mattress. "You never talked about it, but are we gangsters? We aren't supposed to just walk out of Haiti with the box and papers. Don't we need a clearance like an export license from the Haitian authorities. Don't we need something official allowing you to take the box out of Haiti?"

"I think you're right," he admitted as he knelt down beside her. "I know England makes people get clearance if a document is over fifty years old. Only we don't know how old my things are for sure."

Sandy squirmed on the mattress. "Would the Haitian officials have given you a license if you applied for one?"

"It would have taken months for them to issue an export license. Haiti is a troubled land. I didn't dare wait." He wrung his hands. "The Paques didn't trust their government, so why should we foreigners trust it?"

He placed a hand on her shoulder. "I'm sure if we hung around much longer, the government or Ash or the voodoo clowns who were behind that decapitated monkey head would have torn the box right out of my hands."

"But you don't really have any provenance to show

where the box came from. No statement of origin, no shipping manifest...nothing."

"Nothing right this instant, only the box itself. That's plenty and also part of the risk. If I establish origin too soon, some antiquities act could force me to give up the box and the documents. Spain and Italy might both file claims if they heard about it. If Haiti ever gets wind of us sneaking those things out, it could say we were violating their export restrictions."

"Okay, let's not go into that."

"Subject closed."

"Still I feel rotten about you losing your first job as an archaeologist."

"Forget it. The box alone could be worth the loss. And if it hadn't been for the Paques using the Visitors' Tent, Ash would have trumped up something else. From the moment I stepped into his office that morning I could feel he planned to get rid of me. Well, I'm glad to go."

"I know, but I can't help think it shouldn't have happened."

Talbot made himself comfortable on the air mattress and took her arm. "There was no good reason for firing me. Ash is just a bastard."

"You think he'll try to stop us now we've left Haiti?"

"He's smart. Sooner or later he'll learn about that box. I've been thinking he'll try to grab it from me when the *Angora* docks in Miami."

"I wouldn't put it past him. He reminds me of Barney. Is that guy still staring at us?"

"I can't tell what he's looking at. He could be."

"His beady eyes bother me."

"Want to give me a kiss? That should take Barney's mind off what we brought on board."

She offered half a smile. "He'd probably like to know me better." She gave Talbot a long kiss.

"You've sure got his attention." Talbot kissed the nape of her neck. "Only I don't like it."

"He may be annoying, but he's harmless."

"He's scum, and he's not harmless. I see you're carrying copies of three of the papers. Unravel anything?"

"These pages could have been written back in medieval time."

"That's a start."

"I'm having the same trouble you had trying to read the handwriting and trying to figure out what the words meant the way people spoke in the Middle Ages."

She heaved a sigh. "Remember you saw *caballo*, the Spanish word for horse? At first I thought you misread it, had it mixed up with *caballero*, the word for gentleman. But I saw the same word used in another paper that begins *Caro Caballo Mio*, Dear Horse of Mine or My Dear Horse. According to my Castilian Spanish, that's the way you'd start a letter. I don't think it was any different in old Spanish. What's more I saw *caballo*, the word for horse, at the beginning of two other papers." She unfolded a copy of one page and showed him.

"Where does that leave us?"

"Well, My Dear Horse is a literal translation. A freer translation might be My Dear Steed. All three words have masculine endings, so this letter was written to a male, to

My Dear Male Steed. Of course, writing to a steed doesn't make sense. But, if I can substitute the word steed for the word horse, then why can't I substitute the word stud for horse and imagine the letter was to a stud? Or to someone built, perhaps even hung, like a stud?"

"Let me see that." He seized the page and examined it.

She released a peal of laughter. "Don't you get it? The letter was written to My Dear Stud. It's a meaning for *caballo* that's not in the dictionary but which the person receiving the letter shared with the writer. It's all here...in Spanish."

Unable to contain herself, she laughed harder. "That's an earthy, bawdy translation, not exactly a dull, classical one."

"That's your translation. You're saying it's not a manifest listing horses like I first imagined. I don't believe it."

"That's what I think," she said with conviction.

"Incredible." Talbot scratched his head. "But if this is a letter instead of a manifest, what then?"

"I'm getting these vibrations. I think all the documents in the box are a woman's love letters," she said deadpan.

He slapped his thigh then shook her by the shoulders for a moment. "Do you realize what you're saying?"

She took out an orange. "Mind holding these copies while I peel this?"

He accepted two more pages from her. "I don't know. What makes you say they're love letters?"

"What I've pieced together so far." She dug into the fruit, discarding bits of orange peel over the side. "Some of these letters end with the word *amore*, the Italian word for love. One letter ends *Con mucho amore*. The first two are Spanish words followed by the Italian word. With much love. Nice touch, eh?"

She paused, watching his face. "If a smart Spanish woman wanted to curtsy to a sexy Italian, she might dip into his language and pull out a plum, the word for love. Wouldn't that tickle his fancy?"

"It sure would. Remember, I first said that one page might be a manifest dealing with horses? Well, I thought about it some more and considered the exquisite small paintings around the sides of the paper. In the black and white copies they don't look like much, but in the originals the paintings were so lovely, and the colors so beautiful. They reminded me of those gorgeous, illuminated manuscripts which the monks prepared back in medieval times. I began to think these letters were church documents. How wrong could I be?" He slapped his head realizing how wide of the mark he had been. He whistled softly. "I'm getting more and more anxious to reach Miami. Who wrote those love letters?"

"If the woman who wrote them could have a skilled artist paint lovely pictures on pieces of her stationery, she had to hold a high rank, like be from one of the royal families, who were patrons of the arts. She would have the artist decorate blank pages for her and then she would use them up as needed. She had an early version of the decorated stationery women write on today."

He nodded, looking towards the bow of the *Angora* to assure himself Barney was too far away to hear what they were discussing. "This Spanish woman you're speaking of had very fancy notepaper. Anything more?"

"Back in camp, looking at the photographs the Paques brought us of the box, you thought it belonged to Queen Isabella. I think that these letters were also from the Queen. In one letter the writer mentioned *Rex ferd*. You know who that is."

Talbot's face took on a pale, haunted look. "That's got to be King Ferdinand, husband of Queen Isabella. And she was a woman holding the highest rank in the Spanish court. She also knew an Italian whose ship was wrecked off Haiti's coast where the box came to the surface in an earthquake. We're talking about the Queen's love letters." Talbot could feel his spirits rising. Perhaps he had done the right thing in buying the amazing wood box and letters.

"But don't jump to the conclusion she was writing to Columbus just because he had the letters and was Italian. She could have had some other secret Italian lover and Columbus kept those letters over her head." Talbot folded the letters together and paused to gather his thoughts.

"The Queen's love letters are probably worth more than stodgy official documents. And I'm glad the letters may not be written to Columbus. I don't like the idea of the Queen calling him a stud. Stick with *la passione di amore*, and don't translate the word *caballo* as freely as a stud just in case the letters are to Columbus. Calling him a stud makes him sound like he was the Queen's consort when the King was away."

Talbot handed the copy of the one letter back to her. "I like your probing mind. So precise, tying it all together.

He leaped up and performed a little jig in front of the air mattress before sitting down again. *"Amore Amore!* I can't wait to get to Miami with the box full of Queen Isabella's dazzling love letters. What about the signature on those love letters?" His voice was pitched higher than usual.

"Just look." She held up the one copy. "Some letters are unsigned like this one. I can't make heads nor tails out of any of the signatures. They're illegible. And I don't have a specimen of the Queen's signature to compare these with. She wiped away orange juice that dripped down on her chin. "Here, have this." She offered him another piece of orange.

He ate it. "This whole thing makes me shiver." He rocked back and forth on the mattress. "The more you delve into those letters, the more explosive they sound. So far everything fits like the dovetailed corner of a well-made drawer. They're a slice of history, a peek at the way people acted back then." He got up and began to pace back and forth. "Did you notice if the letters were dated?"

"Not one, so I can't tell if there were gaps when she didn't write."

"And nobody's name appears in the salutations. I suppose the writer was being circumspect, trying to conceal to whom she was writing. Besides, she probably liked calling him a *caballo.*"

"Wouldn't it be marvelous if these were love letters from Queen Isabella? If Columbus got hold of them somehow and kept them and the Queen knew he had them, wouldn't that explain the terrific hold he had over her and maybe over King Ferdinand as well?"

"You are thinking blackmail, but I've always admired Columbus. Sure, he needed Isabella to support him, a foreigner, through all four of his turbulent voyages. But these letters may simply reveal her love for him. She could have helped Columbus without being blackmailed into it."

"You're beginning to think she wrote these letters to Columbus. Are you ruling out blackmail?"

"Almost." His thoughts churned.

"Do you want a dull, more classical translation of those letters? I can give you that."

"Don't make a stud out of whomever she was writing to. Love causes people to do and say strange things. Isabella was eighteen years old when she married her cousin Ferdinand. He was a year younger than she was. It was an arranged marriage. The two teenagers hardly knew each other before that. She was a blonde girl with blue-green eyes who didn't marry because she loved Ferdinand. She married him to join two powerful families together."

"That doesn't sound very romantic. It's more like a troubled relationship from the start."

"Perhaps. So what do we have? When she met Columbus in 1486, Isabella had been married to cousin Ferdinand for eighteen years and Columbus' first wife had died the previous year. It's a well-known fact the Queen was much taken with Columbus the widower. Imagine the electricity their first encounter must have generated. Columbus had a commanding presence. Isabella was regal. She was also the key to his coveted expedition. It's said the two of them hit it off immediately. She may have dreamed of him."

"You *are* thinking the letters are to Columbus. Why don't you come right out and say it? Didn't Isabella and her husband turn Columbus down in the beginning?"

"Of course, they sent him to their experts who delayed him and advised against his proposed exploration. Nevertheless the Queen stayed in touch with Columbus. She saw him from time to time and gave him money to live on while the monarchs were making up their minds."

Talbot drew his knees up. "The Queen and Columbus pushed through age forty together. Isn't that the age when life begins? After that, keep your eyes on the support the Queen gave Christopher and ask yourself, could she have done it for love? I thought highly of him. Don't make him out to be a blackmailer or a racy stud. Don't add to the bad things some people say about him already." Talbot glanced up at Barney and saw the man was still working on replacing the cleat.

Talbot turned to Sandy. "For Columbus' first voyage, Queen Isabella got the King's agreement to support the explorer and after the success of that voyage and all the wonderful stories Columbus told about it, the King was won over."

Talbot added, "For Columbus' second voyage in 1493, he commanded a gigantic fleet of seventeen ships carrying a thousand colonists. That voyage was a colossal undertaking the monarchs dropped into the foreigner's lap. It's hard to believe Columbus got such a juicy plum based only on his navigational skills. But while the Queen must have been taken with him, it could have been like being enthralled by any exciting explorer and her support of him would have influenced the King, only such influence didn't make Columbus her stud." Talbot scowled and shook his head.

Sandy's eyes glowed. "I can imagine leaving the hustle and bustle of that crowded seaport in 1493. All those ships with their huge sails snapping in the wind and the town's folk standing on the shore. Women waving their colorful handkerchiefs and little boys running alongside for a ways, playing leapfrog over barrels, cheering the flotilla as it silently glided past."

"Spectacular." Talbot rubbed his chin. "Realize that the colonists were all men! There wasn't a woman among them and none was the settler the monarchs needed. Not a farmer or carpenter or blacksmith. These so-called colonists suffered badly from gold fever.

"Incidentally, the Spaniard, Ponce de León, sailed with Columbus on that voyage. Twenty years later Ponce explored a place he named La Florida (The Flower)."

Sandy perked up. "Too bad Ponce didn't actually discover the fountain of youth."

"Perhaps he did and we just don't know where. What we do know is that Columbus, on that glorious second voyage, took two and a half years and he still didn't bring back from the Orient the great things he promised the Monarchy. Yet the King and Queen, gluttons for punishment, kept right on financing additional voyages. They weren't scatterbrains. They didn't have money to throw around. To give him such support the Queen must have loved him; still that doesn't make him a stud."

"I feel those letters certainly say she loved him. I had

hoped the box was worth what you paid the Paques and worth losing your job over. Love letters from Isabella to Columbus will be worth that and more. They'll bring you a fortune! But you look disappointed."

Talbot smiled. "You're reading too much into those letters. What it comes down to is the Queen thought highly enough of Columbus that she elevated the Italian commoner to Admiral of the Ocean Sea at a time when there was only one other admiral in all of Spain. With that rank and her backing, Columbus could hobnob with royalty, with the Queen. That's all."

"Don't turn your back on those letters."

"Columbus was a hero to me. I'd hate to escape failure by dragging the man's name through the mud. It'd be like hunting animals where, in order to succeed, you have to take a life. I don't like it. Columbus could never have been a blackmailer or the Queen's stud."

"Maybe he was human."

"I still don't like it."

"You're so old-fashioned. Even our illustrious presidents take their sex where they find it."

"From the start I didn't like your vulgar translation of *caballo* and it set me to thinking. Why would the Queen, a woman in her elevated position, and a Spanish woman at that, commit such thoughts to paper? It made me wonder if she wrote them. Columbus was my idol." Talbot hesitated. "I think I may have the answer. The Queen was fond of Columbus. (I think she loved him.) But I can't see her going overboard and writing all that sexy stuff to him without something else pushing her, and I don't mean a sexual frenzy was pushing her. What I believe is that everyone, including the Queen, knew that her husband strayed from the marital bed frequently. Therefore the Queen laid it on thick in her letters to Columbus to give the King a little of his own medicine."

"Maybe she was thinking others would read those letters and she wanted to rub the King's nose in it. You're filling in history's blanks."

"Perhaps; it's more than 500 years ago. And Columbus being a class act, didn't appreciate what she was doing, so he kept those letters in the box away from the prying eyes of catty gossips."

"From what words I can make out, Queen Isabella must not have led a sheltered life. She knew the words."

"Her anger makes those letters very valuable and my explanation keeps them from hurting Columbus. So, question, why did she write those letters? Have I guessed right?"

"You're the expert."

Mulling over his thoughts, Talbot looked at Sandy with vacant eyes.

She studied him. "Sometimes I think you stare at me the way Barney does."

Mention of Barney reminded Talbot he wanted to keep the seaman in sight. He twisted, looking around for the man. Then the pit of Talbot's stomach sank. He made a gurgling sound before finding his voice. "Goddamn it, Barney's disappeared right while we've been sitting here, talking! How could I have let that happen? He was there a minute ago."

A shiny, new cleat gleamed in the place of the old, rusted one. Chips of paint and orange-colored rust marked the spot where the first mate had been working. It was ancient history, a subject about which Talbot thought he knew something and about which he found he was still learning.

Talbot scowled at the closed tool box sitting beside the new cleat. A dirty rag was knotted to the handle of the box and fluttered in the breeze like a torn, unfurled flag.

"That goddamn Barney!" Talbot fumed. He balled a fist and struck his other hand. "That snake has wiggled down through the forward hatch and left his tools behind trying to make us think he's coming right back. Sandy, I'll slide down the way he did. You take the stairs. Hurry!"

She jumped up and dashed across the deck.

Talbot secured the air mattress and rushed forward to look down the hatch. It was empty. Barney had disappeared completely.

Chapter Ten

Barney Is Curious

Barney finished up replacing the old cleat with a bright and shiny, new one and wiped off his hands with a dirty rag. He looked one more time at the two passengers in front of him and cinched his belt tight before gingerly dropping down through the hatch into the dark passageway below. Careful of his revolver, he hitched it around and slithered across the miscellaneous cargo that crowded the whole area. He slowly made his way to the small galley in the reduced light and reached out to grab a battered tin cup and poured in some tomato juice. Grimacing, he swallowed the juice. "Christ, that's sour," he said out loud. "It's like something that dumpy Yardarm would sell." The Yardarm was located on the Miami waterfront. It had a reputation for never throwing anything away, even after it had turned bad.

In the darkened passageway the sound of the engines was clear. One drive shaft ran a bit rough, which was usual. Despite its age it still performed. With the passengers out on deck, this would be a golden opportunity for Barney to take a quick peek to learn why Talbot took special care of the duffel bag. Perhaps it contained something valuable or illegal. There was only one way to find out.

Barney's face hardened as he dragged his lame foot

along the deck to Talbot's cabin. Glancing up and down the corridor, he twisted the doorknob which gave off a harsh squeak. It needed to be dusted with graphite powder that he never had the time to do. He paused. No footsteps sounded in the corridor. There was only the dull throb of the engines.

On opening the cabin door a cool breeze came from the open porthole and blew past Barney. He squinted at the dark cabin. Both bunks were neatly made up. A jumble of things was piled against the hull. Not much for him to see from the doorway. He had to enter the cabin if he was serious and were to find out anything. He looked down the corridor. No one was coming. The young people must have remained on deck, yakking.

The waterproof covering over the duffel bag caught his eye because not everything was protected with extra covering. It was possible the passengers were bringing out something criminal in the duffel bag. Drugs maybe.

Releasing his breath slowly, Barney fingered the gun in his holster. If they were carrying drugs, he should know about it and report it to the captain. But if he were caught snooping, he needed an explanation. A moment later he seemed to have one.

Checking over his shoulder, he darted into the cabin. He left the door open behind him.

Barney hobbled to the porthole, moving as fast as his lame foot allowed. He closed the porthole and dogged down the lugs. Next, he angled over to the duffel bag. As he passed in front of the bunk, he knocked a book to the deck. "Damn." He glanced back at the doorway. No one was there. Bending down, he picked up the book and tossed it onto the bunk.

When he reached the duffel bag, his fingers itched to undo the knots on the outer covering. There were knots that someone who knew nothing about knots, had tied. But what was hidden in the duffel bag?

Heaving the bag up onto the bunk, Barney once more checked over his shoulder. No one was in the doorway. He examined the outer plastic bag that protected the duffel bag within. He could not open it quickly without leaving a trace that showed he had tampered with the plastic.

A noise from behind interrupted him. A rat could be sneaking into the cabin and making the noise. Barney tensed and reached for his gun. He spun around to confront the noise.

No rat.

Talbot's woman appeared out of nowhere. She stood in the corridor, her legs flexed to keep her balance against the mild roll of the ship. Her face was an angry red. She screamed for help.

Barney flinched. His stomach muscles tightened. He had taken too long.

She screamed again. Barney winced. Withdrawing his hand from his gun, he cursed all women and dumped the duffel bag back onto the cabin floor. He grabbed the book lying on the other bunk.

Her body shook with rage. "You thief! Get the hell out of our cabin right now!"

Barney remained outwardly calm and without saying a word hurled the book at the woman, causing her to withdraw. Despite his crippled foot he soon reached the doorway. In his urgent haste he bumped into Sandy as she reappeared blocking his way, and crying out for help.

"What's the matter with you, lil' lady," he asked. "For God's sake, stop that shouting. I can explain everything."

He raised his arm to ward off her fist, at the same time attempting to squeeze by her. "You see," he said holding her wrist, "I thought sea water might come in through the porthole. It's very dangerous to leave it open like that when nobody is in here. A ship could capsize from water pouring in on one side. I've seen it happen." As he spoke, his hand released her wrist and moved over to her shoulder to restrain her. The excuse he had prepared had no effect.

"Get away!" she shouted at him, struggling to shove him off her. "Don't touch me, slime."

Barney blocked another of her blows. His hand slipped down from her shoulder to her breast. "If you'll only let me pass you, I'll be happy to leave...unless you really don't want me to go?" A crafty look crept into his hopeful eyes. "What's the big hurry?" He pressed against her, his foul breath causing her to shudder.

She yelled, "You pig!" and she attempted to scratch him. "Get the hell out of my sight."

Barney's hand slid down further. He reached behind her, seizing her buttocks and jerking her whole body to him. She wildly beat and clawed at him and continued to shriek for help.

"Aw, now, lil' lady, stop all the fuss. Let's us be friends. You know you like a little change once in a while. We all do." He blocked her hands with one arm while still clutching her rear end with the other.

She spit in his face and lowered her head to bite his shoulder. He squirmed away while rubbing where she had spit on him.

Talbot heard Sandy's screams and squeezed through the open hatch in a hurry. One foot caught on the lashing around some cargo and he paused to untangle himself. Once released, he ran to their cabin. "Sandy!" he cried out, "I'm coming! What's the trouble?"

He saw Barney and charged towards the man. "What in God's name are you doing to Sandy?"

"Nuthin', mate. I'm only trying to restrain the lil' woman, is all." He smirked. "I'd leave her in a second if she would let me." Holding onto Sandy for balance, Barney limped to her far side away from Talbot.

"Christ, take your filthy hands away from her, you sick son of a bitch," Talbot roared, but advanced no closer. The seaman's retreat behind Sandy had made Talbot cautious. He saw that the seaman moved well despite his infirmity. He's spoiling for a fight and is about to throw a sucker punch, Talbot thought. If I'm not careful, all I've got to do is to treat this guy like some helpless cripple and he'll floor me.

"We have a little mix-up here. I weren't doin' the lil' lady no harm." Barney offered an old buddy's grin.

To Talbot the grin had the deceptive look of a crocodile lolling in a puddle of muddy water. "So get the hell away from her!" He almost reached Sandy when he detected Barney's body growing taut, ready to lash out.

Talbot jumped to one side when Barney's hand swung up, holding a wrench that he had slipped from his coveralls. Cute, Talbot thought, as he streaked in under the wrench and grabbed the thick wrist with both hands. He twisted hard, forcing Barney to drop the wrench with a crash that could be heard over the throbbing of the engines.

Barney let out a grunt but did not give up. He yanked his arm down hard and fast so that the point of his elbow gave Talbot a vicious jab in the ribs. Talbot winced and had never felt such pain before. He released his hold on the seaman and fell backward tripping over a crate that lay behind him.

"Sandy," he yelled, "get the captain up in the wheelhouse. Tell him it's an emergency. He should leave everything. We need him down here fast. Run!"

She sprinted off.

With his good leg Barney kicked the fallen Talbot. Talbot rolled away to avoid another kick and scrambled to his feet, rubbing his side. He jabbed Barney in the body. The man backed just out of reach.

Without warning, the engines stopped, bringing the ship to an abrupt halt as though the captain had stomped on the brakes. The unexpected loss of forward motion threw both men off balance causing them to fall to the deck. The rasping sounds of the two winded men breathing hard filled the passageway.

Talbot got up first. His body ached. He realized, as he expected, Barney was a crafty street fighter who had the experience of many barroom brawls under his belt. The two men circled each other slowly as they tried to recover from their falls.

They careened towards one another, trying to end the fight fast. When in close, Talbot hit Barney in the stomach. The seaman absorbed the bruising punch and butted Talbot's chin. Talbot staggered back, feeling a sharp pain shoot through his jaw making him dizzy. At the same time he saw that Barney expected him to let down his guard long enough to provide a fatal opening.

With little strength left, Talbot feinted a blow to Barney's stomach and lunged forward. His head smashed into Barney's nose, making a soft, cracking sound. Blood streamed down the seaman's face. He wobbled away, fumbling for his gun.

Talbot drew his machete and looked around to see what he could do to avoid the new threat.

"Hold it, Barney!" the captain's order rang out. "And for chrissakes, get cleaned up. Put some ice on that nose. You, Mr. Talbot, best put your machete away. It's no match for Barney's .45."

"Cap'n, the woman's got everyone upset over nuthin'," Barney protested, pressing a rag to his nose. "Like I told her, I was only in their cabin to close the porthole. Weren't safe to leave it open while they went topside."

"Leave us!" the captain ordered the first mate.

Barney looked at the captain unbelieving, then stomped away. No one seemed to listen to his practised excuse.

"He's lying," Sandy said from behind the captain.

"Sorry about all this, folks." The captain's smile was thin. "But I'll see to it he won't give you any more grief."

"He was in our cabin, touching our things," Sandy

said in a cool voice. "He would have gone through them if I didn't stop him. He was prying into our personal belongings."

"He didn't steal anything," the captain said, "so it's all over."

"Our clothing and personal belongings are private," she persisted, bitterness in her voice. "We expect to keep them that way."

"Really, I assure you it's over. That's the end of it. Barney was curious. He probably wondered what you had in those boxes and that big bag," the captain said in a softer voice, looking around the cabin.

Talbot spoke up, "There's nothing special here if that's what you're saying. Only our clothes, books and in the bag an old box we bought. Archaeologists do that sometimes even when they're not working." He paused to catch his breath.

"That box hold anything good? Priceless treasure maybe?" The captain half-smiled and raised his hand as if to ward off their irritation. "Only kidding."

Talbot opened the porthole. "Papers are all that's in the box, and they're written in a foreign language so we don't know what they say. Sandy speaks the language but she can't make it out. We'll have to wait 'til we get an old dictionary for her. Something to keep her busy on rainy days."

Talbot looked over at the duffel bag and noticed Barney had managed to untie one knot in the waterproof covering. Talbot's jaw tightened. He held in his anger.

"Well, I'll speak to Barney," the captain said. "He's gonna mind his own business."

"Maybe you should think about hiring someone else to take his place?" Talbot said.

"I don't think so. Barney's sailed with me for five years now. Keeps the engines running...usually." The captain smiled. "And, when he takes his turn at the wheel, he holds a pretty fair compass heading; he's always on course. Plus, knowing booze doesn't mix with guns, I don't permit liquor on board. So Barney can't help but keep his battered nose clean while he's out to sea. Good reasons to keep him."

"As long as his big nose stays the hell outa here, no harm's done," Talbot said.

"Guess I'll get a bite to eat before cranking up the engines again. We'll be in the Atlantic but at this speed, it's gonna take us another day and a half to make Nassau."

"What's with Nassau? When we came on board, no one said anything about stopping there. We were supposed to go straight through to Miami," Talbot said.

"Can't help engine trouble." The captain grimaced.

"But why Nassau?"

"We need engine parts and we have to offload cargo. Don't worry, we're not stopping long. Then on to Miami." The captain left without further explanation.

Sandy said, "That Barney is dirt. He's been looking me over ever since we came on board."

"No matter what the captain says about how good the man is with engines, packing a loaded gun makes him dangerous."

"We should get off this wreck at Nassau and away from that guy. We could fly the rest of the way from there."

"What do we use for money? My paycheck won't go that far."

Caressing his neck, she said, "It's a short hop to Miami. It wouldn't cost much and we could use your credit card so we wouldn't need the cash right away."

"What if I haven't any money a month from now when payment falls due? But you're right wanting to get away from Barney. Besides, Ash's people may greet us in Miami. So you fly."

"Not without you."

"It's the only way. I'll see you in Miami. I insist."

She nodded, resigned. "I'll do it but I'm not crazy about the idea."

Talbot sat on his bunk and thought about the stopover in Nassau. He planned to keep a watchful eye out when the ship docked. Ash was smart and he could have learned about the box and radioed the captain to delay.

Talbot decided to find a safe place to hide the duffel bag below deck later, in case someone at Nassau came on board looking for it. At the same time he knew that to keep Barney from sensing how valuable the bag's contents really were, he must appear unconcerned.

Through the remaining daylight hours the *Angora's* tired engines powered the ship at slow speed. At dusk, the engines quit again. In the silence, Talbot searched below deck for a hiding place in which to conceal the duffel bag. He avoided Barney working in the engine room. After a while Talbot quit searching. He could find no satisfactory place to stow the duffel bag and decided there was nothing he could do except wait.

He returned to his bunk, but found he could not sleep. What could he do about the box, he wondered. His teeth bit down on the inside of his lip. He could still think of nothing, but he must not lose the box. The cost of losing his job would be too great.

Chapter Eleven

St. Pierre, Haiti

Before dawn the day after the funeral of the senior Paque, Inspector Canot of the Haitian federal government left Port-au-Prince to drive north all the way to St. Pierre for the first time in his life. A tall, heavyset man in his late forties, the inspector had hair that grew mostly around his prominent ears.

The inspector was trained in the police methods which the United States had provided at no charge. Although he had been experienced in law enforcement for many years before and had no need for further training in the rudiments of police work, his supervisor insisted he take it. He discovered that the foreigners' police methods were far more cumbersome and time-consuming than his own. Instead of rounding up suspects who looked or were acting guilty or needed to be incarcerated, his Yankee training advisor considered other factors. Nor was Canot impressed with the advisor's method of securing a crime scene. Nevertheless, Canot endured the training. The extra pay came in handy.

Driving along the nearly deserted Route 100, Canot was already perspiring from the day's early heat. At last, arriving in the little village of St. Pierre, he followed protocol and paid the mandatory courtesy call on an elderly cleric who must have had exceptional connections down in Port-au-

Prince. Otherwise there was such a shortage of trained police officers that a man of Canot's experience would not have been assigned to this time-consuming effort, to what his Yankee advisor called "investigative policing." A man's death must have struck a sensitive nerve somewhere. Voodooism may have played a part.

After drinking a cup of lukewarm chicory with the local priest and hearing of the murder and robbery, the inspector drove to the outskirts of the quiet village. He walked through a gate that leaned open on broken hinges, his shrewd eyes noting a battered pail that lay rusting along with other trash and weeds. It was the kind of detailed observation his Yankee advisor would have approved.

An old shack, perched on cinder blocks, stood in the back of the yard. More weeds and trash protruded from beneath the shack itself. The inspector frowned. The property was as rundown as the inspector might expect in a poor, remote village not worth bothering about.

On approaching the shanty through the mounds of debris, he scuffed the shine on his polished shoes. He rapped on the side of the building.

"Anyone home?" he asked in his Creole French.

A pregnant black woman opened the front door and stared at him through the screen. She was panting. The exertion of getting up appeared to be too much for her pregnant body.

Canot was brusque. "I've been told Raphael Paque lives here. Get him for me."

She all but closed the door and without speaking

turned away. The inspector stood with the blistering sun on his shoulders. The heat assured the questioning would not take long.

The door opened wider. "I'm Raphael Paque," a dark man said from behind the screen door. He squinted to reduce the glare of sunlight shining into his bloodshot eyes. "What you want?" He eased his bare foot against the screen door.

The inspector's eyes followed the surreptitious move. "Don't waste your time. If I must, I will get in. I'm a Police Inspector from Port-au-Prince." Canot held out his credentials.

"Have a few questions." Inside the shack a naked child lay with children who were dressed in rags. When the front door was shut, they could suffocate in the confined heat. At the very least the children needed something to drink.

Raphael dismissed the inspector's questions with a wave of his hand. "We's in mourning."

"Can't be helped even though this may be a bad time for you. It's police work. Won't take long. I came 'bout another Paque. I guess he's the one who was murdered." The inspector raised an accusing eyebrow.

"What you saying is sick." Raphael shook his head in vigorous denial. "He was my father. Weren't no murder."

"Ah, but your father is dead. That's a fact," the inspector pressed in the officious manner of government employees.

Raphael picked at a sliver of wood on the door. "You know how my father died. It was no murder. Dere's no murderer."

Raucous cries floated down from a pair of sea gulls balanced on the peak of a nearby rooftop. The sounds filled the empty pause.

"The village elders made serious charges. You better go over the whole thing for me."

"Those do-nothing elders. Voodoo people put 'dem up to it. I know all 'bout 'dem. They quick to speak out but they have no feelings. None went to my father when he hurried through the village crying for their help. They never budged. None of 'dem."

"What made him seek help? Who threatened him?"

"No threats. We sold an ugly, old box. It'd been taking up space we needed badly.

"Grandpere loved kids and like to fool with 'dem. He'd take papers from the box and make like he was readin' everything. The kids knew he couldn't see, so he couldn't read. They knew he was only funnin', playin' games to pass the time. The kids would laugh a lot at him showing off."

A guilty look crossed Raphael's grief-stricken face. "We never knew how much he cared about that, so we sold the box with the papers." Raphael glanced down at his rumpled pants, swallowing the lump in his throat. "It gave us more room and money. We meant no harm, but Grandpere took it terrible hard."

Despite the glare from the sun, Raphael lifted his head to look up again. His reddened eyes examined the inspector's paunch through the screen door. The jacket the inspector wore did little to conceal a considerable girth. A civilian could believe the inspector got fat on his government salary.

Canot glanced at his notepad and wrote down a few words before pressing on with his questions. "Where did the robbery take place? Was it right here?" He looked again into Raphael's solemn face, watching closely for the slightest change in expression.

"What you talkin' 'bout? Those foolish elders got no business filling you up with lies like that. There was no robbery. I know that for sure. It's all what the elders like to say. That's what it is."

"What makes you certain? Why would anyone claim your father was murdered?"

"People 'round here have nothing to do. They've got no work 'cept a little fishin'. They like to gossip, have excitement. What happened was some history man from America drove here and bought the box. At the time, Grandpere was out in the village so I couldn't tell him. I knew he'd make a fuss. Only I never expected it to turn out that bad. I should have told him before."

Raphael paused, collecting himself. "The whole family agreed we sell the box. We didn't ask Grandpere because we knew he'd be against it. But in a vote he would be the only one against it. Not enough votes to keep us from selling. That's right, isn't it?"

The inspector waited, watching. His questioning method got all the answers eventually. He let the pause stretch time. "Go on."

"His heart gave out or maybe it was the curse. Many said that's what it was. The curse." Raphael wiped his hand across his eyes. Strain showed on his face. It was clear he felt responsible for what had happened to his father.

But how involved was the man? The inspector looked closely. Was there more to it than Paque was saying?

"Give me the name of the person you said bought what you call a box."

"Monsieur Talbot. Nice American. He and his woman were kind to my wife. The man's what they call an archaeologist. He's in the expedition that has offices in Port-au-Prince. Probably near your police station down there."

The inspector scribbled further in his pad. "Slick as condom jelly," he said coarsely. "That man sweet-talked you right out of your box, didn't he? Tell me, how much he pay you for the box?"

Raphael hesitated. The inspector met Raphael's hesitation with a cold stare that would accept only the truth. "How much?" the inspector. demanded again.

"He pay us two thousand dollars, American."

The inspector sucked air in between his teeth. "That's a 'siderable amount of money when you figure most people on this island don't earn four hundred dollars in a whole year, let alone two thousand. Your father's death was about money. I can see that. Lots and lots of money."

"We're a poor family and Talbot said he's gonna pay us another two thousand American, if he sells the box for enough money. He promised."

"I'd say, don't hold your breath."

"He promised and he is a good young man."

"Easy to promise."

"I believed him."

"Sounds like you people stand to make lots of money. Depends, of course, if you ever hear from the American again." The inspector wiped sweat from his forehead before making further notes.

"We'll hear from the American. Don't worry. I know it. We'll collect two thousand dollars more," Raphael said with a hopeful expression on his face, "and be rich. But no matter how much more we get, we're very sad at what happened to my father. We loved him very much."

"What a family," the inspector observed, shaking his head in disbelief. "I want to know more about the box that a stranger is willing to pay so much for. Tell me about it…"

"What's to tell?" Raphael asked in confusion.

"Weren't you surprised he paid so much?"

"Of course."

"Why would he do that?"

"Monsieur Talbot told me he was an expert. He said the markings on the box made it important."

"But anyone could have put the marks there at anytime. He took a big risk buying it, paying you that much. Why?"

"He said he wanted to be fair with us."

"Maybe he's rich like all Americans?"

"I don't think so."

"Got any pictures of the box?"

"A few," Raphael nodded solemnly. "They show it was old. That's 'bout it."

"I'll look at them." The inspector extended his hand.

Raphael balked. "What for?"

"The pictures. Get me the pictures." The hand remained outstretched.

Raphael walked away from the door. Through the

opening in it the inspector watched the children. They were awake but silent. Watchful. A government man stood close by.

Raphael returned with three photographs.

"What exactly was in this box?" Canot asked, studying the photos one by one.

Raphael shrugged. "Old papers. An old man's dreams. Who could tell if they were more than that? We can't read too well."

"Stop. You can't read at all. Are you quite certain nobody read these papers?"

"No one ever did...It would have spoiled Grandpere's fun. As long as nobody read them, he had his games with the children and his dreams. He just made like he could read."

"I can't understand people plunking down so much money for child's play, not knowing what the papers said 'n all. There's got to be more to it."

"Well," Talbot paid us. He must've known something. He carefully examined everything for a long time. But you don't expect me to tell you more. I did not study the papers. I don't know what he knew or saw. All I know is he paid us the money and he carried the box away."

"You're sure you had no idea what words were on the papers? You have copies of any of them?"

Raphael disappeared from the doorway and returned with photocopies of two pages. He handed them over to the inspector.

The inspector saw the writings were not in French, which was the only language be knew. They were in some foreign language. He took another tack. "You should have shown the box to the authorities down in Port-au-Prince, if it's as old as it looks. They would know about such things or could find out about them."

"Why should I do that? So the government could take it away from us?" Raphael huffed, his voice filled with sarcasm. His face stiffened. "The loss would've hurt Grandpere just as much and our family would have been paid nuthin'."

"Still, you should've told us in Port-au-Prince about the box. One day you people will learn to obey the law. Where did it come from?"

"Can't be sure. It's been around for so long. My father told us according to what he heard it was buried in the sand at the back of a beach not far from here. Only part of it stuck out."

"Washed up on shore, do you think?"

"Probably washed up on shore during a storm if it wasn't sunk too far out. But it was away from the water so maybe somebody carried it off the beach and buried it."

"How old would you say it was?"

"No idea. Talbot thought it could be hundreds and hundreds of years old. He a great man. Knows many things."

"Talbot knows how old it is, but you don't. Is it because it's hard for you to count that high?" the inspector scoffed. "But it was very old, something the government should know about. Did the person who bought it speak to your father?" The inspector's voice became slippery to help Raphael's last answers slide out easily.

"He never saw my father. Talbot bought the box and took it away hours before my father came home. They never met. I told my father about it afterwards."

The inspector closed his note pad and put it away. Pointing to the copies and pictures in his other hand, he said, "I'll make some copies and mail these back to you in a few days."

Raphael shrugged.

"If you think of anything else, call me. Use the same numbers on the telephone that you see on this card. There will be no charge."

Raphael accepted the business card without looking at it.

"One other thing," the inspector said without compassion as he swung back to confront Raphael, who remained with the sun shining in his eyes. "Sounds like you, all by yourself, made the deal with Talbot. By any chance did he pay you a little something extra? For your trouble did you receive a bonus you're not sharing with the rest of the family? Say another fifty dollars or so...American?"

For a fleeting moment the answer passed over Raphael's embarrassed face before his denial. Then he slammed the inside door shut on the inspector.

Canot raised his voice loud enough to be heard through the thin door. "I'll be sure to keep this case open for a while, Mr. Paque."

Walking away from the shack, Canot headed down the lane to question other villagers although it was clear under the new police guidelines, no homicide had taken place for which anyone could be arraigned.

Canot wondered, what about the people of Haiti? Had they lost a valuable piece of their heritage? Was something important enough to revive Haiti's non-existent tourist industry whisked out of the republic? If the foreigner paid two thousand dollars American for the box and the papers and may pay another two thousand, they must be worth a whole lot more. Haiti's loss could be huge. By taking advantage of Haiti's unsettled times, the stranger could have committed a crime against the republic. But deciding what that crime might be was for another government department to make a decision on. It would not be a question that Inspector Canot would look into.

After standing out in the hot sun for much of the early afternoon, questioning other villagers, many of them adherents of voodooism, Canot confirmed that Grandfather Paque died of natural causes beyond a doubt. No one had laid a felonious hand on him. The people had called for an investigation because they wanted the box returned to their village. There was mention of a curse if that did not happen. The new owner had better be careful.

It was troubling that the box and its papers were so valuable they were worth the death of a poor old man. Inspector Canot headed back down to Port-au-Prince with plenty of time to chew the bread and berries his wife had wrapped for him.

A curse upon the new owner of the ancient box and its papers.

Chapter Twelve

Port-au-Prince

The next morning in Port-au-Prince, Inspector Canot completed his report on the deceased Paque and pulled out the address of Southern State Museum from his battered files before driving over to the museum's local headquarters.

When he entered the suite of offices, a slurping sound assailed him from across the room. A man with thin shoulders hunched over a cluttered desk, dividing his attention between running his fingers over a juicy mango and studying a column of figures in a thick ledger. Once in a while the man turned a page and paused to blot a puddle of juice with his dirty shirt sleeve. He appeared to lose track of a number or two in the process. He was probably the bookkeeper.

Canot walked to the desk. Standing in front of the bookkeeper, Canot waited, giving the other man time to find a good place to interrupt what he was doing. When the bookkeeper continued to ignore his visitor, Canot reached across and seized the top of the ledger. In a swift motion, he rotated the hard, stiff cover, slamming it down on the other man's fingers, trapping them between the pages. Canot leaned on the cover with his considerable weight, crushing those fingers among the pages. Canot gave the cover a vigorous push.

"Ow!" the bookkeeper howled. "What the hell do you think you're doing?"

The inspector straightened up, releasing the ledger's cover. "Sorry to have to be so rude, my humble friend, but it appears you have been so busy you never learned that rudeness begets rudeness. You have a guest. Please show me some courtesy. You do have time for that, don't you?"

"I was warned the natives could be a pain in the ass." The bookkeeper extracted his bruised fingers from the ledger and massaged them gently.

"Listen, we Haitians aren't natives, as you so charmingly call us. We're people, like everyone else." Canot moved around behind the other man and headed for the private office beyond.

Getting up, the bookkeeper shouted, "Hold it! Where do you think you're going?"

"To see the man in charge." Canot pointed towards the open door. "Certainly that can't be you."

The bookkeeper attempted to block the inspector. "What do you want to see him about?"

Tired from his long drive the day before, Canot flipped out his police identification. "I'll see whoever is in charge, now."

Ash materialized in the doorway, a cigarette dangling from his lips. "I'll take it, Harris. You can get back to your numbers. He turned to Canot. "I'm Buddy Ash. You wanted to see me about something?"

"Inspector Canot." He flashed his ID card. "May I come in?"

"Yes, of course." Ash nodded and stood aside, then

closed the door behind them. He returned to his desk, gesturing the inspector to take a seat. He placed a report over some magazines that lay on the top of his desk.

"You look warm," Canot observed. "Doesn't our climate agree with you when the electricity goes off?"

Ash shrugged as though the heat were of no consequence. "What exactly brings you to our offices, Inspector?"

"Some questions." Canot glanced around the office. The American's place with its dirt and cobwebs was no better than most offices around the city. "How are your archaeologists doing out at the museum's excavation site?"

"Not as well as our home office in Florida hoped." Buddy Ash took a drag on his cigarette, then exhaled, watching a poorly formed smoke ring hang in the air.

"Do you have a man by the name of Talbot working for you?"

Ash leaned forward, stroking his chin. "Why? Is he in some kind of trouble? Has he caused problems for the police?"

The inspector ignored the questions. "Did you send Talbot up north looking for relics?"

"No, certainly not," Ash said in a puzzled tone, shaking his head. "It's not the way we work. We have a permit covering only the area where our camp is, as you undoubtedly know, Inspector."

"Was Dr. Talbot assigned to look around St. Pierre?"

"I don't know the place but, no, he wasn't assigned there. None of our men are. Not lately. Not ever. And we didn't assign Talbot to any place near there either. Up north, eh?"

"Are you interested in ancient things?"

"You sound skeptical, Inspector, yet that's our whole business. However, there's ancient and there's ancient. How ancient are you talking about?"

"People up in St. Pierre claim the Paques owned an ancient box. They said it was hundreds and hundreds of years old. Does that sound ancient to you?"

"How interesting…if true. Some people say things that are not completely accurate, particularly if they believe they will profit from what they say."

"Still these people strike me as honest. They don't claim to have owned the old box all that time."

"What do they claim?"

"They say it was buried in the sand near the coast. Their ancestors discovered it about a hundred fifty years ago."

"The ones telling this tale didn't find it themselves? I think I'd like to see such a box with my own two eyes before I believed that it was so old. What proof do you have it is as old as they say?"

The inspector slid photographs from an envelope and spread them out on the desk. "Look at these. You're an expert. Venture a guess as to how old the box is."

Ash showed a thin smile of annoyance, then assumed a blank expression before picking up the photos. He brought them close to his eyes, taking his time to examine each one.

Canot noted a glimmer of interest light up Ash's face. It disappeared in a flash.

"I hate to disappoint you," Ash said, handing the pictures back. "They're in black and white. What's more, everything is so tiny. Makes the detail impossible to read. Really, I can't tell you anything. Besides, I prefer not to guess without seeing it." Ash's voice held a note of excitement he was unable to hide completely.

"But an expert would reach for his magnifying glass. Don't you have one?"

"I might have one or two. But not for these pictures. They're much too small."

The inspector heaved a sigh of frustration. He took two photocopies from the envelope and placed them in front from of Ash. "Look at these. They're papers from inside the box. What do you see?"

Ash picked them up and scrutinized them. "Not much I can tell you about these either. They're in a foreign language. Looks like old Spanish, if that's any help. They're handwritten. And that's about all I can say without hiring an expert to translate them." He passed the photocopies back.

"You wouldn't have any idea why your man purchased them?"

Ash choked. "You're telling me Talbot bought these?"

The inspector nodded. "And the box they came in."

"I don't know why Talbot would do such a thing. He's young, inexperienced. Maybe the damn fool bought them as gifts for his female friend."

"I don't think so. Talbot paid thousands of dollars for everything. So he wasn't exactly buying trinkets or souvenirs at those prices. They're more like things my government would want to examine thoroughly. We may be talking about valuable artifacts. You should have turned them over to us. Where do I find this Talbot?"

"I think you'll find he's already cleared out. He and some woman are headed for the States. However, if he took what you say and he didn't get government clearance, he did it on his own. Southern State Museum had absolutely nothing to do with that."

"Mr. Ash, we need your cooperation in finding Dr. Talbot and the box. Otherwise my government will take serious steps against your whole team of archaeologists, as well as against Southern State Museum. Steps you would not like to see us take."

"I understand. Rest assured you'll get our full cooperation on this. Threats aren't necessary."

"Got an address for Talbot in the States?"

"Not that I know of...Oh, wait, I think he lived in New York City with his mother and sister."

"You said there was a woman with him but the New York address is for when he lived with his mother and sister. Did the woman live there as well?"

"I never thought of that. Perhaps the New York address is not too helpful. On the other hand, his mother may be able to give you a better address."

"I'll need a full description of him as well as his New York address."

"Out front, Harris can give you both of those. Locally, Talbot lived at the camp."

"I don't suppose Talbot left a forwarding address?"

"Not that I know of. I'll ask Harris to give you a copy

of Talbot's picture that we keep in our personnel files. I want to be as helpful as I can be."

"I'm sure you do," the inspector said, tongue in cheek. There was nothing more to say.

Ash rose from his desk and escorted the inspector out to the front office, instructing Harris to give the guest a copy of Talbot's picture and the New York City home address.

"Oh, by the way, Inspector, do you mind letting Harris make a copy of your things? Won't take a minute."

"Not at all, even though you didn't seem to think they amounted to much before when you looked at them at your desk."

Ash shrugged. "You never know."

"Well, in case something occurs to you later..." The inspector gave Ash one of his business cards. "Call me anytime you get information."

"Yes," Ash said over his shoulder, returning to his own office, "I'll be sure to do that."

After making the copies, Harris handed the papers and photos back to the inspector who put them in his envelope and departed.

"Well?" Harris asked, entering Ash's office, "learn anything useful from the Inspector?"

"I didn't want to look too interested by asking a lot of fool questions, but I spotted what must have had young Talbot drooling all over himself."

"I thought you told the Inspector you couldn't make out anything?"

"C'mon, now," Ash laughed harshly. "Do I look that

stupid? Please give your boss some credit." He ran his hand through his sweaty hair and sat back to light a cigarette.

"Look at this copy showing the side of the box." He pointed. "In the old days that was the insignia of a Spanish monarch. And because the decoration looks a bit frilly, my guess is the box belonged to a lady monarch. Go back centuries. One woman who was a Spanish monarch was the Queen of the Spains, Queen Isabella.

"She could have given it to Columbus as a keepsake on his return from his first voyage, especially after she heard his imaginative stories of what he had seen. When Columbus sailed on his second voyage to Haiti, he might have brought the box along to show the authority the Spanish throne bestowed on him. For that second trip the Admiral commanded a grand flotilla. In setting up a colony here, the box could have gotten lost."

"Is it possible Talbot could have stumbled onto something that big?" Harris gasped. He moved closer to examine the copies further. He looked over at Ash. "Are you thinking the same thing I am?"

"Who knows? I'm giving you my first guess. I'd like someone to translate the papers that were inside the box. Meanwhile you're going up north to find out what you can. When you finish cooking those numbers and doing a few other things around here, I want you to haul your ass up to St. Pierre. Dig around. Find out what family Talbot bought the box from. What he paid for it. Get a complete description of the other papers. And generally learn whatever you can about the box and the papers and where they came from."

"You're maybe thinking you shouldn't have fired Talbot?" Harris asked.

"Not fired him?" Buddy Ash sputtered. "I should have shot the son of a bitch. He had that firing coming to him."

To show his contempt, Ash jerked his arm up, knocking a pack of cigarettes to the floor. "What the hell, of course he had to go." Ash bent over collecting the scattered cigarettes. "Besides it improves my budget to get rid of him."

"Not by much."

Ash's mood darkened. "He's using up his goddamn beginner's luck. What a waste. But stay out of it. Don't you open your mouth, and go whispering in the Inspector's ear. You got that?"

"Very clear. I won't breathe a word to the Inspector," Harris said. "I don't know why you even think I might say anything to him. Getting back to our friend, Dr. Talbot...firing him so soon after he started working for the museum could wreck his whole career. I was thinking it might be rough on the new guy."

"Don't you think you know it all? Why don't you keep your big nose out of my business?"

Harris grinned, looking unperturbed. "If I keep my nose away, that still leaves me my eyes and ears. They've been open like you asked me. Think the folks in Miami would like to hear about this and how you canned the poor, young joker who just made an important find?"

"We don't know for sure that it's important yet, so shut the hell up. And don't even think about blabbing to Miami if you value your skin. But..." Ash paused. "Why take chances? Let's assume my first impression was correct and the box is important. Maybe we didn't fire Talbot after all…That's it," he said, snapping his fingers, "we didn't dump him like heartless bastards. No, we gave him compassionate home leave. How does that sound?"

"Like you're a very caring manager."

A triumphant expression brightened Ash's face. "I believe I like that. Being in a strange land with a different climate and all, can affect a young man, particularly when his young lady friend has a tough time adjusting, as I've heard that his Sandy was having. Get this, we gave Talbot some extra vacation time to collect himself. Keep him on the payroll. See to it. Fix the books. He may not know it right away, but he acquired the box when he was still a museum employee, so he bought it in behalf of the museum. And if we work it right, he may have acquired the box for our own private little business. We'll see."

"Right." Harris began to laugh, his eyes alight with enthusiasm. "Want me to put through a call to the supply ship? It still hasn't docked in Miami as far as I know. You could talk to Talbot on the ship-to-shore radio. Give him the good news that he really wasn't fired. It was just a little mix-up. He should come back."

"That's exactly the wrong thing to do," Ash said, shaking his head. "He'd know in a second what I'm thinking and he'd disappear with the box. Let's not do anything rash and foolish."

"We could call the ship anyway and tell the skipper to hold Talbot for us."

"Forget that. The ship is too small to guarantee that our radio contact could be kept confidential, especially if the signal starts to break up and we get into a shouting match. We know Talbot is gonna be jumpy. The sound of a call from us will set him running and we'd lose the box. No, I'll call ahead to Miami and get Joey to help take care of this up there at that end."

Harris shrugged. "Just a suggestion. You're the boss."

"I'll catch a flight to Miami later today. The museum owes me a plane ticket and a few days in the States. High time I used them. And don't you spend too much time up at St. Pierre. Get right back and keep an eye on things around here. Tell the men out at camp to keep a lid on whatever they turn up at the excavation. I'll want to be the first to examine everything when I get back."

"Think you'll get Talbot? He acts pretty sharp."

"I'll get the goddamned box is what I'll get. Turn off the chatter now. It's getting on my nerves."

"Well, mon, it looks like this place ain't all one-eyed pirates and bongo drums after all. I'll finish the books." Harris hurried out.

Ash put his feet up on a battered wastepaper basket beside his desk and lit another cigarette. He fingered the copies of the two documents, then searched through his files for the numbers to call at the museum in Miami to get things rolling.

Chapter Thirteen

Preparations For The Reception

Ash stood in the front office studying a report when the telephone rang. He put the report down and rushed back into his own office, stretching across his desk to pick up the receiver.

"Mr. Ash? This is Joey, the guard in Miami. You trying to reach me?"

"That's right, Joey, I was. Give me a second to catch my breath." Ash paused, breathing hard. "How's one of Southern State's finest?"

"Not bad. Doin' okay. You got something you want me to handle?"

"Yes, I tried to reach you earlier because there's a red hot problem tracking your way. One of our guys down here ran off with valuable museum property. We need your expert assistance."

Ash circled around his desk while pressing the phone against his ear. He wiped sweat from his forehead and fell into his chair, propping his feet up on the wastepaper basket.

"Always glad to help out. So tell me what do you want me to do, Mr. Ash?"

"First, I have to impress on you this is very hush hush. You've gotta keep it to yourself. Do you understand?"

"Yessir, I certainly do."

"Our new archaeologist ran off with a valuable, old

wood box that belongs to the museum. The shit pulled a fast one on a couple of the natives down here. He probably thinks we don't know about it. Anyway it gets complicated because it's not exactly from our excavation site. You still there?" Ash covered the phone while he coughed.

"I'm listening. Just tell me what I have to do."

"I'm coming to that. You'll be like moonlighting. I'll take care of your overtime myself. The archaeologist is a young guy by the name of Don Talbot. He never worked for the museum in Miami, so you wouldn't know him. But he and his girlfriend are bringing this antique box into the States on our supply ship, the *Angora.*"

Ash grabbed his chest. He dropped his feet to the floor and swung forward in his seat, resting his elbows on the desk to relieve the pain.

"You want I should meet them at the dock and get the box back for you?" Joey asked.

Ash took his time and lit a cigarette. He waved the smoke away. "That's it in a nutshell," he said having trouble catching his breath. He was sweating. "There are details we can go over when I get up to Miami." His voice sounded strained. "What say I take us to dinner tonight and we talk about the details over a couple juicy steaks and baked potatoes?"

"That's fine by me. Is this Talbot still on our payroll?"

"Sure is. We gave him compassionate home leave and this is how he says thank you. Just terrible." Ash smiled at the phone in his hand. "I'll bring his picture along."

"And a picture of the box he's trying to sneak off with, if you have one. By the way, the museum is changing exhibits today so if you want, I can have them leave room to display this box in?"

Ash smoldered. "No, nothing like that. Don't you understand, this is a confidential matter that you are to keep quiet."

Joey giggled. "Mr. Ash, I was only joking."

"Had me fooled for a minute, but understand I'm talking just the two of us are in on this, very hush hush."

"You know me. I always keep things confidential. Anything I have to do now?"

"Like I said, the young man and his girl are on the *Angora* headed your way, but you know how slow that boat is. You've got lots of time. Don't do anything 'til I get there. I'll be on the next flight out of here. I'm renting a car so I'll pick you up at your place around six-thirty. Still living at the same place?"

"Yep. Three blocks from the museum. Sounds great. See you tonight. I'll have a drink waiting for you."

"Fine. Would you have the operator switch me over to Miss Gurney?"

After a short wait Ash heard the connection being made.

"Miss Gurney speaking."

"Hello, Miss Gurney, this is Buddy Ash down in Port-au-Prince. Haven't forgotten me, have you?"

"Why, no, Mr. Ash. Nice to hear your voice. Something I can help you with?"

"I have to ask you for a big favor. I need you to translate two documents for me. They're in old Spanish and handwritten. I have to have them by tomorrow morning."

"Well, you know I would certainly like to do what I can, Mr. Ash, but this doesn't give me much notice. Does it have to be tomorrow morning?"

"It's a must. Sorry about that, but it's real urgent. You know how that can be. I'll fax copies to you so they'll be in your hands later today. I'll stop by your office in the morning to see what you've made of them. Only it's vital you keep this very confidential for the time being."

"Of course I'll do that. You're in Haiti, you say?"

"Yes, but I'm flying up this afternoon."

"Anything special I should know about these documents?"

"Not an awful lot is known. They were found in a box on the northwestern coast here a long time ago and they're in old Spanish, your specialty. That's it."

"All right. I'll see what I can do. Better look in on me around eleven o'clock."

"Thanks. I'll fax 'em up today and see you tomorrow morning. Very good of you. Adios, Señorita."

"Adios, Señor Ash."

Harris worked over the books in the front office when Ash shouted to him, "Get in here."

"Want me to do something more?"

"I need you to fax these pages to Miss Gurney up at the Miami museum. Send them to her personal. The electric power seems to be back on now so everything's working at the moment."

Harris stood in the doorway, nodding. His face glowed with a warm smile. "Of course you'll save me a bone out of all this, I hope."

"Don't I always? Remember, we have to cut Joey in if this amounts to anything. But let's work on giving Talbot the surprise of his life before you start sniffing around for bones."

Harris threw his boss a mock salute. "Yessir."

"When you finish with the fax machine, if you're ready to go to St. Pierre, you can drop me off at the airport."

In another part of the capital city, the overseas telephone operator put Inspector Canot through to the Florida Department of State located in Tallahassee.

"*Bonjour*, M'sieur Jackson. This is Inspector Canot in Haiti. Are you still preserving Florida's historic resources and handing out permits to excavate state lands?"

"That about covers it," Jackson laughed. "What's up, *mon ami*? How's the mysterious 'high land' that you people call Haiti in your strange language?"

"Haiti needs some reciprocal cooperation. I know this isn't a matter for the State of Florida, but I thought you might still have contacts with the feds in customs. We've got a problem tracking your way."

"You talkin' dope or voodoo dolls?"

"I know the difference between a Drug Enforcement matter and what customs agents like to get their hands on. It's an old box filled with documents. It's a piece of our republic's history."

"Let me guess. No one's authorized taking it out of Haiti, so your culprit is planning to transport unlicensed goods into the States?"

"Something like that. He'll sail into Miami shortly."

"You say something like that. You know U.S. laws can be tricky."

"I'm saying one of your countrymen hoodwinked a Haitian family and walked off with a slice of our heritage. Can you get somebody from the customs department to pick him up? That's all I'm asking." The inspector stirred a mug of hot, black coffee that sat on the desk blotter in front of him.

"I guess I could get one of the feds to confiscate the stuff for you. But why are you interested in this? How much can an old box and documents be worth?"

"A bright, young archaeologist plunked down two thousand American dollars of his own money for them. That makes it of serious interest unless the man's lost his mind. And the head of the archaeology expedition that's working down here, a Mr. Ash, tried to conceal the fact there was something to it. Not much to go on but I've got a feeling about this one." His voice turned ice cold. "Haiti wants it back."

"That's okay with me. Tell me, what does the box look like?"

"I'll do better than that. I'll fax you everything I've got including some views of the box and the documents and a copy of Talbot's picture. He's the guy who ran off with everything. You'll get details about where and when the boat docks, the works. The fed man shouldn't have any trouble." His tired eyes squinted at the steam rising from his coffee mug.

"Okay, my friend, I know you don't want this call to cost you too many gourdes so I'll sit tight until I receive the stuff, then pass it along to the right person."

"You'll have it all within the hour. *Merci biên*, and as

your colleagues say, I owe you one."

"That will be fine, 'cause I'll be traveling down your way one of these days real soon to collect. You coming to the States for the reception of this Talbot?"

"Wouldn't want to miss it. But I can't stay long. In and out. Haiti is hurting. I must get back."

"I'll tell my friend in customs so he can meet you at the dock. It'll probably be a fella by the name of Agent Cole. A good man. He's been around. Give me a call tomorrow. I'll know for sure by then. Maybe he will want to meet you someplace besides at the dock."

"Great. Thanks again."

"Keep in touch, *mon ami.*"

"Will do," Inspector Canot said and hung up. The inspector's tenacity would have impressed his American police trainer.

Chapter Fourteen

Steamy Love Letters

From the fax machine Charlie Jackson carried the copies of the two letters and views of the ancient box down a hall at the State Capitol Building in Tallahassee, Florida. Jackson, a tall, lanky, state government employee, walked whenever he could rather than sit behind his desk. He entered the office of a female employee born in Puerto Rico.

"Señorita Marie, *buenas días*. I hate to disturb you."

She looked up. "Yes, what is it?"

"Could you lend a hand and translate these two pages as best you can? They came in the box you see in these faxes."

Jackson set the facsimiles on her desk. "I'd like to have them pronto. *¿Por favor?*"

"Of course you think I have nothing better to do than work on these things?" she said looking over the copies.

Jackson made a sour face. "I know you move so fast on everything you do, you will be able to squeeze these in with your other work."

"When you say please so nicely, how can I refuse? I'll take a look. No promises. You want to tell me anything about what I'll be translating so I have a clue as to what I'm supposed to be working on or do you prefer to keep me in the dark? This is hardly modern Spanish."

"All I can tell you is that the letters may have been found on the northern coast of Haiti. I know that's not much to go on. They're a couple pages a friend of mine got hold of. Met him at a university seminar." He shrugged. "Nice guy. I'd like to help him out."

"Okay, come back in a couple of hours. I'll see what I can do if I don't have any more interruptions."

"Terrific. Anything you say, Señorita. *Muchas gracias.*" Jackson grinned. He was obvious in noting the time on his watch. "Two hours it shall be."

After looking at his watch many, many times Jackson picked up his phone. "Hello, Marie? Only checking, hon, but the two hours you requested are up. Okay if I stop by your office?"

"I don't know what kind of stupid crap you're trying to pull on me, but, yeah, you better stop by, fast!" There was anger in her voice rather than the usual music.

Jackson walked with long strides down the hall. Entering through her open door, he asked, "All right for me to come in, Señorita?"

"You lecher!" she cried out.

"Got cramps? What's the matter?"

"Thought you were dealing with some foxy lady, didn't you?" She scowled. "Well, that's not me."

"I can't believe this. You serious? Tell me what's your problem."

"These pages...I translated enough words. What I think they mean makes one of them read like a juicy love letter. Parts of it are trash." She sounded embarrassed. Her face looked like she tasted something rotten.

"Listen to me a minute, please. This was on the level. You're a great gal, and I wasn't trying to pull anything on you."

She appeared to calm down. "Tell me again, where'd you get this stuff?"

"From Haiti, where they speak French Creole. I knew enough to see these writings were in Spanish, not French, so I thought of you. End of story. What've you got?"

"What I've got is some wicked lady writing to a horse. At least she calls it...a horse. I believe she's thinking of a macho guy whose appendage resembles that of a horse. Must be kinda prominent at times. And he's servicing the woman with it."

"I had no idea when I gave you those papers. Who is the lady, do you think?"

"You sure this is no joke?"

"I swear." His heart began to pound.

"Well, I haven't figured out who the lady is yet," she said slowly as a new thought appeared to cross her mind.

"You just thought of someone. Who?"

She pursed her lips. "You said these papers came from Haiti. Haiti was first settled by the Spanish. I've studied the markings on the box in that copy of a photograph you gave me. If that's the box, it was a special one constructed for Spanish royalty and there's a chance I know who wrote those letters. It's a wild, far-out guess." She paused. "I'd say if those letters are old enough, Queen Isabella wrote them." Marie put her hand to her mouth to cover the surprise at hearing herself express such a possibility.

Jackson leaned forward as excited as Marie. "*Madre de*

Dios, I'm in awe. That would be something," he said, his face lighting up. "Couldn't get more Spanish than that."

Marie's face grew somber as she sat looking at him. "That's just a guess."

"I understand, but you think that's not good?"

"If I'm right, the Spanish people will hate it when those letters are released, especially at such time the scandal sheets get hold of them. People in Spain would go wild. That one letter is real hot filth."

"You're saying some guy had his way with the Queen?"

"Looks that way, and the Vatican won't like it because she was a good Catholic queen. These letters will ruin her reputation. It's something for you and your friend to think about before going public with your findings."

"Okay, but that means some Spanish official would turn somersaults to keep them out of the press." He collected the fax copies from her desk along with her notes. "I owe you one, Señorita. A very big one."

"If you're talking dirty, forget it. If you're talking dinner, make it soon and I'm not settling for any hamburgers."

"*Adios* and thanks a bunch."

"Keep me posted."

"Sure will."

That evening at Something to Beef About, a Miami restaurant whose reputation rested on its unmatched New York strip steaks, Ash was sipping a third martini when a fit of coughing began. With a look of grave concern, Joey the guard said, "I don't think sitting in the smoking section is such a good idea, Mr. Ash."

Between coughs Ash put out his hand. "It's all right. I'll be fine. Just give me a minute." Further coughing shook his whole body.

"You sure?" Joey asked with alarm.

"A little congestion. That's all. Not used to this good Florida air anymore." He recovered from his coughing and looked over. "See, I'm fine, really." His laugh sounded a bit thin.

"You had me worried for a minute." Concern remained on Joey's face.

"It's nothing. Comes and goes."

"Whatever you say."

"Did you see when the *Angora* is supposed to dock?"

"It's posted on the bulletin board. Tomorrow night around eleven o'clock. A couple of earlier dates have been scratched out."

"Let's be at the pier say two hours before, in case she docks early."

"That's all right with me."

"Wear your guard's uniform and carry a nightstick and a flashlight. Here's a picture of the box we're after. Look for those markings on the lid." Ash pointed.

"What's in it? Is it gonna be heavy?"

"Can't be all that heavy. Only has papers inside."

They interrupted their conversation while the waiter served juicy steaks with baked potatoes split open, their steaming halves filled with melting butter and sour cream. The waiter placed green salads beside the main dishes.

Ash rubbed his hands together and coughed once. "Smells delicious. I'm starved. Let's eat." He drank off his martini in one gulp and slammed the empty cocktail glass down to pick up his fork and steak knife.

The *Angora* took an extra twenty-four hours to sail up along the string of Bahama Islands, stopping numerous times to make engine repairs. At dawn it reached New Providence Island and limped into the port city of Nassau, capital of the Bahama Island group.

* * *

Talbot went up to the bow of the *Angora* and looked ahead as the captain guided the ship into Nassau Harbor and tied up back of a dirty, open air market. The smell of rotting fish mingled with the smell of low tide.

Talbot glanced around. No one stood casually nearby, waiting to come aboard. No trap had been set. Perhaps Ash was unable to move that fast. At least there was no one to hide the wooden box from. Talbot relaxed.

Sandy joined Talbot on deck.

"Let's go ashore and get something to eat." Talbot's voice was loud enough to be overheard by the captain, who was folding his charts and stuffing them in their clear plastic envelopes.

"All set?" Sandy smiled.

"All set," Talbot echoed. "You lock our cabin?"

"Yes, of course." Her face crinkled with an impish grin.

In a booming voice the captain called out to them, "Don't go too far away, you two. We're not staying in port for more than a few hours."

"Only going for some breakfast." Talbot pointed to his

stomach. "If we can find a place that's open. Be back soon."

Talbot helped Sandy hop over the mooring lines Barney had put out and the couple waved to the captain from the dock as they walked away. In one hand Sandy carried a plastic shopping bag containing copies of the letters that were in the ancient box. Some of her clothes were also crammed in.

When they were out of sight of the ship, Talbot said, "Say hello to your folks for me, Sandy. Too bad you're gonna miss the rest of our balmy cruise."

"Wish you were flying with me. Sure you don't want to go? Now that you've spent my savings, you want us to split up."

"You know that's not true. For what I have in mind it's probably best we're splitting up because we'll have a better chance of getting into Miami without attracting a lot of attention.

"The time you spent on that dumpy ship seemed to do you a lot of good. You look much happier than you did back in camp."

She laughed. "I guess it shows I'm glad to get away from creeps like your old boss and Barney. Best of all, I'm excited about those letters you bought. Whatever you do, don't let Barney go near the originals in the wood box. I'm sure he'll come snooping before you dock in Miami."

"Don't worry. I'll never be far from the cabin. How're your legs doin'?"

"Some days they're pretty bad. Today is one of those days. Don't worry. I'll manage." She smiled. They found a taxi to take Sandy to the airport. She waved goodbye.

Talbot returned to the docks. He entered a cafe where he took a seat with a view of the *Angora* and ordered a pastry and a cup of coffee. Consuming them slowly, he watched the ship.

He would remain in the cafe until the captain left to call on the harbor master. Then Talbot would note where Barney was working and avoid him when ducking back on board the ship. That way neither the captain nor Barney would know that she had failed to come back aboard with him. For the rest of the voyage the two men would think Sandy had remained cooped up in her cabin simply to avoid Barney and not cause any friction.

Talbot ordered another cup of coffee and continued to watch the *Angora*.

At eleven o'clock that same morning Ash called on Miss Gurney in her tiny office on the second floor of the Southern State Museum. The office appeared crowded, with bulging files leaving little room for the occupant to move around in. Ash smiled at the woman behind the desk. "Good to see you again, Miss Gurney. Has the museum's leading paleographer been keeping well?"

Miss Gurney was a small woman who wore her hair in an old fashioned bun. A pair of thick reading glasses hung around her neck. She nodded. "Hello, Mr. Ash. I've been keeping quite well. Thank you for inquiring."

"Get my two pages all right?"

"Sure did. No problem." She rose, picking up the two fax copies.

"What would you say if Queen Isabella wrote them?"

She grinned, excited. "Dynamite. Sheer dynamite all

ready to explode. I must tell you the tabloids would have a field day with those letters. The editors would pay a fortune to get their soiled little hands on lurid material like that." She dangled a copy in each hand.

"One is a torrid love letter with a capital 'T'. The other letter is more romantic. You better read my translations of those letters because if I read them aloud, I'd have to wash my mouth out with soap afterwards." She put down the fax copies and handed him her notes.

He read through them quickly. "Takes my breath away," he said laughing. "Sensational. You've got a way with words."

"Not my words at all. I found both letters exciting as hell. Mr. Ash, you have no idea what you have come across."

"Coming from you, that says a lot. Do you think an editor would feel the same way, even though these letters are ancient history?"

"They may have been kept dormant but bear in mind who wrote them. What history. Oh, yes, an editor would love to get his or her hands on these things. Just one editor with an exclusive would pay plenty."

Ash smiled again.

"Reading these letters," Miss Gurney said, "is like listening in on a phone conversation. It's immediate, a spectacular thrill. Here is an adulterous love affair. The writer, a woman, is madly in love. These letters will fascinate people worldwide."

"What're you saying?"

"I figure you have royal love letters written by a

woman who felt free enough to speak her mind and she adored the man she wrote to. Like a moth who couldn't stay away from the bright flame, she was strongly attracted to him. She doesn't hide her attraction. For a Spanish woman not to be more circumspect is highly unusual. The writer has to be high up, a royal person. She writes with such abandon even though the letters are supposed to be private. She was taking a chance. Do you have the originals?"

A broad smile spread over his face. "The wood box pictured in the fax I sent to you could hold a lot of those lewd beauties. All originals. They'll arrive in Miami very soon. But to answer your question, I don't have them right now." He beamed.

"Mr. Ash, look me in the eye. I'd give anything for one of those letters. Anything at all. Why don't you stop by my apartment for dinner after you get them? Tonight, maybe?"

"Sorry, I've already committed to some plans. Otherwise, a dinner at your place sounds good."

"Well, think about it and if you change your mind, give me a call."

"I certainly will."

"If you were to sell those letters…you're talking about a lot of money."

"Let's not count our chickens just yet." His voice softened. "And let's keep this just to ourselves for the time being."

"I most certainly will. You're thinking you maybe don't want to take them public right away?"

"Maybe never."

"A private sale?"

"Perhaps, if the price is right. But keep such thoughts to yourself."

"Happy to do that, and I can all but guarantee those soiled wonders will command a magnificent price. They are an astonishing treasure. I'll put your fax in here with my notes." She handed him an envelope. "I got so wrapped up in those letters, I stayed here after hours last night working on them."

"I appreciate that. You've been a terrific help."

"Kind of you to mention it."

He slipped the envelope under his arm and turned to leave.

She stepped close to him to open the door of the tiny space. Her blouse gave off a sweet perfume when she brushed against him. Offering a warm smile, she said goodbye. Then, lowering her voice, she whispered close to his ear, "Those are some kind of hot letters."

"I'll be in touch, don't you worry," Ash said before he went out into the hall.

"Don't forget me now," she urged with an arch flutter of her eyelids. "I'd love to see the rest of those fascinating letters when they arrive. I know the name of at least one collector who would be very interested in buying them from you. He would come up with the right price, I'm sure. Dealing directly with him in a private sale, you would skip the fee of an agent or of an auctioneer. I could produce a translation that positively sizzled."

"I'll keep what you have said in mind, Miss Gurney. Thanks again and please don't mention this to anyone, particularly around here."

"You already have my word on that." She smiled. Her mouth took a saucy turn. She brushed against his jacket again and left behind a lovely scent of lavender. It was a strong, fresh fragrance, as though she had just dabbed it on before he arrived.

The laugh lines in his face crinkled. He said, "I have options: I could make the letters available to the museum if it wanted to make me its director and I could be an important, much sought-after speaker at professional meetings, or...I can go private with everything. Either way I'd be very rich, leaving my colleagues far behind." It sounded as though his future would become bright as soon as he had his hands on the box and the letters.

When Ash left the confines of Miss Gurney's office, he was so intent on leaving the building that he was looking down at the carpet when he walked right past a longtime associate director of the museum who was also walking down the hall. Ash never noticed the man's mouth drop open as though to greet him and failed to see the look of disappointment on the face of the man whom he had slighted by failing to stop and exchange a few pleasantries.

The associate director looked surprised to see Ash in Miami. He closed his mouth as he watched Ash disappear from sight. The associate director showed no inclination to chase after Ash, who was already going down the steps, two at a time. Ash took out a cigarette and put it between his lips, ready to light up as soon as he stepped outside.

Chapter Fifteen

Missed The Boat

That evening the *Angora* sailed in calm water on the last leg of its voyage. Ahead and off the starboard side, Miami's brilliant skyline marked Florida's coastline shining through the darkness and haze. The navigation lights of a pleasure craft skidded across the *Angora's* bow. On the aft deck Talbot sat in the dark waiting.

Ever since the ship left Nassau, he had lounged out on deck alone. As the trip's last evening approached, the captain had walked past and mentioned not seeing Sandy lately. He asked if she was all right.

"She's resting, that's all," Talbot had answered. "She and Barney won't collide that way. Makes for a smoother trip." The explanation seemed to satisfy the captain. He shrugged and walked away. Later, when he repeated the flimsy explanation to Barney, the seaman made a face showing his disbelief.

While Talbot sat out on deck in the subdued evening light, Barney scuttled below and tried the door to Talbot's cabin. It was locked. He rattled the doorknob several times. No voice told him to go away. Still, it was possible for the young woman to be in there. Talbot might have locked the door when he went up on deck. Or, she could have locked the door herself from the inside and didn't answer in order not to be disturbed. But there was a third possibility. She wasn't there at all and hadn't been ever since the ship left Nassau. If Barney managed to enter the cabin, he would have no excuse if she was actually lying down in the cabin.

Barney rejoined the captain in the wheelhouse, saying nothing about Sandy. Instead, he lifted the passkeys hanging on a hook out of the captain's line of sight. Barney wrapped a handkerchief around the keys which kept them from jangling in his pocket when he sidled off. He looked and confirmed that Talbot was still up on deck. Barney went below. He would learn what Talbot was hiding.

As the ship drew close to home port, Talbot took out a small flashlight and, as best he could, checked the ship's position on a map he spread before him. The *Angora* would be sailing past a spit of land called Government Cut very soon. It marked an entry to the Port of Miami. Time for him to get moving if he was not to risk meeting Ash when the *Angora* docked. Talbot folded his map and put it away before slipping below to change into his wetsuit.

In the deserted passageway he stopped short. He saw that his cabin door stood open. He was certain he had locked it before going up on deck. Someone had sneaked in. It could only be as Sandy had predicted. Barney.

Taking a deep breath, Talbot withdrew his machete. He approached his cabin quietly and paused for a moment outside the door, listening for a sound from within the cabin.

Nothing.

With his free hand, Talbot eased the door open wide.

Still no noise came from within.

He charged through the doorway into the dark cabin. At first he saw little. "What in hell..." His voice trailed off as his eyes adjusted to the darkness. Barney's figure sat at one end of a bunk. Talbot flipped on the wall switch to confront the first mate. The duffel bag containing Talbot's ancient box rested across the man's legs. He had been caught red-handed. Barney's eyes were fixed on the bag. Talbot's sudden appearance did not seem to concern the first mate. The seaman's steady gaze was blank. He was neither startled nor embarrassed. Talbot had a premonition. Warily he drew near the motionless figure and reached out to press on the side of Barney's neck. He felt for the man's carotid artery.

There was no pulse.

What could have happened, Talbot wondered. Perhaps a heart attack? He saw the outer, waterproof covering was rolled down and the drawstrings that closed the duffel bag inside were exposed and untied. He noticed Barney's hands were covered with little red dots of blood. The palm of one hand was bloody. Long thin scratches ran along the arm.

Talbot looked closer. Tiny metal barbs were imbedded in the drawstrings. The barbs glistened razor-sharp. They must be soaked in a fast-acting poison, Talbot thought, killing nosy Barney who had untied the knots in the dark. The first mate had taken a chance, but paid the price.

Putting away his machete, Talbot donned his wetsuit. As he did so he remembered the arrogant taxi driver who drove both Sandy and him from camp down to the dock in Port-au-Prince. That driver was probably a member of a voodoo cult. The barbs confirmed he had been the one to plant them in the drawstrings. No wonder he took so long to load their things into the trunk of the taxi before driving away from camp. And no wonder the taxi driver appeared hostile and silent. He was waiting for Talbot to handle the drawstrings.

Talbot thought of the voodoo woman who had strung up the decapitated monkey head as a warning. She was more than a religious fanatic. She was an accomplice to murder.

Talbot patted down Barney's corpse and almost kept the dead man's gun, but at the last moment he left it untouched in its holster. With great caution Talbot used the seaman's pliers and screwdriver to close the drawstrings and retie the duffel bag.

Talbot might have left a note denying he was a killer but knew his only hope was to turn the duffel bag and the barbs over to the police for examination once he got the ancient box and letters to the right person.

Glancing around the cabin for the last time, he started to grab a book but stopped and left all his books behind. He turned off the light and locked the cabin door when he left.

On deck, Talbot lashed the duffel bag to the inflated air mattress and slipped his machete into a plastic bag that contained his clothes. He lashed the second bag onto the air mattress as well and gave each rope a hard tug to test all was secure. Then he used a broom to hold the mattress away from the hull as he lowered the mattress over the side.

As soon as the mattress hit the water, he released both

the broom and the rope allowing them to sail back out of sight in the dark as the ship continued on course.

"Well, here goes," he muttered, clambering over the side and letting himself fall backwards into the water. Once clear of the ship's screws he swam back along the wake and located the air mattress bobbing on the surface. He kept a low profile in the water as he coiled the ropes and tossed them onto the mattress. His black wetsuit merged with the water's nighttime color. He was invisible. Sweating, heart pounding, his throat felt dry though he was surrounded by water. He felt exhilarated.

He checked and saw that the two bags were secured to the mattress. He turned it towards shore and headed towwards shore. His strong breast stroke caused hardly a ripple. He nudged the mattress forward with his chin and noticed when he ran his tongue across his lips, they tasted of salt.

The *Angora*'s navigation lights faded in the distance, then disappeared. He realized he had never said goodbye to the captain. Not that it mattered. What was important was how soon the captain would miss him and Barney. Talbot chuckled aloud thinking of how angry someone like Ash, would be on meeting the *Angora* when it docked and discovered the ancient box was gone. It would not be a happy welcome. Talbot could care less and laughed at the thought.

Talbot swam, wondering who would be the first to find Barney's body. The Miami police would not take long to begin their hunt for him and Sandy. He pushed the air mattress faster.

The low, throbbing noise of a powerful boat engine and the strains of music reached out. Water was a good conductor of sound. A cigarette boat raced towards Talbot less than a hundred yards away. It would be close and he had no time to swim far enough away to be safe.

Two people sat in the boat, nestled together, enjoying the tranquil night. Neither looked in Talbot's direction. The boat swept by Talbot, missing him, but causing swells to ripple out and wash over him. Not until the boat was well past did he begin to swim again.

A soggy paper carton brushed against his face. He pushed it aside and focused on the point where he intended to go ashore. Another boat approached. He grasped the mattress to support him. while he sank lower in the water. A dead fish floated in front of his eyes. A piece of waterlogged plastic rubbed against him. He eased them both away.

The second boat came closer and almost hit him before racing by. When it was a safe distance past, he gave the mattress an extra push. Then he swam to catch up with it. He gave the mattress another strong shove and followed. He repeated the effort several more times before his breathing became too labored and he used the breast stroke once more.

The skin of a half-eaten grapefruit bumped his cheek. He batted it out of his way and pressed on. The wetsuit kept him warm but it was also taking extra energy to swim. Despite his fatigue he did not climb on the mattress. Instead he rubbed his eyes, hoping to come to the shore soon.

At last his feet touched bottom. Repressing the urge to

run out of the water with the bag in his arms, he held onto the mattress to keep a low silhouette. His legs propelled him through the shallow water into the beach. Once he reached dry sand he clawed his way through seagrass and stood up. Hurrying over pieces of driftwood, he raised his fist high over his head. He was so elated he wanted to shout. It was a marvelous feeling. He had brought his box and the letters into the States, and no one was there to take his priceless treasures from him.

Standing on a dock in the Port of Miami, Ash smoked a cigarette and squinted into the night trying to pierce the haze. "The *Angora* should be sailing past Government Cut about now. Can't be much longer. You ready to jump aboard?"

Joey stood beside him in a guard's uniform. The man glanced up from a copy of Talbot's picture he was studying. "All ready. Otherwise I'd be hunting for another job in the morning." His eyes twinkled. "Right?"

"You're right," Ash said. "Uh, oh, we've got company." Ash inclined his head back toward the two men who were approaching the dock from the car park. "Maybe we even got a fight on our hands."

"Who are they?"

"I've seen the one guy before. He's Inspector Canot. Works for the Haitian government. I didn't expect to see him up here, though. He's out of his jurisdiction. Don't know the other man."

"They after the box, too? If they are, I'll move fast and hop on board ahead of them as soon as the ship's close enough to the dock. There's nothing like a little competition."

Ash flicked his cigarette butt into the water and shoved his hands in his pockets. Visibly upset, he glared at the inspector as the two men walked up. "Well, what a surprise, Inspector." His voice was clipped. "Have you lost your way?"

The inspector's little eyes grew even smaller as he stared at Ash. "When I come to recover my country's heritage, that's not losing my way, Mr. Ash."

Surveying the growing number, Ash threw up his hands and groaned. "This makes quite a large welcoming committee. But let's get something straight. The Southern State Museum leased the *Angora*. At the moment it's still our supply ship and we don't want outsiders forcing their way on board." He stepped close to the inspector. "Is that clear? Otherwise it could get ugly."

"Ash, before you get carried away by your own importance, this is Agent Cole of U.S. Customs," Canot said clenching his teeth. "You may be about to commit a crime by interfering with an agent of the law."

"You're the one who is interfering if you set foot on our ship," Ash growled. "There's no contraband on board the *Angora*, if that's what Mr. Cole is here for."

Looking grim, the inspector said, "Not true. Your ship fled Haiti carrying an ancient box and documents that are a very valuable part of our country's culture. You never obtained government clearance to do that. I order you to give everything back to Haiti before you get any deeper in trouble."

Ash's face became sullen, obstinate. "Stay off our ship. That's fair warning."

In the next moment the *Angora* floated silently out of the haze, its bow pointed towards the dock. Both engines were in neutral. The ship's momentum carried it forward as its speed fell off. Slowly it drifted to the dock. Only the captain appeared on deck. He strode towards the bow and picked up a hawser to heave to the dock.

"Looks like the captain has no one on board to give him a helping hand," Ash said shaking his head. "Why is he working alone? What's going on?" Ash ran to grab the line and loop it over a stanchion.

Once Ash secured the bow line the captain returned to the engines and pivoted off that line bringing the ship parallel with the dock.

Joey stepped to the edge of the dock and prepared to jump. Then, despite some awkwardness, he leapt onto the ship as it bumped against the piling making a screeching. noise. For a moment he teetered. Recovering his balance, he pulled himself up over the ship's railing and dashed below. The corridor below deck was empty. He hurried to the cabin he was told was occupied by Talbot and Sandy. He rapped on the door. Nothing happened. He tried the door but it was locked.

While he stood pounding on the door, Agent Cole joined him. "Open up in there," Joey shouted. He turned to Cole. "I'm afraid the birds have flown. Why don't you go up and get us a key from the captain? He must have a spare."

"Be back in a minute." Cole hurried past both the inspector and Ash, who were rushing up.

Bearing a key, Cole reappeared minutes later in the passageway. "The captain hasn't seen anyone lately and doesn't know where his first mate is. The captain found this key. He hopes it'll work." Cole squeezed in front of Joey to unlock the door and yanked it open. Everyone crowded into the dark cabin.

Joey was first to speak. "Hey, you," he said to the still figure on the bunk. "What's going on? Snap out of it!"

"That's not possible," Cole exclaimed advancing to the bunk as the lights were switched on. "This man is dead."

Joey and Agent Cole approached the body to examine it. "Don't touch anything," Cole admonished.

"What are the scratches on his arm?" Joey pointed.

"And these little dots of dry blood on his hands," Ash asked lighting a cigarette. "He must've been handling barbed wire."

Cole added, "Those marks could be from fish hooks. Happens if you're not careful."

"Looks more like someone jabbed pins into him as if he was a voodoo doll," Ash said.

"Only I'd bet those fish hooks or pins or whatever had poison on them," Cole said pursing his lips. "This man looks like he's been poisoned to death, murdered."

At that moment the body toppled backward like a sack of potatoes falling from a truck.

"Terrible. And where is Talbot or his lady friend?" Ash asked with a disgusted look on his face. "Why did they have to murder this poor sailor?" He coughed while taking stock of the cabin.

Joey watched Ash coughing and bending over as if feeling severe pain. "Better take it easy, Mr. Ash."

Ash waved off the admonition. "More important," he said straightening up, "where the hell is the wood box? I've looked around but I don't see it anywhere."

Ash coughed harder. He looked at what Talbot left behind. Suitcases and several cardboard boxes rested against the ship's hull. There was nothing resembling the wood box in the cabin. "Goddamn, that greedy Talbot stole our box. He thinks he can get away with that."

Holding his hand over his nose, Joey said, "Think I'll go up and get some fresh air. I'm not comfortable near the smell of death."

Ash's face hardened. "Why don't you tell the captain what we've found down here. Ask him if he can guess where Talbot and Sandy might have left the ship. I'm going to talk with the Inspector for a minute."

Ash discreetly signaled the inspector to step out into the passageway with him away from Cole. "Inspector, I don't know how you feel about this," he said in a low voice, "but it looks like this will take more of our time and effort than either of us figured on."

Inspector Canot smiled his agreement.

"What would you say if I proposed that we work on it, just the two of us together? Keep it all to ourselves, so to speak. See what we can do as partners? It's something I've had in the back of my mind since I saw you come down to the dock. No museum. No Haitian government. On the other hand, if we don't do that, neither of us will get the credit we deserve for all the trouble we will be put to. So, what do you say? Just the two of us?"

The inspector stroked his chin. "I don't know. I'd have

to think about it, but I suppose we can try it for one day before I have to get back to Port-au-Prince and file my report and my expense account. Perhaps when we leave this ship, we should all go someplace and over a cup of coffee talk about what to do next ?"

"That's fine with me. There's an all-night diner three blocks down on White Street." He nodded in the direction. "I'll join you there in a couple of minutes," he said and clapped the inspector on the back.

Chapter Sixteen

The Manhunt Begins

Talbot carefully looked around the beach to make sure no one was watching him. When he felt certain he was alone, he went back to his air mattress and dragged it farther up on the shore. Bending over, he untied the ropes and lifted the two bags onto the sand. From the one bag he pulled out his machete and dry clothes. He stripped off his wetsuit. The chill in the salt air raised goose bumps on his bare skin.

He cut a piece of cloth from that bag and reaching into the other bag past the outer waterproof covering, he wrapped the extra piece around the dangerous draw strings. Next, he dug a hole and dropped his wet suit into it. He let the air out of the mattress before throwing it into the hole. Anticipation made his hands tremble as he buried those things and covered them with sand. He felt like a pirate ready to leave his lair carrying his booty.

With the duffel bag slung over his shoulder he hiked almost a mile to a public street. He walked along that street for a half hour before a taxi picked him up. He instructed the driver to take him directly to the Miami International Airport.

At that hour the taxi encountered no traffic and sped across the city. When it arrived at the airport departures curb, Talbot got out and lifted the bag onto his shoulder, refusing the porters who came up offering their services.

He believed it was too soon for the Miami police to be looking for him, so he made himself conspicuous as he explored the terminal building. He walked up to several ticket counters along the main concourse and asked for flight information. He also collected their timetables. Later, he bought a magazine from a newsstand and stood in several different locations reading it.

Afterwards, he strolled the concourse one last time, then wandered out through a side exit. Across the street in the multi-tiered parking complex he spied a pair of headlights flick on and off. Sandy was waiting for him. She waved from her side window. He hurried to her and heaved the duffel bag onto the back seat of the car before climbing in.

"No jellyfish pester you while you swam in the moonlight?" Sandy asked, kissing him hard on the lips.

"The swimming was great. No trouble." He pulled her slender body to him and returned her kiss with a fierce one of his own. "How are your legs holding up tonight?"

"No change." She stroked his face, running two fingers along his cheek. "Miss me?"

He delayed his reply, as though thinking hard about what answer to give.

"Well, don't hurt yourself answering too quickly," she said.

He had the annoyed reaction to his teasing that he sought and he laughed. "I like it when I get a rise out of you. Yes, I missed you." He leaned over and kissed her again. "My fabulous box is now in the country. But," he went on in a serious voice, "Barney is dead."

Her face paled. She stared at him for several moments in stunned silence. "Oh, Don, were you involved in his death, by any chance?"

"If you're asking did I do it? No, I had absolutely nothing to do with it. Do you remember the taxi driver who drove us down to the *Angora* in Port-au-Prince? Near as I can figure, he must have been one of those voodoo bastards and worked poisoned barbs into the drawstrings at the top of my duffel bag. By the way, those barbs are still imbedded in the drawstrings, so be real careful and don't touch them. Better yet, stay away from the bag altogether."

"Don't worry."

"Tonight while I was sitting up on deck, Barney must have sneaked into our cabin, pulled down the waterproof outer wrapping that covers the duffel bag and untied the drawstrings that had the poisoned barbs stuck in them. When I reached him, his body was sagging on my bunk with the bag lying across his legs. His one arm was cut up and his hands punctured. Drops of blood spotted his clothes. It was no voodoo ritual sacrifice using dumb animals this time. The man was murdered. Poor guy. I didn't like Barney but that's way too high a price for him to pay for being curious. So much for the captain's promise to keep Barney out of our cabin."

"How awful. It gives me the chills." She shivered.

"Puts us in a jam," he said. "The police will think we're the murderers. They'll hunt us down."

"That's rotten." Her lips trembled and tears welled up

in her eyes. "Their investigation has to show we're innocent of any wrongdoing."

He winced. "Not after I've just thrown the duffel bag with the barbs in the back seat of this car. It's the best evidence of what happened and the police don't know a thing about it."

"We're not criminals. We've done nothing wrong."

"The police will be looking for us anyway. We're stuck right in the middle. Good thing I have the box."

"At least we're safe for now. Must we talk about it anymore?"

"Not tonight. I noticed you got us some transportation."

"Belongs to Dad. Have to bring it back in the morning." She hesitated. "I'm sorry to be the one to tell you. Your sister called my folks. The night before we left Haiti on the *Angora*, your mother died in her sleep. She's already buried."

Talbot was silent for a while his head bowed. "It hurts. I'll never repay her for all she's done."

"She only wanted your success and happiness. You'll soon have them with the ancient box and the letters."

After awhile Sandy broke into the silence to ask, "Don, how're you doing?"

His voice cracked. "My mother deserved better."

"She'd want you to go on," Sandy said softly.

"I know, but I wanted to do things for her." He drifted off into silence.

Later he asked, "Did you do any more work on the letters?"

She smiled. "I was waiting for you to ask. In a letter I'm

now reading, the Queen calls him by a name that looks like Chris."

"Finally a name."

"She comes right out and says she misses Chris. I sense she hungered for him when the King was off fighting some battle. She wanted her darling Chris. Dreamed of him in bed with her and was brokenhearted without him. She hears his deep voice at night. Her love for him reaches to the heavens. Love was in the air she breathed. She's tender one minute. The next, she's the practical chorus girl asking when he's going to bring her the delicate silks he promised."

"You're making real headway, but I can't get all that enthused." Talbot frowned. "Calling him a stud doesn't make Columbus the man I admired. He's like a lover boy servicing a passionate, oversexed woman. I knew he must've charmed the Queen, only I never thought of him as her gigolo. I just can't swallow Columbus carrying on with the Queen. I'll look at that a long time before I accept it."

"You're upset with the news about your mom. Columbus could be both an explorer and the Queen's intimate."

"I wanted the whole world to see those letters. Mom would have been proud of me. Now I'm not sure I can do it. The letters make Columbus appear too quick to get in the sack, and they sully all he did."

"I still believe he's great despite the gleam in his eye."

"I'm thinking of destroying those letters."

She gave him a pained expression. "Well, sleep on it. Want to see my surprise for you?"

"Yes, of course."

"My legs feel lousy. You have to drive, sailor."

"What's this sailor thing? You have a boat?"

Her face lit up. "What did you expect? I have a thirty-footer. Two diesels. She's moored over on the Miami River. I spent much of the day with my folks. Said you had some time off and would be along. Dad borrowed the boat for us to have a little vacation."

"Sounds wonderful." He reached across and hugged her.

She arched an eyebrow. "Is that it? Don't I at least rate another kiss?"

"I ought to smother you in kisses, but let's get the hell out of here before some cop comes along asking what we're doing. We've hung around long enough."

"The thing is, the boat belongs to a friend of my Dad. It has to be back in three days."

* * *

"Damn," Ash said standing on the dock with Joey. "It's so frustrating. Earlier today I showed two samples of the documents inside the box to some publishers and gave them Miss Gurney's translation notes. They're all excited. Already throwing big numbers around if I would let them release excerpts. But I don't have squat. We've got to find that box!" Ash's voice was harsh.

"Don't worry. It's only a temporary delay. That's all. Anyone could understand that. We'll get the stuff back soon. I'm certain we will." Joey looked as confident as he sounded.

"Hope you're right." Ash balled his fist. After I built

their hopes up I can't keep those people dangling very long. Don't want to let them get away."

"I was standing beside the captain when he called the Miami police. They'll be here soon to check out the dead body and hunt for the Talbots. You told me those two are short of cash so they won't get far. Besides, the box is too big to hide so if Talbot travels on public transportation, the police will latch on to him fast. Don't worry."

"I'm worrying like hell. If the police arrest him before we get the box, it could finish us by tying up the box and the papers a long time. I want Talbot but I want what he's got of ours more and I want it right now."

"We'll have to beat the cops to him. That's all."

"Let's go drink some coffee with the Inspector and the customs guy."

Ash and Joey drove to the all-night diner and joined Agent Cole and Inspector Canot at a booth. Ash announced, "Joey spoke to the captain. Tell 'em."

"Well," Joey said, "the captain saw the woman and Talbot leave the *Angora* very early this morning in Nassau. They went for breakfast but he never saw them return and he never saw her again. He thinks she probably flew from Nassau to Miami, leaving Talbot on the boat to make it look good."

Ash and Joey ordered coffee. When it was served, Ash took a sip and turned to Agent Cole. "Joey used to work for the Miami Police Department. What say Mr. Cole, you and Joey check out the terminals tonight. Cover the planes, buses and trains? I'll make it worth your while."

Cole replied, "We can give it a try, anyway. Things are

quiet in the city at this time of night so it should go fast."

"Fine. Right after you finish a terminal, call me or Inspector Canot. I'm staying in the same hotel he is. Here's where you call," Ash said, showing the telephone number on his room key. "Keep us posted. If you get a lead, call us right then so we can follow it up while it's still hot. Any questions?"

Both Joey and Agent Cole shook their heads. "You'll be hearing from us soon," Cole said. The two men finished their coffee and left.

When they were alone, Ash said to the inspector, "I've been wondering what great interest Haiti has in all this?"

"No mystery. Its tourist business is shot to hell. The box and the documents could revive it."

"With all the trouble in your republic, do you really believe anything could bring back tourism?"

"I have faith Haiti will recover. Give us time and some attractions in addition to our spectacular beaches and water. I have faith in Aristede."

Ash laughed. "It will take more than the box to turn things around." He hesitated. "The translations that the Tallahassee woman gave you and the one I got make the letters sound pretty wild. If you could decide that the box and the Columbus letters don't need to go back to Haiti, then I see no reason to hand them over to my museum either. Know what I'm saying? You and I could let a private party buy them from us. It's something for you to think about. You don't have to give me your answer right away."

"Time we got some sleep before the phone starts to ring. I'll think about what you've said."

"That's all I ask. Can I give you a lift back to the hotel?"

"Thanks just the same. I have a car."

"See you at the hotel in the morning. Give it some thought."

"I will," the inspector said.

Chapter Seventeen

Waterproof

The following morning on the power boat Sandy's father had borrowed for them, Talbot yawned and stretched. "We've got work to do. I'll give you a New York City address for Juan de Silvo. You'll fax him copies of everything. He'll help us."

"Who is he?"

"A good friend I roomed with at the university. He took over his father's shop and knows the antique business like the expert he is. I'll have him check the authenticity of everything. If he can verify their age, he'll give us an advance."

She raised her eyebrows. "After spending that money to buy the box and letters, do you have any doubts they're authentic?"

"I've said it before. I used my best judgment at the time I bought them from the Paques. But it's never too late, if I'm wrong, I'll stop sending good money after bad."

"How about the age of the parchment the letters were written on and the ink? Does he have the equipment and the expertise to determine how old they are?"

"It's his business. He has everything he needs to test all that, even to test a sliver off the box. You'll mail the sliver to him."

"But to test those things, won't he need an original letter, too, not just a fax copy?"

"I'm afraid so, and I'm going to hate to express an original to him. But I kept one out of the bag just for that, and he'll need only a few particles of the paint and a few of the vellum the letter is written on. While you're out I want you to fax a copy of all our stuff to de Silvo."

"Fax him copies of the copies you made in Haiti?"

"Yes, and include a copy of the pictures of the wood box. The police are probably out looking for us by now. Perhaps Ash is, also. So, be careful. Don't take any unnecessary chances. Find a couple stores that have fax machines for the public to use. If you send small batches from different places, you won't be there long enough to attract attention."

She frowned. "You're going to ask de Silvo to translate the letters all over again, aren't you?"

"Yes, of course. Don't be upset."

"Something the matter with my translations?"

"C'mon, don't be so angry. Nothing's the matter with them. They tell us a lot. Only, two or three heads are better than one. Besides, he's got professionals, two paleographers he can tap for this. They're expert not only on real ancient writings but also on documents that were written as recently as five hundred years ago."

"Well, he better hurry 'cause we can't hide out for very long. Our time's going fast."

"Two short days left. Juan will move on this stuff. He has to."

"What are you going to do with the box and the set of original papers? Keeping valuable things like that on board this boat is a terrible risk."

"I know." He smiled. "When you get back from faxing that stuff, I'll show you an old smuggler's trick."

* * *

Talbot used a pair of pliers to extract the poisoned barbs from the drawstrings. He soaked and wiped the evil barbs clean several times. Careful not to cut himself, he inserted them back into the drawstrings. He also wrapped a small boat anchor in an old bed comforter and stuffed the added weight into the duffel bag. He placed the whole thing back into the plastic outer bag. Finally, he sealed the outer bag with a waterproof cement.

He started the engines and let them idle. Out on deck he disconnected the electric and water lines that were hooked up to the boat and tossed them onto the dock. He left in place the bow and stern lines holding the boat fast to its slip. After he was satisfied the engines were thoroughly warmed up he turned them off.

In late morning Sandy's father brought her back to the boat. He chatted briefly with Talbot and hoped they would enjoy their short vacation. He didn't stay. When Sandy descended into the galley, she found Talbot had prepared lunch. "You ought to do this more often. It looks good."

He laughed. "Nothing fancy, and while you were gone I telephoned de Silvo. He told me he received everything you faxed to him and as I expected, he'll help, starting right away."

"You went off the boat?"

"I had to talk to Juan. I wanted to make sure he wasn't away someplace and would do the work for us. I found a public phone on the other side of the parking lot over there. Besides, I haven't shaved in a while and I wore dark glasses with my baseball cap pulled down over my hair. No one recognized me in the time it took me to make the call."

"What did he say?"

"He's happy to help and likes our ideas about Columbus and Isabella. He believes it's possible the Queen was as attracted as we think. He mentioned that Diego, a son of Columbus, married the niece of King Ferdinand. The families had to be close for that to happen."

"How wonderful. Pieces keep fitting together."

"He also pointed out that King Ferdinand was the one in the family with the reputation of philanderer, not Queen Isabella. She was said to be a plain woman, kind of sulky, out of sorts much of the time, not the most likely candidate for a torrid love affair."

"Maybe, if someone like Columbus gave her extra attention, he would win over such a woman all the more easily."

"In the letters she sure makes it sound like he won her over."

Sandy asked what Talbot had done to protect the box. He told her he had cleaned off each barb thoroughly and added an anchor to give the bag more weight. "That way the current won't drag the bag away. I also waterproofed the bag. Now watch."

He tied one end of a short rope to the bag and the other end to a wooden float and demonstrated how with the bag lying on the river bottom, the rope extended up just enough to hold the float out of sight below the water's surface.

He lowered the whole rig into the water close to the dock where no boat traffic passed and where no one would observe him while he was hiding the bag. He also showed her that he could reach over the side of the boat with a grappling hook to probe for the rope and recover the bag in short order.

"Now it doesn't matter how much anybody searches the boat, he won't find the box on board."

She laughed. "You're a great smuggler. I like it. Just don't forget to haul it in when we leave."

The couple sat down to eat lunch. As they ate, Sandy showed him an old Spanish dictionary she had purchased that morning from a used book store. "This should help me," she said, waving it in his face. "It's ancient enough."

"Keep at it, my love."

With the battered dictionary before her, Sandy worked after lunch, translating a copy of one of the letters. Talbot put the other copies into a plastic shopping bag and filled the rest of the bag with potato chips. He stowed it on a cabinet shelf over the galley stove.

Sandy called to him, "What if the U.S. government says we smuggled these papers into the country?"

"Keep your mind on translating. We'll work something out. As long as we've got the original papers stashed away where no one can find 'em, people will go slow in pressing charges against us. They won't risk losing these historical documents forever."

"I hope you're right." She gave him a weak smile.

"They say possession is nine-tenths of the law."

"I wouldn't count on it in a murder case."

* * *

At the Federal Office Building in Miami, Agent Cole handed the phone to the inspector. "It's for you. It's Ash."

"Inspector Canot speaking."

"Inspector? This is Buddy Ash. Any word?"

"No luck so far. During the night Cole and Joey reported in. They didn't get much information and I didn't get much sleep. They did say Talbot had been there at the airport and they confirmed that the woman flew in from Nassau yesterday like the captain suspected. She used a credit card. That says Talbot is short of cash, otherwise she wouldn't risk revealing her identity with the card. The Miami police are now climbing all over your supply ship."

"Okay. Can we meet in my room at the hotel, say about two-thirty this afternoon so we can work out what we're going to do next?"

"We don't need meetings. We need action. We need to find the box and those letters."

"Of course. That's what the meeting will be about. I'll have something definite for you by then, Inspector. Something you'll like very much. Trust me."

"Hope so."

"I guarantee you'll like it. Talk to you later."

Inspector Canot turned to Cole. "Go over that again for me."

"Talbot was definitely at the airport last night. People saw him walking around there. The lady at the newsstand recognized his picture right away. But I couldn't find any record of him buying a ticket out of there. He didn't use a credit card in his own name, and his name wasn't on any passenger list. And he wasn't seen at either the train or bus station."

"Did you guys check all the foreign and domestic flights out of here?"

"The works, but as you know, while he needs to show his passport to fly out of the country to Mexico or South America, on a domestic flight he doesn't have to show anything. He could have given a false name and flown without our knowing it."

"Nobody remembers selling him a ticket?"

"It's early times. Most of the airline personnel on duty last night haven't reported in for work yet today so we didn't have much luck showing Talbot's picture around for that purpose. But we have them watching for his credit card and the one the young lady used."

"Right. That was good work with the woman at the newsstand. Did you contact the taxi companies?"

"After phoning a few, we got lucky. A cab picked up a fare carrying a large bag on his shoulder. The driver said he picked up the passenger walking along a street on Dodge Island where we guessed Talbot might land. The island lies along the main channel the *Angora* would have passed through coming into the Port of Miami. The cabbie picked Talbot up about the time the *Angora* docked."

"Where'd the cab take him?"

Cole smiled. "Straight to the Miami International

Airport. He was dry as a bone. The bag he carried was wrapped in plastic. The box must be inside."

"Great, he's clearly traced to the airport. Is that the end of the trail?"

"Until we hear differently from one of the airlines. But I don't believe he flew out of there. Too obvious. He only wants us to think he did. I'm gonna catch some sleep. See you later."

"Will you and Joey be here this afternoon?"

"I know I'll be there."

"Thanks, Cole."

Ash drove slowly along the street, his head bent low as he craned his neck to read the house numbers of the apartment buildings he passed. He pulled over and parked. Entering a clean, polished vestibule, he read the name Martinez posted opposite the intercom for Apartment 2C. Martinez was the surname Ash had pulled from Talbot's personnel file back in Haiti, the one to notify in the event of an emergency. This had to be the address of Sandy's parents.

A brash, confident Ash pressed the buzzer.

A tired, male Latino voice answered. "*Sí?* Who is it?"

"I'm Buddy Ash from Southern State Museum. Mr. Talbot gave your name to contact in an emergency. I must talk to you. It will only take a minute or two. It's very urgent."

The Latino voice grew irritable. "I know who you are. We have nothing to talk about, Señor Ash."

"Stop it, please. I am not calling on my personal behalf and I don't care what your daughter might have told you about me. But you have to see me for her sake. Give me a couple of minutes. That's all I ask."

"*Venga.*" The reluctant voice contained suspicion.

Ash chuckled. Mr. Martinez was in for a shock. A buzzer sounded at the door frame. Ash quickly stepped into the carpeted lobby and hurried up the stairs, smoothing his hair and straightening his gray jacket. Breathing heavily, he wasted no time going down the hall to Apartment 2C. When he rang the doorbell, an older man opened the door slightly, leaving the security chain in place. A Latino peered out. "Señor, you said there is some emergency involving my daughter?"

Ash hesitated. "Yes, an emergency." The hesitation made Ash sound unsure. The pause seemed to cause Martinez to grow more wary than he already had been. As the door started to close, Ash stopped it with his foot.

"Señor, take your foot away now or I call the police." Martinez pushed hard to close the door.

Ash's foot did not budge. "Give me a moment," he demanded. "That's all I ask. Your daughter is in deep trouble. Talbot's behavior is hurting her...and will possibly involve you. You must do something."

"I've already talked to my daughter. She tells me the box belongs to Talbot. A Haitian family sold it to him. Talbot paid good money to buy it. She said it's perfectly legal and I believe her. Take your foot away."

"Sir," Ash said without moving his foot, "I'm not talking about any box. I don't care what Talbot bought and paid for." He paused. "I know you're a good father and want to be loyal to your daughter, but I must talk to you about something altogether different, something that could do her great harm. Did she tell you Talbot was acting kinda strange so we gave him a little time off to recover? He used it to sail up here on the museum's supply ship and committed murder along the way."

Martinez frowned. "*Madre de Dios,* what are you saying he did?"

Mrs. Martinez appeared behind her husband, her eyes filled with concern. "Carlos, what is it? What does this man want?"

"He's with Don's museum. He's saying something about Don and Sandy."

Mrs. Martinez examined Ash more closely. "What's wrong?"

"You folks don't want me standing out here in the hall, talking about your daughter and murder. Please, let me come in. I will only take a minute."

Martinez shrugged his shoulders in defeat and slid the chain off the door. "Go to your right." He spoke in a subdued voice and pointed the way. "We'll sit in the living room, *por favor,* and tell us what you are talking about."

"I'm Talbot's boss at the archaeological dig down in Haiti that the Southern State Museum is sponsoring."

"Yes, yes. We know that."

"Do you folks mind if I light up my cigarette?"

"Neither of us smoke. We would not appreciate the smell in our apartment."

Ash shrugged and placed an unlit cigarette in his mouth.

"How is our daughter mixed up in a murder?"

"I hate to be the one to tell you. Believe me, I don't like to interfere in the personal life of anyone, but she's with a man who has been acting peculiar. We thought he could use some time off to get his head straightened out." Ash held the look of concern on his face during the long pause that followed his remarks.

Mrs. Martinez looked uncomfortable. The plain woman's hands fussed with her shapeless dress. Her breathing was shallow.

"What are you driving at exactly? What is it about Talbot's personal life you cannot leave personal? What needed to be sorted out?" A tic over the left eye of Martinez began to throb.

Ash sat down, looking from one to the other. "I'm not going into the details but your daughter and Talbot are prime suspects in a murder case. The police are out hunting for them. They're dangerous felons wanted for murder."

Mrs. Martinez lost the color in her face. "I can't believe it," she said and shivered. "They have their whole lives in front of them. They aren't killers."

Martinez watched the eyes of Ash determinedly. "How do you know this? Did you see the actual murder happen so you are certain of what you're telling us?" His face barely concealed the apprehension that must lie within.

"No, I wasn't aboard the *Angora* when it happened. But they were known to be the only ones to occupy the cabin where the murder occurred. Your daughter will probably be charged as a murderer or as a co-conspirator. That's why I have to see the two of them and see whether they want the museum attorney to be present when the police question them."

Mrs. Martinez fled from the room with anguish frozen on her face and tears streaming down her cheeks.

Martinez watched her depart, then turned back to Ash. A sadness came over him. "You're saying our daughter is with a murderer? The police are after them?"

"I appreciate how you must feel." Ash spoke softly. He almost had his quarry.

"No, you can't...ever," Martinez said shaking his head.

"It's got to be a terrible shock. But if you know where they are hiding out, you must tell me."

"They aren't hiding out. They just don't want anyone to disturb them. They want a bit of privacy and now you ask me to divulge where they're at." Martinez raised a trembling hand to turn the accusation away. "There's got to be a mistake, some other answer than this horrible disgrace. What do you want?"

"For myself? I don't want a thing. But Talbot is another matter. He needs help. I must find him before he harms your daughter and harms himself further."

Martinez squirmed. "I don't understand."

"Don't treat this like a test of your loyalty to Talbot." Ash gritted his teeth. "At least let me talk to him before the police are able to catch him. You know where he is hiding out. He's in trouble. You can save him."

Martinez tried to control his agitated body. His trembling lips had difficulty forming coherent words. "I tell you, Talbot is not hiding. He and Sandy are off having a little vacation," he said.

Emphasizing the seriousness of what he had to say, Ash leaned towards Martinez. "One more thing, you asked did I see the murder actually take place. Well, I saw the first mate of the *Angora* was dead when the supply ship docked here in Miami. The sailor had been alive when the ship left Nassau after a quick stopover. It was clear he had been poisoned. Not stabbed, not shot, but murdered all the same. A sordid murder. We know Talbot did it because no one else went into the cabin. Don't you see? If you harbor a murderer, you become a criminal yourself. But you're no criminal. Don't become one. Please, you've got to tell me where Talbot is."

The figure of Martinez crumbled. "You say my daughter is involved, but it doesn't sound as though she did anything wrong."

Ash nodded. "Oh, but she did."

Martinez appeared wide-eyed at the accusation.

Ash said, "She is a co-conspirator for harboring a criminal, just like you're doing by not telling me where Talbot is. You're misguided. I must find out where he is if I am to bring him the professional care he desperately needs."

Martinez stared at Ash for a long time as if trying to make up his mind. He fidgeted in his seat. His fingers rapped the table top. He hesitated once as though about to speak but said nothing. At last he blurted out, "I shouldn't be telling you, but this morning I dropped my daughter off at a Miami River pier…If you see them, tell them I will help in any way I can. They need only ask."

Martinez gave Ash the exact dock number where the pair was staying on their borrowed boat. He said he was certain Ash would find Talbot on board. Then the despairing man got up from his seat and escorted his unwelcome guest to the door. The two men did not shake hands nor speak further before Martinez let Ash out of the apartment.

Once Ash left, Martinez looked bewildered by the whole episode as he hurried back to the bedroom he shared with his wife. He found her body sprawled across their bed. He released a long, keening wail as he bent over to look more closely at the mother of their only child. She mumbled something he could not understand. Looking bewildered by the whole episode, he fled to the kitchen and brought back ice cubes wrapped in a dishcloth. He rearranged her body on the bed to make her comfortable.

On unsteady legs he rushed to the living room telephone and called for an emergency ambulance, then he returned to the bedroom to look in on his wife. She seemed to be resting peacefully. He went to the kitchen and armed himself with a butcher's knife. Pacing back and forth in the kitchen stabbing the air with the weapon, he waited.

Martinez put down the knife while he walked to a closet and put on his jacket. He concealed the knife by slipping it up his sleeve and held it in place with a strong elastic band. When the ambulance crew arrived, he watched them minister to his wife and put her on a stretcher to take her to the hospital.

Martinez went down and got into his car. He found it would not start. He telephoned a nearby service station. The mechanic who came out after a short delay, said the trouble was that the parking lights had been left on overnight and had run the battery down. The car was soon started. Martinez withdrew his knife and placed it on the seat beside him and drove to the Emergency Room of the Ryan Memorial Hospital. He learned his wife would recover fully and be released in the morning. He got back in his car and headed for the Miami River. He talked to himself most of the way, recounting his meeting with Ash.

* * *

Talbot pointed to the bag of things Sandy purchased while she had been away from the boat during the morning. "It's time," he said, "we wrote our own letters to Columbus."

He reached into the bag and pulled out stationery that looked old and pens that contained brown ink. In one pen the ink was black.

"Are you expecting trouble? You act so jumpy, as though it isn't safe staying here."

"Only taking precautions. We have some very valuable things that many people would like to get their hands on so I have good reason to seem jumpy. We're going to do everything possible to prevent anyone from stealing my treasure."

"But nobody even knows this boat is here except for my father, and he isn't going to broadcast where we are to anyone."

Talbot screwed up his face. "How about the owner of this boat and his friends? They must know where this boat is. And there could be others. I would prefer they not come out and get a look at our faces. Our faces could already be shown around. We don't know when the police will put out a bulletin charging us with crimes and quite probably carrying our pictures. And Ash is around somewhere. I can feel it."

"I hope not."

"All the same, let's take a few extra precautions. For starters, we'll dummy up some letters and tape them to the wall here. Nothing fancy. The bogus ones will delay an intruder, give him something to question and leave him less time to think about where we've hidden the real ones."

"I can't imitate the Queen's handwriting."

"It doesn't matter. No one around here knows what the real thing looks like."

"Then what?"

"I think we'll go ashore, hoping no one will recognize us. We'll buy a few things to disguise this boat. Paint, stencils…"

"But we can't paint it. This boat isn't ours."

He laughed. "Don't worry. We won't paint it. We'll get lots of masking tape to cover the old name and serial numbers. Then we'll paint a new name and serial number on the tape. Later, before we give the boat back, we peel off the tape and the new paint along with it. We've got to do whatever we can think of to protect the box for the next couple days until de Silvo gets word to us."

"Okay, give me the stationery so I can write some Spanish, señor."

An hour later when he and Sandy had prepared their versions of letters, they taped them to a wall of the salon and left the boat to go shopping.

In New York City de Silvo studied the copies of the letters Sandy had faxed to him. Knowing old Spanish very well, he quickly grasped the gist of the letters and placed a telephone call to the Spanish Embassy in Washington, D.C. Following a short delay the operator at the embassy switchboard said, "Connecting you with the attaché now."

"Hello?"

"Good day, sir. I'm Juan de Silvo, owner of a New York City shop dealing in rare antiques. I have some things you will find most important to your country."

"Yes?"

"I realize we have never met, but in the course of my business a batch of love letters has come into my hands. They were written long ago in an archaic Spanish."

"Love letters," a voice scoffed. "Of what possible interest could such letters be to me, even if they are in old Spanish?"

"These letters date back to the late 1400's. It's likely Queen Isabella wrote them."

"Sounds like you should send them to the *Biblioteca Nacional*, our national library in Madrid. The girl at our switchboard can give you the address."

"No. The problem is that the letters are in very poor taste, less than queenly. I am calling you to find out if the Spanish government wants to examine such letters before they are released to the general public?"

The attaché sounded amused. "This strikes me as rather vague and strange. Pardon me for treating it lightly. I am sure you are well-meaning, but it is impossible for me to say one way or the other without first seeing what you are talking about. May I at least look at copies?"

"Of course. I understand. This must seem weird coming out of nowhere from a stranger. However, I am willing to fax copies of two of these letters to you. Let me emphasize that if the letters distress you as much as I believe they will, be prepared to send them off to the right people in Madrid without delay. There is no time to lose because these letters will be released to the public very soon unless your country requests otherwise."

"I look forward to receiving copies of these letters, Mr. de Silvo? That is your name?"

"It is."

"Believe me, if they are what you say, I shall treat them seriously. But we get calls like this from time to time. They no longer excite us. If your letters are in old Spanish, I shall need to have an expert look them over. That will take time. Let's leave it that I shall be in touch with you as circumstances dictate."

"That's all I ask. I'll fax you these copies right now with my telephone number."

"Fine. Do that."

"One other thing. If you decide the letters are to be taken seriously, have the Madrid authorities send me a copy of the Queen's handwriting. They can do that quicker than I can hunt through my files here."

"I'll have them send you what they can. But before that, let's see what you send to me."

"Thank you for your time." You old fart, de Silvo added under his breath.

"De nada. You're welcome. *Muchas gracias* for the courtesy of your call."

* * *

Shortly after Sandy and Talbot left their boat to make some purchases, Joey drove up to the slip Ash had specified. He parked his car near the dock and sank down in his seat, chewing on a stale piece of gum. Confronting a murderer, if one lay in wait on board the boat, was not the kind of work Joey normally handled.

The boat appeared quiet and vacant. Joey left his car and ambled cautiously onto the dock. He glanced around. No one seemed to pay any attention to this stranger. He leaned over, grabbing the ladder to climb down onto the stern of the boat. He knocked several times on the door to the salon and rattled the doorknob. It was locked. That the door was locked probably meant the boat was not occupied at the moment.

Joey returned to his car. From the trunk he took out a steel bar used to change tires and he hid it under his jacket as he walked back to the boat. He looked around again. No one seemed to pay any attention. He wedged the bar between the door frame and the door. With a sharp snap he forced the door open. He hurried inside, closed the door and stood still in the salon, barely breathing as he listened. His stomach made unfamiliar noises. This was definitely not his line of work. Could the murderer be hiding, locked up in this boat?

Joey stared at handwritten letters taped to the wall

opposite him. Perhaps Talbot had been studying them. Still he had been careless to leave them out in plain sight like this. Joey stepped closer to the letters. They were in a foreign language and must be the ones Ash is looking for, but where was the box Ash said the letters came in? Ash wanted that, too.

Collecting the letters off the wall before going any further, Joey piled them on the coffee table in the center of the salon and stripped off the tape sticking to each before going further.

He ransacked the salon, pulling out drawers and dumping them on the deck. He opened the cabinets above and pulled their contents out. He overturned furniture not secured to the deck and moved everything he could.

With a flashlight in hand he crawled beneath the main deck, hunting for the box in the cramped area around the engines where the air smelled. He crouched down in the quiet. Only the sound of water sloshing against the hull could be heard. He shoved oil cans and rags out of his way. His breathing became ragged as he finished his search around the engines.

Joey searched further but found no sign of the box. Yet, with the letters in plain sight, the box should be close by unless...Talbot had taken the box with him. Joey stepped outside and climbed up onto the bridge. He pulled apart two built-in cabinets but found no old, wooden box.

Climbing back down and walking along one side of the boat, he searched it from bow to stern. Baffled, his shirt soaked with sweat, he did the same on the other side of the boat. He found no sign of the box. But what did he know about boats? If the box was on board, it could be hidden in a place he knew nothing about.

At least he need not go to Ash empty-handed. He returned to the salon and gathered up the batch of letters he had removed from the wall. He stuffed them into a bag and took one last look around the salon before leaving.

Back in the car he again sank down in the driver's seat. His pulse was racing. He heaved a great sigh of relief and massaged his gums. He had come away without being murdered.

Chapter Eighteen

The Cupboard Was Bare

A t mid-afternoon Ash relaxed in his hotel room, sprawled out in an easy chair, one arm draped over the back. He swirled ice cubes around in a half-finished drink and watched the television which was set on low volume. Smoke from his lighted cigarette drifted up from an ashtray on the small table beside him.

The telephone rang, intruding on his thoughts. He pulled it to him and listened. "By all means, c'mon right up, Inspector." A smug look spread across his face as he put the receiver back down. He pressed the remote control to turn off the television.

A minute later he heard a soft knock and opened the door. "Come in, come in, Inspector. Glad you could make it. You look tired."

"I am. Right after lunch I took a short nap but I'm still walking in my sleep. All night long the men kept calling me with their reports. Talbot's not here. He's not there. Drove me nuts and I lost a lot of sleep."

"Make yourself comfortable. Want a drink?"

"Just a soft drink; diet, if you have one."

"Of course," Ash said, passing him a can and a glass filled with ice. "Can we get right to it? Last night we said it would be to our mutual advantage to pool our resources. Just the two of us. Remember that?"

The inspector nodded. "I remember you saying it."

"You feel the box belongs to Haiti. It's part of your republic's heritage. I understand that."

"It's not complicated."

"And I say Southern State Museum owns it because our employee, Talbot, bought the box for us. Then the museum uncovered its real value with no help from Haiti. Since we took over, the box has been under our protection."

"You call that protection? The box is gone. And before that, the box and its contents were taken out of the Republic of Haiti by a murderer without government clearance."

"So let's forget all that. We're pooling our resources, right?" Ash tried to look sincere. He smiled.

The inspector's shrug of his shoulders was noncommittal as he tugged his jacket down.

"Let that go for the moment. Did anything come out of last night's hunt?"

"They found others who saw Talbot at the airport. They even came across a woman who answered his questions about flight times. It's tantalizing."

"That tells us little. He was at the airport, which we already knew."

"The fact people clearly saw him last night confirms he wanted to be seen so we'd think he flew out of there." The inspector shifted in his seat.

Ash beamed, taking a puff on his cigarette. He blew his smoke away from the inspector. "I assure you that you are absolutely right."

"Thanks for your vote of confidence." The inspector

bowed his head in mock gratitude. "Cole also thinks Talbot is still lurking in Miami somewhere."

"Good news, Inspector, I know for a fact Talbot is here. I visited Martinez today. He is the father of the woman with Talbot. Oh, don't look so surprised." He laughed. "We had the address in our files. Martinez lives right here in Miami. After I twisted the father's arm he told me where the two of them are holed up." His voice became hard. "Before I go any further, are we in this together?"

The inspector shrugged again. "We're in it together."

"That's great, partner." He patted the inspector on his shoulder. "They're on the Miami River in a boat her father borrowed. It's not far from the airport. Cute, eh?" He began coughing so hard he bent at the waist, his body shuddering.

The inspector looked alarmed. "Can I do anything?"

Ash wiped his mouth with a handkerchief and gasped, "No, thanks."

"I'm impressed you found out about Talbot that fast. So, why are we sitting around?"

"Easy does it. There's no rush. Help yourself to the macadamia nuts I just opened. I've sent Joey to the boat in his guard uniform. He's a big guy. He'll grab this Talbot and the box. I've been waiting to settle things with you before we go out to the stadium to meet Joey."

"Then, let's go!" The inspector sprang up from his seat, splashing his drink on the rug.

"In a moment. I tell you, we've got time." Coughing again, he raised his hand signaling the inspector to stay put. He caught his breath and mopped his face with his handkerchief. "You have contacts in Haiti you can call and get an official clearance for the box and the documents. I'll sell the stuff off privately and you needn't touch a thing. You simply collect a nice piece of the action. How does that suit you?" The pain in his chest slowly subsided.

The inspector's eyes were half-closed. "I'm thinking it might work unless the value of the box is too tempting for you." Canot looked at Ash skeptically.

"If you get the clearances, you'll receive a big piece of the mouth-watering pie. I'll see to it. Guaranteed."

The inspector offered a lazy smile. "Nothing's certain in this life."

Ash grabbed his chest and winced. "Jesus, what the hell's the matter with you anyway? Don't you trust me?"

"No reason I should. Your American money says it all, 'In God We Trust.' It makes no mention of trusting anyone with the name of Ash."

Ash shook his head in disgust and lit another cigarette. "What're you trying to pull?"

"I don't like my partner to pull anything on me. That's all."

"Being vague, saying nothing's certain, is not the way to do it."

The inspector asked, "Can we see how Joey made out? Let's talk more about this after we see the box and its documents."

Ash recovered his good humor and clapped the inspector on the back. "Of course. And for the record, I'll say it again: Cooperate and there's a great future in store for us."

"I look forward to it," the inspector said, hurrying to the door.

Half an hour later Ash and the inspector drove up to the empty stadium. Both men jumped out and rushed to the only other car in the parking lot.

Joey met them holding a bag in one hand.

"What happened?"

"Sorry, Mr. Ash. I've got to tell you right off: Talbot wasn't on the boat, and I didn't find that wood box."

Ash bared his teeth "Goddamnit to hell! Where could it be? I don't care so much about Talbot."

"I looked everywhere but I never saw the box. There could be places on the boat I may have missed. I don't know much about boats."

"You search everywhere, including around the engines, real good?"

"Best I was able. Far as I know it's not there. I figured maybe Talbot took it with him, trying to sell it."

"Not necessarily, and he wouldn't have taken it with him on a first meeting. But if the box wasn't on the boat and he wasn't lugging it around, that only leaves…"

"It's off the boat and in the Miami River," the inspector said softly.

"You think he threw it away?"

"Hardly."

"No, he wouldn't do that," Joey agreed.

A cunning glint appeared in Ash's eyes. "Talbot can be too smart for his own good. Tell me, Joey, was there a line hanging off the bow or the stern of the boat that could have been tied to the box underwater?"

"I never noticed. Told you I don't know much about boats. Geez, I'm sorry." He looked crestfallen.

"It's okay. What's in the bag?" Ash asked.

"I found quite a few letters taped to the wall. I took 'em all down. They were in some kind of a foreign language which was like what you said." The guard took the papers out of the bag and handed them to Ash.

Ash riffled through them in a hurry. "Christ, these are nothing like the samples. No drawings on them at all. These are phony," he wheezed. "Inspector, take a look."

Inspector Canot glanced at them and shook his head. "You're right. They're nothing like what we're looking for. Certainly none of the originals look like the copies we have."

"So, let's get the hell over to the boat ourselves and do a real search. Joey, you lead the way. We'll follow in my car." He sounded impatient.

The three men drove off, headed for the Miami River.

Chapter Nineteen

Madrid, Spain

I n Madrid, where it is five hours later than on the east coast of the United States, Señor Moreno returned to his office after dining early at a nearby restaurant. Alicia stood up and followed her boss into his office.

He looked up. Pausing a moment before speaking. He viewed the striking baubles that adorned his secretary's glowing health. Gold rings dangled from her ear lobes. Other bands of the lustrous yellow metal encircled her wrist and fingers. Like her Spanish ancestors, she had a love for the opulent bullion.

"Yes?" he asked.

"Paolo wishes to see you, soonest." She flashed her engaging smile.

"Of course." Moreno's voice sounded dry and weary. "He does not realize how everything has piled up and the sole reason for my return this evening was to catch up on my work and *not* to spend time with him." He pointed to the many papers and reports crowding his desk, some about to fall off. "I really don't know if I can spare him the time."

Alicia offered a patient smile as though she had heard this a thousand times. "Does that mean you want me to show him in, if he will hurry?"

Moreno looked at the way his secretary wore her thick, black hair tied in the back with a soft, red velvet bow. "Alicia, Alicia, what am I to do with you?" He clasped his hands under his chin. "I get no sympathy. Already I am losing the pleasant glow from the enchanting wine that accompanied my delicious dinner. Yes, tell him to make it quick. And you go home. Take a hot bath, relax. I shall not need you *here* anymore this evening. Think of me working late." There was a twinkle in his eyes.

Minutes later Moreno's assistant knocked and entered. "This had better be important."

"Sir, I assure you it is." Paolo's hands fidgeted. "You remember your last trip to Rome?"

Moreno grunted. "How could I forget, but let's not play twenty questions. I remember His Excellency saying Spain was not to become involved in unfavorable publicity during the next few weeks. Coming from the cardinal that was a very strict order. It includes you. That a problem?"

"No, sir, not for me." His assistant smirked. "But there is a problem. It involves matters both of the heart and of our government."

"What kind of nonsense are you spouting tonight? Don't waste anymore of my time reciting silly tales. I have more important business."

"This is not a silly tale. We have received copies of two letters written by Queen Isabella."

"Ancient history. Send them to one of our libraries here in the city." He shifted in his seat and opened a file. His eyes flicked up. "You still here? Something else bothering you?" He raised a querulous eyebrow.

The assistant squirmed. "These are not any old letters. Nor are they the official decrees of a staid queen. One letter smolders with the red hot coals of great passion. In it the Queen writes she has found ecstasy. She expresses carnal delight. The Queen is not queenly. The woman's obscene. I read a rough translation. She dipped her pen in filth. She will touch off a national scandal Spain will never live down. She will attract the terrible publicity His Holiness warned would not be tolerated."

"To whom did she write these infamous letters?"

"The translations were done in confidence. The two scholars who prepared them said they were only speculating but they thought about it and guessed she wrote them to the Italian, Christopher Columbus. They believe the Admiral must have been as bold on land as he was at sea."

"Goddamnit! What a time for such letters to surface. The publicity will have the Vatican seething. The Pope will cancel his visit or regret his visit if these come to light while he is in Madrid. Off the record, I must say I liked Columbus."

"Apparently the Queen felt even stronger about him."

"What do we know about him?"

"His detractors say he was a rapist and a pillager."

"Christ, Paolo, it was the men under Columbus who committed the actual rapes and did the pillaging. The troublemakers ignore the fact that the motley crews were foisted on him and later the greedy passengers were also pushed on him. Everyone was hungry for gold and was wilder than any of the poor Indians they met in the New

World. None of that was the fault of Columbus. The Queen must have known him better."

"And said she loved him."

"She realized Columbus was a good man."

"She overlooked he was a mere commoner."

Moreno rose from his chair to pace up and down. He wasn't through talking. Perhaps it was the evening's wine. "Even today some detractors accuse Columbus of bringing typhoid fever to the New World. At the time I'm sure no one gave a thought to the ships the King furnished or whether they carried typhoid germs. Those old ships must have had ticks crawling on the rats as well as all over the crews, biting, spreading germs. You can't blame Columbus for what he was handed to explore with."

"If I could interrupt…"

Moreno motioned his assistant to be quiet. "Because the Town of Palos was indebted to King Ferdinand, the King had the town provide Columbus with two old ships, the *Pinta* and the *Niña*. Columbus rented the *Santa Maria* himself for the first voyage. Columbus was stuck with junk, rat-infested junk. The ships were little more than rafts with sails, held together by crude, hand-forged nails. They were caravels, suited by their shallow drafts, to explore in water that wasn't deep. They carried crews of little more than two dozen men apiece. Ferdinand treated Columbus as if Columbus was the King's cheap lottery ticket. Wager a couple broken-down ships on the explorer and maybe the King would win a big prize."

"Yessir," Paolo said.

"Those voyages were no lark. Out on the empty ocean

the crews must have feared what might happen. Would they get back alive? The only thing stronger than their serious concerns was their hunger for gold. They hoped to fill their pockets with it."

"Yessir. But we can't ignore the Queen's letters. They won't dry up and blow away just because we want them to. They are steaming evidence of the Queen's erotic feelings. People will heap foul oaths on her and our country."

"Those in high places have been indiscreet before, but this is too much and at such a bad time. Where are the letters?"

"I have copies right here and rough translations of the old Spanish." He placed them in Moreno's hands.

Reading a translation, Moreno's eyes opened wide in astonishment. "Absolutely scandalous. How could a woman in her position write such garbage to Columbus and why do the Americans revere Columbus when he never set foot on their soil?"

"But they say he discovered America."

"Bah, a fairy tale for children. Back in 1492 the American continent was unknown to Europe and though Columbus never discovered America, he got things started. The American Indians wouldn't have done that. They never ventured very far out into the Atlantic Ocean so they weren't about to bring the Old World to the New. He did that with the help of our country's financing. That's why he's famous."

The assistant's face turned red. He pointed to the translation. "You have the real hot letter, sir. The other is a romantic love note. But there may be other letters more indelicate."

Moreno's hand wiped his face. "The Admiral must have bowled Her Highness over. She was one worked-up female."

"With lots of time on her hands to get really worked up."

"Our women's marital infidelity never was something to be taken lightly. Propriety! No matter how women behaved, if it wasn't with propriety, they were punished. Scandalous! But she got away with it. Certainly an ordinary *señorita* would have been banished from her Spanish family for acting in such a despicable manner, but people in high places were always treated differently. It used to be that royalty could do no wrong except in the eyes of other gossiping royalty. Could the Queen have been so angry at her husband's philandering that she sought revenge by taking up with that Italian?"

Moreno looked at his assistant. "Do we know for certain the Queen wrote these letters?"

"We're almost positive. We have a copy of a picture of the box the letters came in. It's convincing. And the paintings which decorate those letters could only be done by a very skilled artist, the type of artist who would be commissioned by royalty. The things she writes also confirm it in their way."

"How about the handwriting? Did you compare it with documents the Queen is known to have written and signed?"

"Not yet. No time."

"Get in touch with the *Palacio de Bibliotecas y Museos* right away and get copies of a couple documents you are absolutely positive were written or signed by Isabella. But use caution. A lot of it. No leaks to the press. None!"

"At once," the assistant said, collecting in his trembling hands the papers from Moreno's desk.

"And where the Christ are the originals of all this garbage?"

"They sent us these copies from our embassy in Washington, D.C., in the States."

"I know where Washington is. Now listen to me, please, before I lose control." Moreno's fists gripped the sides of his desk top. "Where are the originals? The originals!"

"In Miami, Florida. We don't know exactly. Our embassy in Washington sent us these copies they received from someone in New York City." Paolo shrugged away going into further detail. "It gets complicated."

"Shit! Uncomplicate it. I give you whatever authority you need, but see to it. You, personally." Moreno pounded on his desk. "Clamp a tight lid on the letters for at least three to four weeks. And I mean goddamn tight. Those letters must not leak out to poison our relations with the Vatican before or during the Papal visit."

The assistant's head bobbed up and down. "Yessir, I'll see to it right away." He was about to leave the office when Moreno stopped him with a further thought.

Moreno snickered. "Paolo, don't forget what the cardinal said. Breathe in and out."

"Yessir," he bowed his head, "in and out."

"One more thing." Moreno's eyes clouded over. "Maybe you should request our library to make up samples in a different handwriting that will cause the person in the States to think it is the Queen's writing. Put together something clever you can fax to Washington to confuse things for a day or. two. The confusion won't last longer than that because they must have books in the States with samples of her handwriting. But they may not refer to them right away."

Moreno sank back in his chair. "Get hopping on this. God, what a way to finish my night," he said out loud as much as to anotherwise empty office. No wonder the Queen carried Columbus all those years when he was making wild promises he never kept and was making all those mistakes. Had it not been for her support, Columbus would have been replaced in a flash by a competent Spanish captain. She must have been rubbing the King's nose in his many infidelities with every voyage Columbus made.

Moreno went straight home this night and did not stop by Alicia's apartment along the way. There was no twinkle in his eyes. Paolo had better clean up the mess.

Chapter Twenty

Hurried Departure

B y the time Ash, the inspector and Joey drove away
from the stadium and headed for the Miami River,
Talbot and Sandy had finished shopping and were
returning to their boat.

As the two of them approached the boat, Talbot
grasped Sandy's elbow. "I see we've had a visitor or two.
The chair on the afterdeck has been moved. Wait here." He
took a deep breath, feeling his chest tighten.

Setting his shopping bags down, he stepped on board
and picked up the machete he kept hidden beneath an old
towel outside the salon door. He looked at the split door
frame.

"Somebody's broken in," he yelled to Sandy. "I'm
going inside to look around. Why don't you wait on the
bench for a minute." He strapped on his machete.

"Be careful. Someone could still be in there."

Talbot waved to show he heard her. He exercised caution entering the salon and saw their bogus letters had been
stripped off the wall. Everything was in shambles. The cabinet drawers were pulled out and dumped on the deck. The
closets and lockers were opened and emptied, all in a fruitless attempt to find what was not there. He looked in the
engine compartment. Tools and equipment had been
thrown around. Oil cans were bashed in, causing them to

leak. Talbot could have laughed at the futility of the intruder's efforts if it were not for the mess. He went back outside and signaled Sandy to come aboard.

When she saw the upheaval, she put her hands to her face. "Oh, God, I hate the slime who did this. Is anything of ours missing?"

Talbot gave a bitter laugh. "Only the worthless letters we hung up on the wall. At least that tells us who's responsible. The idiot missed the copies hiding under the potato chips."

"It must have been Ash. I wish we could report the louse to the police." She grimaced.

"Never mind. It's high time we cleared out of here. Hope we haven't waited too long."

She began to pick up some things lying on the deck and put them away.

"Let's forget that stuff for now. We've got to leave right away and keep moving."

"You sure?"

"I'm sure. Time's running out."

"Don't forget your wood box in the river."

"I won't. Gonna fish it out right now. Then I'll crank up the engines." He gave her a hug. "Feel like casting off the lines? Your legs not giving you trouble?"

"Don't you worry about me. I'm fine." She pouted. "Only, I'm mad as hell at whoever wrecked this place."

"Let's move fast. Leave everything as is. We can tidy things up later. Cast off the lines and pull the bumpers up on deck when I tell you." He lifted her chin and kissed her quickly. "Let's go."

Her face brightened as she hurried out on deck and went to the bow. Talbot leaned over the side and hooked onto the rope attached to the duffel bag. He found the extra weight of the anchor he had put inside the bag slowed him down as he dragged it through the water. When it neared the surface he strained to pull it up. Sweating profusely, he hadn't expected it to take such an effort.

Sandy saw him struggling and called back, "Want me to help?"

He grunted, "Thanks, but I've got it."

He hoisted the duffel bag onto the deck and carried it dripping wet into the salon. Damn, this thing is heavy, he thought, and it smells of the river. Moments later he rushed topside to start the engines. They came to life on the first try. He opened the throttles, thinking they sounded warm enough that they wouldn't conk out if called on to deliver full power in a hurry.

Sandy stood watching for his signal. When he motioned to cast off the bow line, she bent over and untied the thick rope. Then she hurried back pulling in the rubber bumpers as she went by. Reaching the boat's midsection, she unhitched the two spring lines. A single rope now held them to the dock. As she acted quickly, her one leg slipped and buckled under her. She recovered and hobbled to the stern to release the last rope.

At that moment she spied two cars speeding into the adjoining parking lot and skid to a halt. Their doors slammed shut after three men scrambled out.

Favoring her leg, she dropped to her knees to undo the stern line. Her hands shook as she strained to untie the knot, but it was stiff from days of holding the boat in its slip. She winced. Pain seemed to shoot up through her legs. Though she tugged hard on the knot it did not loosen.

She recognized Ash among the men sprinting down the pathway to the dock. "Oh, no," she cried. In desperation she clawed at the unyielding knot, praying out loud she could pry the stubborn line free. Her eyes blurred with tears as she scratched and pulled, scraping her fingers raw without undoing the knot. With a look of despair she turned to Talbot. "Don," she shouted, "I need you down here right now! I'm sorry but I have really tried and I can't untie the stern line. *Help me!*"

She waved her arms in a frenzied attempt to catch his attention over the noise of the twin engines. "Don! I'm stuck. This damn rope won't budge!" She looked desperate.

At last he turned and was dumbfounded to see her plight.

The three men thundered onto the end of the long, wooden dock. The leader stumbled, causing those behind him to break stride. They grabbed him and helped him to regain his balance. He straightened.

"Coming," Talbot yelled, shifting one engine into slow forward gear. The single engine began to pull the bow around to head out into the river. Drawing his machete, Talbot leaped down the steps, two at a time.

Inching away from the dock, the boat took up the slack in the stern line. Ash sprinted around a garbage bin in front of their slip. Joey ran close behind.

Tension on the taut line increased. Talbot bent over and

hacked at the line, growing tighter still. As Ash reached out to grab the boat, the rope parted. Under severe tension, the end of the severed rope snapped back, striking Talbot in the head, knocking him unconscious. Slowly the boat continued to draw away from the dock.

An exhausted Sandy sank down beside Talbot's still form. She pushed the hair back from in front of his face and with one finger traced the outline of his birthmark.

"Oh, Don, wake up," she whispered. "I need you."

His eyelids fluttered. "What the hell are you so rudely staring at?" he demanded in a weak voice.

"At my handsome prince, that's who." She helped him to stand and make their way to the bridge.

Looking back at Ash, Sandy's face gave no hint of her loathing of the man for firing Talbot and treating them so callously.

Ash glowered and raised his fist at Talbot. "Goddamn you. Come back with that box! It belongs to the museum. That's the truth." Ash and the other two men standing beside him watched the boat draw away at a rate that was agonizingly slow. "Bring that box back!"

Talbot shook off his dizziness and shoved the other throttle into the forward position. He gunned both engines and as the boat charged towards the middle of the river, he spun the wheel hard to starboard. Picking up speed, the boat heeled over and raced downstream towards the Intracoastal Waterway and the Atlantic Ocean beyond.

Ash raged, "We've got to catch that crook. That's all there is to it."

"We will," Inspector Canot said. "Agent Cole probably

knows someone in the United States Coast Guard who can help us out."

"I certainly hope so."

"It would also be nice if we had that boat's serial number. Anybody remember it?" the inspector asked.

"I guess I do. I'll write it down," Joey said. He wrote on a slip of paper and handed it over to Ash. He looked at his wrist watch. "I'm sorry, Mr. Ash, but I have to go now. This thing is taking more time than I bargained for."

"What?" Ash grabbed the man's arm. "You can't quit now. Don't leave. You saw that we're getting close. This is a critical time. We missed them only by a slim margin. Stick 'round a little while longer. We need you here."

"Sorry. I can't. I have certain hours on the schedule. I have to get back to the museum. I could lose my job by being late. You know how that is." He detached his arm from Ash's grasp.

"Stay!"

"I can't."

"What the hell you talking about?" Ash fumed. "You saw how close we came, almost nailed that guy." Ash paused, letting his face soften as he gave Joey a friendly pat on the back. "Talbot won't get far. It won't take us much longer to bring him in. Stick around."

Joey shrugged. "I'm really sorry. You'll have to contact my boss about that. If he says it's okay, I'll come right back."

Ash shook his head. His voice became hard. "You know I can't do that. This is highly confidential. You better go ahead. Don't want you to lose your job on account of me."

"Sure wish I could stay longer to help you out."

"Yeah, just remember this is very hush-hush, god-damnit, so keep your lip buttoned up tight."

Joey gave the two men a goodbye salute, then walked down the dock. As he got into his car, another vehicle drove up alongside. The inspector and Ash were looking downstream and never noticed an enraged Señor Carlos Martinez climb out of the car that just arrived. Armed with the knife he brought from his kitchen, Martinez headed straight for the two men on the dock.

Joey rolled down his window and shouted, "Look out! This guy's got a knife."

Neither Ash nor the inspector heard as Martinez hurried along the dock. He was almost upon them when Ash, out the corner of his eye, saw the raving man for the first time. In a swift, reflex movement, Ash stepped aside avoiding the knife plunging towards him. As he did so, he stepped beyond the narrow portion of the dock that separated him from its edge. His shoe, seeking solid footing where there was none, stepped into space. Arms windmilling through the air, he tumbled into the Miami River and sank into the murky depths that flowed over his gurgle of surprise and fright.

Joey jumped out of his car and ran down to the dock. With the inspector's help he wrestled Martinez to the ground and pried the knife loose.

"Ash is destroying my daughter and young Talbot," Martinez yelled. "Let me up." He lashed out at the two men who held him. "That liar put my wife in the hospital."

"Take it easy," Joey said, restraining him. "Don't do

something you'll regret for the rest of your life. We'll hold onto the knife." He pried it loose and held it at his side.

"Best go home now and forget the whole thing," the inspector added.

Martinez tore himself out of their hands. "I'll get that no-good bastard yet," he mumbled, as he strode back to his car.

Ash floated to the river's surface, sputtering and gagging. He appeared unhurt, drifting downstream in the sluggish current, but a fit of coughing made it difficult for him to keep his head above water. With slow, weak strokes he splashed his way to shore.

Joey and the inspector ran down the bank. At the river's edge they grabbed and pulled him onto shore, where he sank to the ground breathing hard.

"Hope you didn't drink any of that filth," Canot said.

Ash gulped. "A little. Where's the raging bull? Is that silly man still around?"

Canot shook his head. "Don't worry, he left. We held onto his knife. What was that all about?"

"He's the father of the woman who was hiding down here." Ash wiped the dirty water from his face. "Guess he had second thoughts." Ash coughed up river water as he began to take off some of his wet clothes.

Handing him a towel, Joey said, "I don't know who this belongs to. It was hanging over a bench up on the dock. Now I've got to get back to the museum. Glad that guy didn't stab you, Mr. Ash. Had me worried."

"Okay, Joey, stay in touch." Ash sat on the ground wringing water out of his underwear as best he could while keeping it on. Joey hurried away.

Ash glanced around. "I'm glad my swim didn't draw a crowd." He looked downriver. "Are they gone?"

Canot said, "Talbot and the boat? Yeah, long gone. We're back to square one."

"Don't go negative on me. They borrowed that boat, so they're on a short leash. They aren't going to sail far away to Canada or anywhere like that."

"Then the Coast Guard can track them from the air. Its helicopters patrol this area all the time."

"That's what I'm thinking. Get Agent Cole to contact his man in the Coast Guard." Ash twisted his pants and shirt to remove some of the water. "Meanwhile I could stand a smoke. You got any dry cigarettes?"

"Sorry," Canot said. "Can you drive in those wet clothes?"

"We'll sure find out real soon. I have to empty out the water from my shoes first." Ash took off one shoe. "Son of a bitch polluted river. Get a whiff of me. I stink like a god-damn bag lady." He poured the water from his other shoe and squeezed water out of his jacket.

* * *

On board their boat, Sandy joined Talbot at the wheel. "That was awful close. Thanks for cutting us loose." She kissed him on the cheek. "It's like we're fugitives."

The boat powered downstream, raising a turbulent wake behind them.

Sandy looked back. "We're really moving." She was still shaking. "That could have been a disaster back there."

"Close call, all right." He laughed and leaned over to kiss her. "That's life on the run. How're you feeling?"

She rubbed her bare arms. "Still shaky after that. And your old boss gives me the creeps. I can't figure out how he located us so fast."

"I was wondering how in hell he did that myself." Talbot noticed the small river boats they passed were bobbing up and down on his wake. He throttled back. "I hate to say it, but your dad is the one who could have told them."

"Don't go blaming this on him." She put her hands on her hips in defiance. "You know as well as I that he wouldn't tell them. Besides no one at the museum ever heard of my father. They wouldn't know enough to contact him."

Talbot wagged his finger at her. "Sorry, that's not quite true. My application for a job was in the personnel files back in the Port-au-Prince office. It had your family's address in it. When I signed on I gave it to them to contact in an emergency. The accountant Harris had the file and must have shown it to Ash."

"I don't believe my father would ever sell us out. Not to Ash. Not to anyone. No way." She appeared steadfast in her conviction.

"I don't know how Ash wormed it out of him. It may not have been pretty. But I'm sure that's the weak link. Not your father but the personnel file leading Ash to your father."

"Not my father. Never."

"It's okay. Just remember your dad was the only one who knew about us and where we were."

"Well, how about Mr. Juarez who owns the boat? He knew."

"He only knew where his boat was. He didn't know us. I'm telling you, it's okay. Give your dad a call when we tie up tonight. Make sure he's all right. I wouldn't put anything past Ash."

"I planned to call my dad anyway to tell him not to worry. We'll get the boat back to Mr. Juarez when our time is up. But I'm worried about my dad."

"Great. Now do you want to tidy things up down below? Nothing fancy. I'd help you but we should put a little distance between us and Ash. Then we'll anchor to tape over the ship's name and serial numbers. That'll make it a bit harder for anyone to spot us. I hope."

"Aye, aye," she smiled and added, "My dad didn't do it."

"If you say so. Only I hope for your dad's sake, he wasn't as stubborn as you are."

Sandy went below.

Talbot continued to cruise down the Miami River while trying to puzzle out how Ash might have gotten Sandy's father to divulge their whereabouts. The boat passed several Haitian freighters that were tied up along the river. Their decks were piled high with used bicycles, worn-out mattresses, discarded refrigerators and old lumber. Talbot could not imagine what was stored below deck. Whatever it was seemed to interfere with the safe operation of their bilge pumps, for the freighters sat dangerously low in the water.

In the salon, Sandy wiped off the mud on the duffel bag

and dragged it in a locker. Then she began straightening up the mess. She righted overturned chairs and slid drawers back into place after putting their contents in order as best she could. The bag topped with potato chips was less full but the copies of the letters remained intact. She put it up on the shelf, fretting over her dad.

Once they had sailed out of the Miami River into Biscayne Bay, Talbot changed course, heading south to follow the Intracoastal Waterway along Florida's southeastern tip. He began to worry again about what could have forced Sandy's father to divulge their location to Ash. He knew her father wouldn't succumb easily.

Farther along, Talbot turned into shallow water. When the depth gauge read four feet, he shut the engines down and dropped anchor.

After showing Sandy how she could help, he changed into swimming trunks and jumped off the stern into the water. It came up to his chest, but didn't feel as cool as the night before.

Sandy reached down and handed him a roll of masking tape. He covered the old name and the serial numbers with it and sprayed paint over stencils purchased earlier. He created a different name and numbers on the tape. When he was finished, he handed her what remained and swam away from the boat. He turned and admired his handiwork. He gave it a thumbs up and waved for Sandy to join him in the water.

Later they clambered back on board the boat, feeling refreshed.

When they got into their clothes, they lashed two beach

chairs to the forward deck, put up a blue awning, and flew an old, red flag from the stern. Their attempts to alter the boat's appearance were done.

Soon they were out sailing in the Intracoastal Waterway again, headed south at a leisurely speed.

At dusk a helicopter circled overhead. Probably looking us over through their binoculars, Talbot thought. Maybe they would be fooled for a time but there was nothing more he could think to do to disguise the boat. He felt uneasy.

Until the helicopter disappeared in the distance, Talbot delayed switching on his navigation lights. What would the pilot of the helicopter report, he wondered, and to whom? Talbot steered their borrowed boat into the Gray Marina for the night. They tied the boat up. To buy a few things for their supper, Sandy dug into the little money she had borrowed from her father. She also paid their docking fee in advance so they were free to slip away when morning dawned. They returned in the dark to their boat.

While she cleaned up after their supper, Talbot took the duffel bag out of the locker, adjusted the length of the rope attached to it and lowered it over the side. He positioned it close to the dock as he had done before.

"Sandy, we're all set for the moment. I'm going ashore to call de Silvo in New York City to get an update. Care to come along?"

"Yes, I can call my folks. Let Dad know that we and the boat are all right and I can learn how he's doing."

Chapter Twenty-One

The Letters

"Hello, Juan? This morning you told me you received in good shape all the copies Sandy faxed to you. Did you spot anything interesting?"

"Whoa, whoa. Not so fast, *amigo*. You make my poor head ache. My people are giving it top priority, but they haven't been working on the letters for a full day yet. However, there's only one word for what they have gotten out of the letters so far.: "Fantastic!"

"Really?" Talbot's face lighted up. "I can't tell you how good that makes me feel. What impression do the letters leave your people with?"

"Ah, that is something incredible. Two of my part-time women who are expert in the old Spanish have been doing the translations for me. They were both so intrigued by the material they didn't stop. Not for coffee. Not for lunch. Not even to go to the ladies room for a smoke. They kept on working. Most unusual. I've got a couple tired assistants on my hands with their eyeballs hanging out. But the letters thrilled them at the same time they made these ladies laugh. I gulped when I heard what the women told me. These letters are goddamn hot. More than what you told me to expect."

"What did your women say? Were they blushing?"

De Silvo laughed. "Not these women. Maybe they're too old, too blasé. Who knows? Actually, they're both married so they tried not to show it affected them that way. Mind you, they haven't translated everything yet and already they've learned some sexy Spanish words that didn't used to be in their vocabularies."

Unable to stand still Talbot shifted his weight from one foot to the other as though he needed to be standing before a urinal in a men's room. "What did you figure out about the writer?" Stress resonated in his voice.

"Let me say the letters have the sound of a Spanish noble woman. Although her vocabulary often slips below the belt, the letters suggest the writer was probably in the royal family. They reveal a very passionate female who had strong feelings for the guy who received the letters. What else can I tell you about them except I wish I had such a woman crazy about me?" He chuckled.

"Could the letters have been written to Columbus?"

"That's an enormous jump, but that's what they look like."

"Finding the box in Haiti, about where Columbus lost the *Santa Maria*, doesn't that confirm to whom the letters were written?" Talbot insisted.

"I concede it increases the chances the letters were written to Columbus. Yet, it's not the same as having his name spelled out on them. For now I'm saying the letters may have been written to him. After all, he was a seafaring man with an eye for the ladies. Don't forget on his first voyage to the New World he sailed in the company of an adventuresome trio of females."

Talbot frowned. "Don't hand me that. The crews were all men."

"I'm talking about the ships. In Spanish the ending for female nouns is the letter 'a.' Each ship had a name that ended in that letter. The *Santa Maria* was the Saint Mary. The *Pinta* was the painted lady. Finally, the *Niña* was the little girl. So you see, females all."

"Anything else?"

"*Amigo*, I know you're pissing in your pants with excitement, trying to nail everything down, but take it one step at a time. My staff is giving priority to determining the age of these things. I've been in touch with a contact who works in the National Library in Madrid. See if he had any thoughts on this. He had important news."

Talbot sensed trouble. "Was it good news or bad?"

"I don't know how to tell you. I didn't want to but I know I have to. This friend recalled reading in the archives over there, a fragment of a diary written back in the year 1492. Something strange was going on in the Royal Court at that time. That set me to thinking. Right away I hunted out a copy of Queen Isabella's handwriting in my library. The handwriting didn't match any in the letters. Your letters are all forgeries! Fakes! Done by not one person but by two different people. Sorry, I just had to tell you."

Talbot's mouth dropped open. He gasped. "That's incredible—and you weren't going to say anything to me. That means I got stung by the Paques down in Haiti. I feel sick. Are you sure two people wrote the letters?"

"I apologize for not catching it sooner. Anyway, after comparing the handwriting over and over I'm absolutely certain they are forgeries and both my assistants agree. The Queen did not write those vulgar letters. And get this. I received a sample of handwriting from some cretin over in Madrid's National Library claiming it was the Queen's handwriting."

"And..."

"I'm sorry, the sample from Spain's library didn't match anything either. It didn't match that of the two people who wrote those letters and it didn't match the Queen's. They're not bad as forgeries go. Nothing clumsy about them."

Talbot's tanned face turned a very pale white. For a time he was unable to breathe. He squeezed the receiver almost hard enough to break it and sobbed. "Hell, that's an awful kick in the head. I counted on those letters. Are you positive your sample is authentic?"

"No question about it. Please forgive me."

Talbot gulped, "There goes a tremendous link with the past and, with it, all my dreams of becoming more than just another archaeologist. I've lost everything."

"I am sorry, *amigo*. But don't throw those forgeries away. They're old and have interesting art work decorating them, and they could be worth a bit of change for shedding light on another period in time. For example, the forgers comment on the lives of serfs, vassals, and peasants. Their toil. Snaring rabbits, picking berries. They echo the bowing and scraping of that period and vibrate with medieval passions. Also, hold onto the box. It came from the same period."

Talbot's face twisted in agony. Fired from his job and

broke. No chance now to make up for that. Nor could he avoid the embarrassment. He had gambled and suffered a whopping loss. Feeling clammy and miserable, he slumped against the wall of the booth. All he had were bits and pieces. Consolation prizes, chicken feed. Fighting to pull himself together, he swung around and stood upright.

His thoughts floundered as he sought a convincing explanation. Firmly grasping the receiver, he panted, "Listen, Juan, I say you've got something wrong. Look closely at the truth."

"*Amigo*, I've already done that, many times."

"Have you considered how the King needed gold to support his armies? The King could even have encouraged the Queen to write those letters just to keep Columbus nearby. Columbus hung around the court for over six years. That's a long time. The Queen must have been crazy about Columbus, and when he was away, she wrote those letters to him. The letters must have been lost in Haiti by Columbus. How else could they get there, especially if they were forged? Columbus didn't think those letters were forged if he received them."

Talbot continued, "Your problem is you're not convinced the way I am that the Queen truly loved Christopher. Take her marriage to King Ferdinand. Do you think they were a devoted couple enjoying the connubial bliss of a happy marriage? Nonsense! They met only two days before they got married. Two days in which to get to know each other and complete their mating dance before they got hitched. There were no loving arms and warm embraces. They didn't marry for love, so she was a woman waiting to fall in love."

"That may be true enough but it doesn't change the letters."

"Listen to me. Ferdinand's affairs with other women were so flagrant that a lot of people knew of his peccadilloes. History books recorded his tendency to transgress. I'm certain that kept Queen Isabella from worrying she might fall in love with Columbus, even though Spaniards demanded their women behave themselves and act decorously."

Talbot raised his voice. "Remember Columbus promised the Queen lots of the terrific, smooth fabric called silk to replace the coarse European woolens she wore. How could a woman not love such a wonderful guy? The Queen had to be heads over heels in love with him."

"They are forgeries. Let the bad news sink in."

"Hell, are you overlooking the lyrical quality of the words in some of those letters?"

"It doesn't matter. They weren't her words. I'm thinking they may have simply coincided with what was actually going on at the time."

Talbot shook his head. "Columbus promised her sacks of hard-to-get spices."

Talbot recalled reading that, in medieval days, European meals were as dull and unvarying as the meals fed to pet dogs today. Moreover, without refrigeration, medieval food often smelled bad and tasted rotten. On the other hand, exotic spices not only could conceal such off-putting smells and tastes but also could give variety to any meal. Clearly, a merchant would be able to sell a shipload of Oriental spices in Europe for ten times what he paid for them in Asia. After a single trip to the Far East he could become rich if…he could get to the Orient and back alive.

Talbot said, "Don Cristóbal Colón promised the Queen those wonderful things. Now you're telling me they were mere friends? No way. Columbus had too much going for him. No doubt in my mind. She was in love with him and bound to write to him of that love."

"Maybe she was in love with him. I'm not saying she wasn't. What I'm saying is she didn't write those letters."

"Tell me what you saw in those writings. What did they look like?"

"Not much to tell. Although the vellum suffered minor deterioration the writing was untouched. Both handwritings in the letters are the well-formed scribbles of the day, the usual loops and swirls, broad strokes and tight little squiggles, a bunch of hen scratchings. They aren't your ornate Latin calligraphy. They even have a touch of the cramped scrawl to them like the Queen's."

"There you just said it. They're like the Queen's."

"*Amigo*, it doesn't matter. They are goddamn forgeries."

"Before you go, you want to put a figure on what the box and the letters are now worth?"

"Hold your horses, *amigo mio*, don't be in such a damn hurry. As soon as I have the complete story, I'll quote you a price that's higher than what I can give you at this point, when I must allow for so many uncertainties."

"We don't have much time. Others are trying to snatch from us the only things that'll save my career. Sandy and I had to leave our slip on the Miami River in a hurry. Ash, the manager of the museum's expedition in Haiti, and two other men, came charging down on us there. They didn't draw guns when we pulled away so either I'm not a murder suspect or none of them was a cop. But that's how close the other side is. We've got to hurry. There's no time to waste."

"I'm not wasting time. By the way, you didn't tell me how you got these things out of Haiti. What's the story?"

"We sailed them out."

"No government clearance?"

"Nothing like that. Besides, you say they're forgeries."

"You've got a big problem."

"I know. Even Sandy pointed that out to me."

"Haiti will maybe make a claim. Perhaps Spain will, too."

"For forgeries? I don't think so."

"And you've got no provenance, nothing to show where these forgeries originated, other than maybe a bill of sale that's signed with an x by people who can't read."

"That's why I came to a problem-solver." Talbot nodded at the phone while his feet fidgeted.

"Not that it is the most difficult problem to be solved, but you've definitely got one. And, of course, today many people don't like Columbus. That means a smaller market for the old box and the letters."

"You're beginning to sound like a pawn broker trying to shave the price. No matter what critics say, for me Columbus remains a brave and courageous man. He took a tremendous risk. What if one of the rumors about the ocean had been true? In fact, you don't need rumors. As far as we know, he was lucky to avoid the disasters that mariners experience at sea, such as scurvy. Call it luck. Call it skill.

Columbus accomplished something stupendous. He crossed the Atlantic Ocean and returned to Spain alive. Overlook whatever bad is said about him and consider Elvis Presley fans. They celebrate Elvis for his accomplishments in music and entertainment. They don't whine about his mistakes. We should treat Columbus the same way."

"I'm sure there must be collectors out there who would love to buy those forgeries. Although you may have to sell the letters and the box privately if you wish to tap into that market and you'll get a lower price."

"There you go again attempting to knock the price down."

"Please call me back in about twenty-four hours. I should know more. I've only given you part of the picture. I could have some good news for you by then."

"Okay." Talbot frowned. "Only I can't take too much more news, good or bad. Talk to you soon."

"*Adios, amigo.*"

Talbot hung up. His face held a troubled look. When he stepped out, Sandy entered the phone booth. She stood talking for a long time. After finishing her call, she left the booth crying. Talbot hurried to her side and put his arm around her. "Hey, what's the matter?"

"Mama's in the hospital, and it's all my fault."

"What's wrong with your mother?" Talbot asked.

"She may have suffered a stroke. The doctors have to perform more tests. I'll tell you about it when we get back on board the boat."

"C'mon, what're you saying?"

"Later, when we get back to the boat. I'll tell you," she sobbed. "I just want to sit down."

"Well, I don't mean to have you feel worse, but the news from my friend in New York City wasn't good. He's compared the handwriting with an authentic one. I've got forgeries. I'll get some money for them, probably enough to repay you, but that's it."

Sandy wiped her eyes and looked up. "It was like you figured. Ash took the address of where my folks live from the files. He gave my folks a story and they let him in the apartment. He said I'm traveling with a felon, which hurt Mom. She left the room and collapsed. That's when the doctors believe she may have suffered a little stroke."

"Will she recover and be all right?"

"The doctors feel she has a good chance."

"So what was it Ash said that got her upset?"

"Not my mother alone. It affected my dad as well. What happened was Ash told my folks we were murderers. Ash then changed his story. I was traveling with a murderer. It was more than my mother could handle. She fled from the room. Ash kept on with my father saying he could get us a lawyer the museum would pay for but first he had to talk to us. That's how he wormed our location out of my dad. I should have told Dad why we really had come back to the States when I had the chance. That makes what happened my fault," she sobbed.

Talbot stared at her wide-eyed. "I was the one who asked you to tell your mom and dad we're on vacation and not to say anything about me getting fired. Don't blame yourself. I should have told you to warn them."

"Well, you were right. Ash wangled the information out of my father."

"Your dad wouldn't have told him where we were if he had known what Ash was up to."

"Looking back, Dad didn't think Ash even bothered to tell him what motive you had to kill Barney. My dad is terribly sorry about letting Ash make a fool of him. He wanted me to tell you he apologizes for making trouble and hopes we get a little time by ourselves away from Ash. If there's anything Dad can do for us, he said he'd be only too happy to do it. Just let him know."

Talbot patted her hand. "Try to put it out of your mind. It's over. Let's bunk down. We're getting up early tomorrow and slipping out of here before the others who are docked here are awake to see whether we sailed north or south."

Chapter Twenty-Two

On the Run

I n fitful sleep Talbot writhed and tossed through the night. An hour before dawn he was awake in his tangled sheets, planning the day's cruise north to Palm Beach. He could take the boat up through the sheltered Intracoastal Waterway. But once past Miami, he would have to go slow. The reduced speed maintained on the waterway protected waterfront homes from destructive wakes left by speeding boats and gave ample time to raise the many bridges strung out over the waterway. Or, he could sail out to the Atlantic Ocean and head north at whatever speed he chose and mingle with the sport fishing boats.

When he could no longer bear lying in his bunk, Talbot got up and dressed. Stepping out on deck, he found everything dripping wet from the thick, morning fog.

In preparation for an early departure he hauled in the duffel bag and dragged it into the salon where he wiped it off and stowed it away in a locker. He yawned and started the engines. Their muffled sound roused Sandy. She dressed as he disconnected the water line and the electrical line. He climbed up to the flying bridge, where visibility was better over the low-lying fog. From there he operated one set of the dual controls as Sandy cast off.

The boat glided across the marina's still water, leaving

behind a few ripples that soon smoothed out and disappeared. Except for the soft rumble of the engines at slow speed the early morning was quiet. Talbot wondered if de Silvo would finish today and what good news could de Silvo provide?

Sandy coiled the ropes up and put the bumpers away in their racks. Talbot rubbed his eyes. Nobody was stirring aboard the boats that remained secured to the marina docks. He turned north, following the Intracoastal Waterway channel markers back up towards Miami.

Sandy joined him on the bridge.

"Everything secure?" he asked.

She nodded, a sweet smile on her face. "Before I fell asleep last night I thought about what you said. I'm really sorry for you about the letters." She frowned. "Are you doubling back the way we came?"

"Only a bit. When we draw opposite Miami, I'll change course and head out to sea. North on the ocean we'll be more flexible."

"You don't expect anyone will notice us out there?"

"That's the idea, and we won't be as confined as on the waterway." He tried not to show his concern.

"I'm going down to the galley. Would you like some hot, fresh coffee?"

"Sure would." He blew on his fingers to warm them.

Sandy went below while Talbot looked ahead through his field glasses and jotted down the number of the next channel marker. He checked it against his chart to determine exactly where they were and penciled in a course he planned to take. But as his eyes ranged over the chart, his mind jumped to the letters. He inflated his lungs with fresh air. Sonofabitch, he thought, can they all be forgeries? De Silvo could be mistaken about what was authentic.

Sandy reappeared with a mug of hot coffee she handed up to him.

"Smells good. Thanks," he said as she left for the galley again.

Moments later she came back with a mug of coffee for herself and climbed up to stand beside him.

"I'm not sure the letters are counterfeit. When you got up last night, what did you find in the letters you worked on?"

Her mouth pursed. "They're all chopped up. The handwriting is hard to read, and I can't find a lot of the words in the dictionary I bought yesterday, but I made out some things."

Sandy smiled. "The writer devoted an entire letter to some man who entered her chambers one evening and removed his cape. She was sitting close to a small stove, sewing and had a heavy blanket around her. Earlier, she had dismissed the help. Her husband was away with his army for the whole week."

Sandy looked closely at Talbot. "Are you listening?"

He nodded.

"Well, the woman noticed her visitor was growing chilly and invited him to sit closer so she could share her blanket. He saw she was dressed for bed. She picked up a scented puff used to perfume her pillow and dabbed it on her neck. The man leaned over and told her how good she smelled. She turned the statue of the Blessed Mother to face the wall."

Talbot nodded again. "Was there more?"

"Soon her visitor became warm under the blanket and shed the rest of his outerwear. She offered him a chicken leg that lay in a warming dish on the stove. The man chewed on the leg while she spoke of exchanging rings with him. He did not think it wise and finished the leg. Putting down the bone, he wiped his hands on his handkerchief."

"A true gentleman, not wiping his hands on his pants. He knew how to behave in the Queen's chambers."

"The Queen began to feel chilly herself. The man held her close. One thing led to another and that was it. End of the letter."

"Does it help to assume that Queen Isabella is writing about an evening alone with Columbus?"

"It's a whole lot easier. I can figure out what the Queen was getting at. For example, we know that Columbus went on a journey through unknown waters. In another letter the Queen hopes an instrument her lover navigates by is reliable. I bet she was referring to a compass."

"She probably was. Back then it was still a new gadget, the latest thing to steer by when sailing out of sight of land, particularly on a cloudy day or a rainy night when there were no stars in the sky. Sailing by a compass must have seemed like magic and was something to write about."

Sandy took a sip of her coffee. "In that same letter the writer hoped her man would be sailing on the new breed of ships called the caravel. I guess it was a small ship that didn't sit very deep in the water. It must have been ideal for exploring close in to shore."

"Too bad the Queen got her wish. Caravel-built hulls

were different than the hulls of other sailing vessels. Their bottom planks were butted each against the other, edge to edge, rather than the planks overlapping as they did on most ships. That could have made caulking of seams more difficult for the *Santa Maria*. That could have been part of the problem when it foundered on the barrier reef off Haiti's shores."

"The writer scribbled about *amore* and how an Italian, or the love of an Italian, thrilled her. She raved about how being with him was like being presented with a bag of gold. I got the feeling gold turned her on. She and the King must have needed plenty of it to pay their armies while fighting against the Muslims."

Talbot nodded. "The King and Queen weren't the only ones needing gold. All of Europe suffered a gold famine back then. Commerce was growing. So was the need for gold coins to make trading easier. Gold made a great currency. It didn't wear out like paper did, and it didn't tarnish."

"Anyway that's what I translated last night, fitting bits and pieces together, making leaps across words and phrases I couldn't translate and ignoring the penmanship when I couldn't decipher it."

Talbot gave her a thumb's up. "But it's too bad de Silvo thinks they're all forged." At that moment the sound of a helicopter reached them and grew louder. The aircraft flew low over their boat before circling away.

Talbot looked somber as he watched the aircraft turn back towards Miami. "I wonder if it's keeping an eye on us?"

"Hope not. It's probably looking for drug traffic.

Besides, our boat doesn't look the same as when we started out. That and the fog should make them wonder if this is the same boat."

"Maybe. In another hour we'll be sailing in the ocean among the chartered fishing boats. Then we'll set you up with fishing gear so we will look like everyone else out there." He could think of nothing else to do. His stomach tightened with concern.

"Think I'll go down and fix us some breakfast."

"No rush. I'm not hungry."

"Keeps me busy, and you have to eat."

* * *

Ash rose from his hotel bed shortly after eight A.M. which was late for him. He had spent much of the previous night at the hotel bar with the inspector discussing the need to find Talbot before the police located the man. Ash also talked at length about how he and the inspector could personally profit from their joint venture.

After Ash ordered breakfast from room service he lighted his second cigarette of the day. It started a fit of coughing. When he recovered, he showered and shaved. As his meal arrived, the ring of his phone startled him.

"Not waking you, I hope," Inspector Canot said.

"Hold it, I've got to sign this." He took the check and scribbled his signature on it. "Inspector, I've already bathed and dressed, so don't worry about waking me. What's on your mind?"

"Agent Cole's contact in the Coast Guard says he

believes Talbot is already on the move this early in the morning. Can't be certain with the fog. The boat is headed back up here to Miami. The Coast Guard will monitor its progress."

Passing his hand over his face, Ash swallowed. "What the hell is he coming back up here for? Why pull a crazy stunt like that?" He began to cough.

"Perhaps he thinks his disguise has us fooled."

Ash brought his coughing under control. "I don't believe it. He's pulling something. Maybe he's going to visit her father. Do you think we should rent a boat to intercept him?"

"The Coast Guard is a bit fuzzy about the identification. We'd better hold off a while to be sure it's the right boat before we rent one of our own."

"How about the Miami police? They hot on his trail yet?"

"From what I hear they're lagging a couple steps behind us. Can you meet me in the lobby in half an hour? I'd like to say goodbye before I leave for Haiti."

"What do you mean, goodbye?"

"Like I told you last night, I have to get back to Port-au-Prince today. But you'll catch Talbot before very long, so you don't need me. Just don't forget me when you get the old box and the letters."

"I wouldn't think of it. See you downstairs in half an hour." Ash crossed the room and stood in front of the mirror. He gazed at his reflection and smiled at the image of a mature executive about to embark on another day of making wise decisions and issuing important commands. This might be the day that millions of dollars of ancient treasure fell into his hands.

Ash stood preening for a few moments more before sitting down to finish his cigarette and cup of coffee.

Less than thirty minutes later he sauntered across the lobby. He shook hands and bid Canot goodbye. He watched the inspector settle his bill at the desk and ride off in a taxi.

But the inspector did not leave Miami. He transferred his luggage to another hotel and spent the rest of the morning at poolside, sunning, napping and occasionally consuming light refreshment. But he spent most of the time playing a recorder his American police training officer had given him. The night before he had strapped it beneath his shirt and recorded Ash's conversation at the bar. The recorded voice was very clear as he played the tape over and over. He smiled, sipping his drink, and hummed an old tune sounding like a cat purring.

Out on the ocean, Talbot sailed north hugging the shoreline of Florida's east coast and staying out of the Gulf Stream's rough water where it flowed close in to shore. He was beginning to warm up and was ready to shed his light jacket. He noticed the haze was burning off fast and visibility was improving. A container ship passed by, headed in the opposite direction. Probably bound for South America, he thought. Overhead, white cumulus clouds boiled up in the blue sky. Was de Silvo finished, he wondered.

He nibbled at a toasted cinnamon bagel and looked back at Miami's mammoth luxury liners tied up to a long pier awaiting their next pleasure cruise. He wondered what Ash was doing. Then his thoughts turned to the collection of Spanish letters and who might buy them. The next thing he knew, the morning haze had completely disappeared, promising the day would be warm and clear.

An empty oil tanker sitting high in the water slipped past without a sound. A short time later Talbot heard the steady thunder of a jet plane's climb-out over the ocean from the Fort Lauderdale airport. The aircraft gleamed in the sun until it became a speck in the sky, too small to see.

In the distance a police helicopter flew north, swooping low over the beaches, showing no interest in their boat. Two sport fishing boats sailed out from shore. Talbot hoped the fish were biting and that many more small craft would join him off the coast at West Palm Beach. Bits of waterlogged debris floated by. Talbot referred to his chart and saw that Boca Raton and Boynton were the next small cities they would come to before they drew opposite Palm Beach.

Later in the morning he sighted the skyline of West Balm Beach and called down to Sandy, "Want to see where the fat cats hibernate?"

She joined him on the bridge and he said, "That's Lake Worth, part of the Intracoastal Waterway that runs along Palm Beach between the city and the ocean."

"We going in?"

"Not yet. Much too early."

She put her hands on her hips. "Am I going to miss the thrill of shopping the famous Worth Avenue stores of Palm Beach?"

"Most likely." He laughed. "We'll stay out here on the ocean, cruising back and forth among the charter fishing boats as long as the fish are biting. By the time the fish quit, the expensive shops will be closed. Why don't you hop down to the after deck and work on your tan? You could sit holding a fishing pole in your hands, looking like you expect to hook a big one."

"Wouldn't you be surprised if I did actually land one big enough to cook for our supper?"

"Sorry, that won't happen. We have no bait."

* * *

At the Federal Office Building in Miami a Coast Guard employee left another message on the empty desk which Inspector Canot used during his brief stay in the city. The message reported that Talbot's boat was out on the Atlantic Ocean, approaching Palm Beach. Throughout the day, reports on where Talbot's craft was located, accumulated on the courtesy desk that had been used by the inspector.

In the quiet of mid-afternoon Ash wandered up to the unoccupied desk and helped himself to the stack of messages. He read through them, then left the building in a hurry.

Later in the afternoon the inspector appeared at the desk, looking rested. He collected the messages that lay on top of the desk and took his time studying them. He inquired of others in the large room and learned that a man noticeable for his coughing had gone through the messages some time ago and rushed out.

The inspector telephoned Charlie Jackson in Tallahassee and informed him Talbot must still have the box. He described the boat including the false serial number and its amended name as reported by the Coast Guard.

Talbot would probably anchor for the night in the shallow water of the Intracoastal Waterway at West Palm Beach.

The inspector said he would appreciate it if Jackson spoke with his Coast Guard friend and asked for him to continue his good help. The inspector added he had made an interesting tape the previous evening. Ash did not realize his dishonest proposal of a conspiracy to cheat Haiti and Southern State Museum out of the box and its contents had been recorded. The inspector mentioned he would turn copies of the tape over to the proper authorities. He was about to return to Haiti.

Jackson assured the inspector he would seek the further cooperation of the Coast Guard.

"How about getting the police force to go out to Talbot's boat tonight?" Canot asked. "The police might find a murder suspect they are looking for."

"I'll take care of that as well, thanks."

Chapter Twenty-Three

The Intruder

Perched on top of a tall, wooden piling, a brown pelican surveyed the Intracoastal Waterway. The ungainly bird waited patiently until, swooping low, barely skimming the water, it snared an unsuspecting fish that broke the water's surface. Though the sun had set, the still air remained hot and sticky.

Buddy Ash sat in a rented car parked nearby. Its windows were open to vent the cigarette smoke that threatened to blind him. Occasionally he raised his binoculars to watch Talbot's boat. The red flag, which the Coast Guard had reported was flying from the stern, helped him keep track of the boat.

With growing excitement he watched the craft leave the ocean and sail into the waterway. The boat passed not far from where he sat, then turned out of the channel into shallow water. A figure dropped an anchor off the bow and a second anchor off the stern. Ash recognized Talbot.

Talbot's figure went back inside the cabin. Three night lights lit up, marking the boat's position. In the approaching darkness Talbot appeared on deck again carrying a large sack. He walked around to the far side of the boat and out of sight.

Minutes passed.

Talbot reappeared and picked up a second bundle that inflated to become a rubber raft. He lifted the raft over the side and tied it to the stern before returning to the cabin.

Ash did not see the figure again until it came out dressed in different clothes. Ash watched the figure climb down into the inflatable raft and row ashore. The raft was tied up alongside several skiffs secured to the dock. Above the dock hung a sign offering bait and diesel fuel for sale. Talbot went inside the shack at the end of the dock. When he came out, it was completely dark. He stood in the lighted doorway for a moment. A flashlight came on in his hand. The light bobbed and then disappeared as Talbot walked inland.

Ash snapped his cigarette out the open window and started his car. Grinning in anticipation, he drove over to the bait shack and parked the car. He placed a sharp hunting knife beneath his jacket before getting out of the car.

Perspiration dripped from Talbot's body by the time he located a public telephone booth several blocks in from the bait shack. He shined his flashlight on the booth and saw the folding door was shut. The day's heat was trapped inside. It would be like a steam bath in there, he thought. Though already sweaty, he needed privacy for his call and entered the booth, pulling the door shut tight behind him. The cloying, humid air felt even warmer than he expected. His nose wrinkled at the sour smell of something left on the floor of the booth.

He dialed de Silvo, requesting the telephone operator to reverse the charges. The phone gave off a busy signal. Talbot opened the door of the booth and breathed in the cooler, outside air while waiting. He placed the call again. The line was still busy. After a further wait he tried once more before his call was accepted.

"Juan, you must be sitting right at the phone. It's been so busy. Excuse me for reversing the charges, but I didn't want to carry around a pocketful of change."

"No problem, *amigo*. And of course you're right. I am sitting on top of my phone. Any minute now I expect an urgent call to come in about the age of your things."

"Do you have any word for me now? You said to call in twenty-four hours."

"The letters are still safe?"

"Of course."

"Good."

"What's good about it? Sandy and I were shocked at your bad news. Are you now taking that back and no longer saying the letters are forgeries? Is that the good news you promised last night?"

"Not exactly. The letters expressed forbidden love between a queen and her dream man. Like I mentioned before, some letters are very naughty. However, in one letter the writer says the man we believe to be Columbus makes her feel like a whole person, not merely a male's chattel."

De Silvo interrupted the telephone conversation to speak to someone who was with him. After a muffled discussion de Silvo said to Talbot, "It's sweet how the romance blossoms in those letters. Putting aside the pornographic ones, the rest are very tender. They mention King Ferdinand was often away with his army and left the

Queen when she was going through her change in life and wasn't feeling well."

De Silvo paused to sip a cold drink. "I agree with you that sometime during the six years before Columbus sailed on his first voyage under the Spanish flag the Queen may have fallen in love with him."

"Can you trace that love growing in the letters?"

"Oh, yes, the letters are quite touching, beautifully written."

"Damn!" Talbot's fist pounded the small shelf beneath the phone. His mouth felt parched as a dusty road. His throat tightened. He had to ask. "Let's leave the diced onions and get right to the cooking. Are you going to say the letters are not forgeries after all?"

"Forgeries?" De Silvo's voice sounded thoughtful. "They were forgeries. But never mind. I have some good news."

Talbot stammered, "How can that be? If the letters are forgeries, the Queen didn't write them. Columbus wasn't the horny sailor the letters made him out to be. The courageous visionary can still be my hero. Is that your good news?"

"Partly. But there is plenty more. This morning I received a next-day delivery from you of an original letter. Magnificent. I liked the feel of the old vellum on which it was written."

"What do you mean? All the letters were written on old vellum."

"I'm getting at something else. The vellum on which that letter was forged dates back to the 1400's. If every letter was written on the same vellum, which I'm thinking is a pretty safe bet, a flock of sheep from that time period must have given the hides off their backs for those forgeries. They're valuable if all are on ancient vellum."

"I looked 'em all over pretty carefully and didn't catch any major differences. Every letter appeared to be written on the same ancient parchment, some on the 'hair' side and some on the 'flesh' side. So?"

"One of my workers took a few sample particles of the actual vellum and a few particles of the ink and of the paint that decorated the original letter to test their age. I just received a preliminary report over the phone. They date back to the late 1400's. Also, the age of the box checks out."

"What the hell are you trying to tell me?"

"Don't be discouraged. Let's begin with the little paintings that adorn many of the letters. They were done in the style of the illuminated manuscripts the monks painted in the 1400's. Even though the copies are only in black and white they have fine detail, the same as the one original you sent me. Such excellent art could only mean royalty was involved. The nobles in court were the patrons of the arts, supporting them. If the original letters are preserved as well as they appear to be in my copies, they are in marvelous condition."

"And?" Talbot felt restless.

"The letters, all prepared in the late 1400's, weren't done yesterday by some clever counterfeiting ring out to make a fast buck. Probably a couple of lowly scribes sat hunched over their benches preparing the letters for their masters. Judging from the photos, the box looks like it has to be around the same age as the letters or somewhat older."

Streams of perspiration flooded down Talbot's face. Using the side of his hand as a squeegee, he scraped his forehead dry. "You're telling me everything is valuable on account of its age? Is that your good news?"

"That's also part of it."

"The Paques weren't alive in the 1400's. They couldn't have been mixed up in the forgeries. That makes me feel better."

"*Amigo*, there must be more. Give me a scenario that fits the facts. You're the archaeologist."

"I need a second to open the door a crack. It's stifling in here." He pushed the door open and held the phone to his ear.

"All right," Talbot said, "I think of the 1400's and imagine how the high and mighty Spanish nobles of the royal court must have felt. Those titled aristocrats would have been lying awake nights thinking the grasping foreign mariner was stealing their birthrights away. And they would have puked on the decision of their majesties to engage Columbus to hunt for a new route to the wondrous Orient and its gold."

Talbot began to smile, thinking.

"What's more," he added, "the nobles would have wondered how the crown had the nerve to waste money on exploration when it had armies to support."

"I agree," said de Silvo.

"Finally, the nobles must have feared the get-rich-quick scheme of Columbus might actually succeed. The nobles' hatred festered, leading them to plot against Columbus. That was the something strange that was going on in 1492, which your Spanish friend read about in the fragment of the diary in the Madrid library. Remember this was during the days of Machiavelli when false words were spoken in high places."

Talbot's voice rose. "At their secret meetings the nobles must have been desperate, craving something to destroy Columbus in the eyes of the royal family and the church. What better way to do that than to whip up gossip with love letters from a married Spanish woman."

De Silvo chuckled. "Perhaps these scurrilous love letters were hatched by the court noblemen. Interesting."

Talbot shifted the telephone to his other hand. "To add to the credibility and stir public imagination further, the plotters sought to store those letters in a receptacle that would support, even enhance, their scheme. The box they stole from the Queen was just the ticket. Don't you see? This whole thing was nothing but a way to set tongues wagging, and not so incidentally, to bring down Columbus."

Talbot wiped his sweating hand on his shirt, but could not control his feet to keep them from fidgeting. "I know I'm right. I can feel it. That explanation is the only thing that makes sense."

De Silvo said, "Tell me how you explain the box containing all those forged letters winding up in Haiti? You used to believe Columbus was the one who brought them over. Your thinking must have changed. How did they get to Haiti?"

"The master or captain of the *Santa Maria* that sank off Haiti's coast would have been in on the plot. He must have been the culprit who brought them along. It's the only way that makes any sense to me. During the trip across the Atlantic he could have hidden the box on the stern deck in the cabin he had right next to Columbus. The master would have expected to produce the box in Spain at the end of the return voyage and claim that Columbus in the muddle of disembarking, forgot to offload it.

"Doesn't that explain it?" Talbot asked. "And the plot was to make it appear Columbus carried the Queen's love letters around with him in the royal box to protect them from prying eyes. The noblemen probably expected the contents of the letters to get out not only to the royal family and to the church, but to leak out to the public through what the servants might overhear and pass along. That would ruin the reputation of my hero Columbus. But when the *Santa Maria* was shipwrecked on one of Haiti's barrier reefs, the ship's master didn't dare transfer the box to the *Niña*, the only ship that remained. That ship was too small to squeeze another thing on to it other than Columbus himself and his immediate belongings. Unable to sneak the box back to Spain, the ship's master buried it on the beach near St. Pierre. To make it worse, the greedy master volunteered to stay behind in Haiti with many of his crew to hunt for gold. He planned to wait until the second voyage of Columbus swung by to pick him up."

Talbot hurried on, "Of course, it cost the ship's master his life, like it did all those who remained behind in Haiti on the first voyage. The stolen box and the bogus letters never got to do their dirty work and the Admiral was spared the torture of a Spanish Inquisition that would have forced him to 'confess' a love affair whether one existed or not." Talbot smiled. "The rest I got from the Paques. The box remained buried until a massive earthquake unearthed it in 1842 and my Haitian family came across it. Their find didn't amount to much for them because nobody in that French-Creole speaking family could read anything, let alone read the old Spanish language. That poor family held the find of the century in its hands for over 150 years and never knew it. The letters languished in the box unrecognized for what they were until I bought them though you say they were forged."

De Silvo's voice filled with awe. "Not bad for a young archaeologist, *amigo*. Such an explanation makes what you've acquired quite extraordinary…even priceless, though they are forgeries. And you're not so naive about Columbus."

Talbot grinned in the dark. "It all fits. But, Juan, I've still got a big problem with all you've told me. When the bogus letters failed to show up at the end of the first voyage, Columbus still had three more voyages that needed to be outfitted. Huge expenses had to be met. Long before the fourth voyage it must have been clear to the monarchy that Columbus would never discover a new route to the fabulous Orient nor bring back the huge quantities of gold, spices and silks he promised. Why keep on bankrolling him?"

"I have no answers for that, *amigo*. It does seem strange." His voice trailed off. "Call me if you have any ideas."

Realizing he was speaking into a dead phone, Talbot hung up and stepped out into the fresh, night air.

In the bait shack Talbot told the proprietor he was taking his rubber raft out to the boat but would probably come back later that night. The man assured him he would still be open because he had rented out one of his skiffs to someone visiting a nearby boat.

Talbot grew uneasy and rushed to the window. He looked out. His eyes bulged. The only boat in sight was his own. Some stranger was visiting it. He tried to swallow. The knot in his stomach tightened further. Who had rowed out there, he worried. Not the police, for there was no police car parked in front of the bait shack. He had a premonition. He had to get out to Sandy fast.

Chapter Twenty-Four

An Unwelcome Reception

T albot dashed to his rubber raft and untied it. Jamming the oars in place, he rowed frantically, turning around several times as he went, checking that he was going in the right direction. All the while he thought about the forged letters and the relationship Columbus must have had with Queen Isabella and King Ferdinand. Were the letters truly forged?

Drawing near, he lifted the oars out of the water. As the raft drifted close, he noticed the boat Mr. Martinez had borrowed for them was all dark. What could have happened? Had the generator failed? Did the fuses blow? The boat had been running so well. Talbot hoped it was nothing serious. He wanted to return the boat in as good condition as when he got it. Somehow Ash must have caused the problem.

The raft bumped into the stern of the borrowed boat. Talbot scowled at the strange dory tied up there. Ash had to be on board.

Sitting motionless, Talbot held the oars out of the water and listened. He heard only the whisper of waves sloshing against the hull of their boat. He decided against calling out to Sandy in case she was hiding from Ash and dared not answer.

As quietly as possible he boarded the boat and paused

on the after deck, listening again. The sound of an approaching motor caused him to balance himself. The wake of the other craft set off small waves that lifted and rocked the deck on which he was standing.

When the sound of the motor faded, he looked at the dark salon. From the outside it had the deserted appearance of a haunted house. Water splashing against the hull was the only sound.

Advancing to the salon door, his shoulder brushed against wind chimes that hung from the exterior wall. They gave off a melodious murmur loud enough to reveal his presence. The partly open door was an invitation to enter. He hesitated. No voices came from within. Suspicion flooded his mind. Someone was in there. He could feel it. But why no lights? No sound coming from within?

In the silence he realized he was holding his breath. His heart beat rapidly as he stepped closer to the open door. Crouching down, he took out the machete that lay concealed alongside the entrance. He smelled cigarette smoke. Ash was in there. Was the man lurking behind the door, waiting to ambush him? Talbot stretched his hand through the open doorway and groped for the wall switch.

Sandy shouted, "Don, look out! Run!"

His body stiffened and his startled gaze darted around the room as the fluorescent lights blinked on. He stood disbelieving. The place was in shambles. Piles of potato chips and photostats were scattered over a table. More lay on the deck. Chairs were overturned. Cabinet doors were open, their contents pulled out onto the deck.

Sandy sat against the far wall. Her feet were tied to a

bench that was bolted to the deck. Her hands were bound in front of her. She pressed them against her cheek that was discolored and bruised where Ash must have hit her. Her eyes were puffy. Tears spilled down her face.

Ash stood beside her. Smoke rose from a lighted cigarette hanging from the corner of his mouth. He held a knife to the throat of his hostage and put down his cigarette.

Talbot groaned. "You miserable creep, get away from Sandy!"

Ash bowed his head in a mock salute "Hello, ugly fledgling. What kept you so long? Usually you're in such a damn hurry. But tonight you took your sweet time getting here. I'm sick and tired of waiting." Ash laughed scornfully.

A wracking cough interrupted Ash's laugh, causing the hand holding the knife to become unsteady. "If I had known how long I had to wait, I would have had Sandy fix me a drink. I'm thirsty."

With the passing of another boat the salon heaved, causing the cigarette to roll to the table's edge. Grabbing it before it fell off, Ash took another puff, then put it back down where it had already blackened the surface.

Talbot's face was grim. "You're sick. Haven't you hurt Sandy enough? Let her go."

In a somber voice Ash whispered to Sandy, "You stupid witch, tell Talbot to stop talking such ridiculous nonsense. He knows what I'm here for and I'm not letting you go till I get it." With a flick of his wrist he drew a blood-red line across her throat.

Fear seemed to grip her.

Talbot raised his machete.

"Hold it." Ash placed his knife against Sandy's throat again.

She looked close to fainting.

Talbot halted. Visibly shaken by the other man's cruelty, he yelled, "Leave her alone!"

In a high-pitched voice Ash ordered, "Quit your stalling, goddamnit. Do exactly as I say. Your Sandy's life depends on it. Get over there." He pointed.

Looking first at Sandy, then back to Ash, Talbot stepped further into the room. His pulse raced. "Are you mad?" There was scorn in his shocked voice. "What the hell's wrong with you?"

"With me? Why nothing at all," Ash hooted.

"Then let her go."

"Don't waste time. And before things get out of hand turn your machete around and put it on the table, handle first. Do it nice and slow."

"Don, don't do it," Sandy wailed, squirming and yanking on the rope that gripped her ankles. "No, Don, don't do what he says."

Again the knife cut into her throat. Blood seeped into the new cut.

Talbot suppressed the urge to rush the deranged man and set his weapon down as ordered. Stepping back, he displayed empty hands.

Ash picked up the machete in his free hand and hefted it. "Too dangerous. This thing has got to go." Holding it by its handle, he placed the point on the deck and stuck his foot in the middle of the blade. He stomped down with his full weight snapping the blade in half, leaving two broken pieces on the deck. He thrust his knife against Sandy's throat once more as he snorted in derision. "That silly weapon isn't good for much anymore, is it?"

Talbot did not respond to the taunting.

Ash continued, "You used to be in such a hurry, unable to control your ambition. Well," he confided, clearing his throat, "you've got company. Now there's two of us. I'm also in a hurry. I want the box and the original batch of letters. Not *mañana* but right now!"

What Ash intended to say next was lost in a fit of coughing. When he recovered, his face had a pallor that had not been there before. He gasped for air. "Give me everything right this minute or I start carving Sandy up, but good." He laughed. "What's it to be?"

Talbot heard the anger in Ash's voice and agonized in his own mind what to do. "If you hurt Sandy, they'll put you behind bars. Those letters won't do you much good then."

"Spare me," Ash sneered. "I'd simply explain to everyone who asks that the clumsy bitch had an accident. That's what I'd call it. I'd say she slipped and fell on this knife while cutting up some kindling. No crime. I'd pay somebody to be a responsible witness who would make my story airtight." He looked pleased.

Talbot was unnerved at how mentally disturbed Ash had become. How far would the man go?

Ash growled, "If I said she fell on a knife that happened to kill her, naturally you'd try to twist the whole thing around and call it murder. But who'd listen? Killing poor ol' Barney makes you a murderer yourself. Also, you stole the museum's valuable property. So, you're a murderer and a thief, hardly in a position to accuse me of anything."

Ash reached across the table and fingered copies of the letters that were mixed in with the potato chips which lay strewn across the table. "This idiot Sandy showed me these copies, thinking I would be foolish enough to take them and go. I'm an expert. Where are the originals? Quick or my knife takes real action."

"You're wasting your time. They're not worth killing over. I just got off the phone with an expert in New York City. He said they're forgeries."

"I don't believe it. That's a load of crap," Ash snarled. One side of his mouth screwed up. "You'd say anything to save your precious papers. Better tell me where you stashed them." He made a violent motion with the hand holding the knife against Sandy's throat.

She screamed, her eyes dilating in fright. Again the knife cut into her slightly. The blade glinted in the light, ready to go deeper. Blood seeped into the new opening. Her neck turned red with blood.

"She's bleeding, you ass!"

"I'm losing my patience," Ash rasped, ignoring Talbot's concern.

"All right." Talbot was in despair. "You can have the box and the papers. Give me a chance to get them. Meanwhile, take the knife away from Sandy."

"I'll take it away when I'm damn good and ready. Where the hell you hiding everything? I'll get the stuff myself." He struggled to control a hacking cough. His chest heaved and his face turned a vivid crimson. When the coughing subsided, he picked up his cigarette and took a last puff before mashing out the glowing embers on the table top. "Where exactly is the box?"

"It's outside, concealed under water. A rope with a float attached to one end is tied to a duffel bag that it's in. I have to snag the rope and the float with a grappling hook which I keep outside on deck."

"Smart ass," Ash applauded facetiously. "So, that's where you hid it. I wondered when you anchored here, what you were doing on that side of the boat. Now I know. Anyway I'm not having you out there, yelling for help. I'll get the hook myself. Tell me exactly where to use it."

"The bag is submerged in the water opposite the wheel-house. You can't miss it."

"Hand me that other rope and turn around. Careful." Ash appeared to have his rage barely under control. "Remember, one wrong move and I stick Sandy. She won't like it, so move, ugly fledgling!"

Talbot stared at the steel blade against Sandy's throat before he turned away and laid on the deck, face down. Before tying a noose in the rope, Ash clenched the knife between his teeth. Then he ordered Talbot to lift his head slowly up off the deck and tilt it backwards. When Talbot did as directed, Ash slipped the noose over the young man's head and pulled the noose snug.

Next, he directed Talbot to extend both arms behind him and to bend his lower legs back towards the arms.

Ash was watchful as Talbot complied. He tied the younger man's hands and doubled legs with the length of rope he used on the neck. When he finished, his captive resembled a chicken trussed up in a supermarket display case. "I think you'll stay put for a while," Ash growled.

As soon as Ash hurried out on deck for the grappling hook, Talbot strained to loosen the rope. Unable to make any headway, he rocked his body from side to side. After several attempts he rolled over onto his back. He collected his breath and rolled over onto his stomach. He repeated the moves over and over, edging closer to Sandy.

When she saw what he was attempting, she pleaded in a low voice, "Oh, hurry, Don. Hurry."

"Shh, shh," he panted and exerted every muscle in an attempt to move quickly. Perspiration drenched his face and body. His breathing was strained and uneven. The taut rope cut into his wrists and ankles.

Sandy bit her lip, watching him approach. "You're getting closer. Keep going." Her whole body shook.

Talbot heard Ash out on deck in the dark, wheezing and muttering to himself as the man probed back and forth through the water, searching with the grappling hook. Apparently on the first try Ash failed to snag the line that was fastened to the weighted duffel bag. Ash's curse raged through the open door.

Meanwhile, Talbot bumped against Sandy's legs. He twisted around to raise himself to his knees and leaned against her. He did not know how long he could hold that position before the boat rocked again and caused him to lose his balance. "Take hold and loosen the rope on my wrists first," he whispered with sweat stinging his eyes.

Her hands reached out. "You did great. I can feel the rope, but," she groaned, "I can't untie it."

"Sandy, you've got to try! Ash is liable to do anything when he comes back. Try real hard."

"I am trying," she sobbed, "but I don't have the strength." Her eyes flashed. Tugging and pulling, she tore at the rope, her mouth set in a grim line, her fingers raw and bleeding. "I think I'm getting it."

He felt the rope loosen slightly. "Keep going." He felt it loosen some more. At the same time he heard Ash's joyful roar.

"Quick, the man must have hooked the rope. He'll be in here any minute."

"I am being as quick as I can." Sandy tugged feverishly on Talbot's loosened rope.

The loud, wheezing sounds told them Ash was laboring to haul the bag through the water. Talbot thought the warm air and the extreme effort Ash had to make, must be sapping the man's energy.

"Ash has our duffel bag, all right. He must be pulling it to the surface." Talbot tensed.

A dull thud sounded. Talbot thought, the bag was out of the water and hitting against the hull. Sandy worked harder on Talbot's loosened rope.

The squishing noise of a wet mass plopping down onto the deck announced the arrival of the duffel bag on board. Ash sounded jubilant. There came the sound of the man collapsing on top of the bag. The exertion demanded rest.

"Don, your hands are free," Sandy whispered. "What are you going to do? There's no time to untie your legs."

"I don't know, but we can't stay together like this." With the help of his free hands he dragged himself away.

Before passing the two pieces of his broken machete that lay on the deck, Talbot grabbed the handle that had part of the blade attached to it. He moved on to the spot where he had been before and slipped the broken piece of machete beneath him at the moment Ash appeared in the doorway.

The elated man's chest labored as he clung to the doorframe for support. He pointed back outside. "That bag is too goddamn heavy."

After a brief pause Ash wiped the sweat from his face and went back out. Moments later, he tugged his soggy prize inside, leaving a wet trail behind him. He walked to the middle of the salon displaying his triumph. "Tough luck, you two," he gloated, coughing hard and rubbing his chest.

He knelt down and untied the rope that was attached to the float. He rolled the waterproof outer wrapping down from the duffel bag within and began to untie the knots on the drawstrings around the opening of the duffel bag. Looking at Sandy, he crowed, "A man's got to persevere." He laughed and turned to Talbot lying on the deck. "Hiding the box in the water was pretty clever of you."

Ash's pants were dripping wet. Blotches of color from his exertion covered his face. He opened his mouth letting in more air that his lungs strained like overworked bellows to have. Not looking at his hands, he continued to untie the knots on the draw strings. "Remember there's always somebody a bit smarter than you, ugly fledgling."

Talbot asked, "How did you find us here?"

Ash beamed. "Oh, I have my contacts. The U.S. Coast Guard kept its eye on you sailing back and forth. This afternoon I drove up from Miami and kept track of you myself from shore. Most of the time I only had to keep an eye out for the red flag hanging off the stern of your boat. Made it real easy for me." He snickered. His fingers tore at the drawstrings.

Looking at Talbot lying on the deck, Ash appeared not to notice that one part of the machete was no longer in sight. Drenched in sweat, Ash began to cough, nonstop. All the while his fingers with the eagerness of a hungry pup gobbling its food, snatched and clawed at the knots on the drawstrings of the duffel bag.

Talbot watched their captor's face take on a strange pallor. "Don't do that," he shouted in alarm. "Leave the bag alone!"

Ash glared at him and picked up his knife to point it at Talbot. "Goddamn it. Shut the hell up!"

Sandy said, "Mr. Ash, you re not well. You should see a doctor."

"Shut up, I told you." He rubbed his hand across his face. Without looking at what he was doing he went back to untying the knots. Moments later he glanced down at his hands. Blood trickled from them onto the deck. Tiny holes appeared on his hands. Scratches showed up around his wrists and arms. "Son of a bitch," he screamed. The puddle of his blood on the deck was widening. He looked at the drawstrings. "There's little barbs hidden in these strings. Lots of them." Recognition dawned in his eyes. "They're poisoned barbs. They're cutting and poisoning me the same way they cut and poisoned Barney on the *Angora* until they killed him. No wonder you handed this stuff over to me. You did it to get rid of me."

"No, no, that's not it," Sandy cried out.

"Never mind, bitch," he snarled at Sandy. "You started this." Turning his back on Talbot, he stood up and walked slowly towards her with his finger fondling the sharp edge of his knife blade. His intent was evident.

"Wait a minute," Sandy pleaded. "Listen to me." The determined warmth in her voice sought to calm him. "It's not what you think. Take it easy. You're not poisoned. You're not going to die either."

"Bullshit! Look at how the barbs have already ripped into me," he said, holding his hands before her. "You murderers are stalling me, hoping the poison on the barbs will soon do its dirty work so you two can have the box to yourselves."

While Ash moved towards Sandy, Talbot tugged the broken machete out from beneath him and clamped it between his teeth. With the agility born of need he slid across the deck behind Ash without making a sound.

Looking Ash straight in the eye, Sandy gave no hint of what Talbot was doing. Dragging her words out, she said, "You've got to listen to me. Please, Mr. Ash."

Ash said in a thick, husky voice, "I told you to shut up. I know stalling when I hear it."

Sandy ignored Ash's demand and kept talking to him, her eyes never straying from his.

Talbot stood up awkwardly and took the broken

machete from between his teeth. He took a deep breath and using all his strength, he lunged, hammering Ash's knife hand with the broken machete.

The unexpected blow knocked Ash's knife to the deck. He whirled around. His eyes bulged at the sight of his captive close behind him, standing bolt upright with his head tilted back by the noose around his neck. Ash could see Talbot's legs were still tied, but somehow Talbot was armed with the broken machete.

Ash backed away, retreating to the duffel tag. His battered hand was turning blue. "If I'm going to die," he shouted, "I'm dumping the box overboard. It won't be much good to anybody then." With bloody hands he lifted the heavy bag up in his arms, favoring his swollen hand. His neck muscles stood out from the strain. He choked and gasped for breath.

"Mr. Ash, it's no good," Sandy sobbed.

"Wait," Talbot implored, as he yelled at his former boss.

Ash faltered as he attempted to raise the bag higher with trembling hands. Unable to lift it up over his head, he wobbled under the load and headed for the doorway. Violent coughing wracked his body almost causing him to let go of the bag.

"Don't you listen? Drop it," Talbot shouted in alarm. "Don't make it kill you."

Anxiety showed in Sandy's eyes. She cried out, "Please stop."

As though in a heavy sea, Ash lurched off-balance in a circular direction. "If I'm not getting these papers, nobody is," he gasped.

Clinging to the duffel bag, he reached the exit and lost his balance. In trying to recover, he let go of the bag and crashed into the door. He fell to the deck clutching his chest. His mouth hung open. His lips were peeled back, exposing rotted teeth. His crumpled body lay still as the duffel bag beside him. He was dead.

Sandy turned away, weeping. "Oh, no. How horrible."

Talbot called to her, "It's all over. I'll get rid of the rope around my legs and help you in a second." He untied his legs and ran to Sandy. He cut her loose and they hugged each other like the desperate pair they were. Part of the rope still hung from in back of him where it was tied to his neck.

Gradually Sandy's weeping subsided, but the strain and fear remained etched on her face. She slipped the rope over Talbot's head and threw it away. "I can't bear to look. Could you cover Ash's body?"

Talbot placed a blanket over the corpse. "I repeat, there was no poison on those barbs. I admit I had murderous thoughts but I'm no murderer. I cleaned off every one of the barbs thoroughly. They could still scratch anyone who blindly untied the strings like Ash did, but there was no poison on them. Leaving them in the drawstrings protected my property. It was like putting up a barbed wire fence around my stuff to prevent trespassing. Besides, scratches won't kill you. People trying to commit suicide have slashed their wrists far worse than Ash was cut and they lived.

"He must have suffered a massive coronary, but he brought it all on himself. We have nothing to feel guilty about."

She nodded.

"How about we go sit outside?" he asked.

Together they walked out to the stern deck and huddled in the dark, watching the Palm Beach lights flicker in the distance. He pulled her close and held her tight for a long time.

She broke the silence. "You going ashore to call the police?"

"In a minute." He looked at the luminous face on his watch. "I may call de Silvo first."

"Haven't we been through enough? What more can he say?"

"Well, there are some loose ends. Why did the Spanish monarchy support Columbus through more than one voyage? I think I have an answer for which there is evidence. I want to get Juan's opinion."

"Whatever he says, you'll always be my guy. I love you."

Their lips met in a kiss.

"And I love you very, very much." He stood. "I'll leave Ash's dinghy tied to the stern so the police can see it when they get here." He shrugged. "Try to get some rest. It could be a long night."

He cracked his knuckles and leaned over to kiss her once more before leaving. He dashed away looking excited.

Chapter Twenty-Five

An Explanation

As Talbot rowed to shore, he could not keep his legs still. He kept thinking about what he would say to de Silvo. If the letters were forged, it must have been part of a plot of the conniving, cutthroat nobles in the royal court. They badly wanted Columbus to fail, fearing if he returned with his ships brimming over with gold, silk and spices, he would be a wonderful hero. He would not have failed.

The short trip into shore ended. Talbot clambered onto the dock and scurried inland. At first the interior of the telephone booth felt cooler than earlier. That quickly changed after he pulled the folding door shut behind him. He sat down and dialed. In his haste, his finger slipped and he dialed a wrong number. He redialed. The connection was made.

He panted, "Hello, Juan? If I sound nervous, I am. Death nearly did us in. Since I spoke to you last, my old boss sneaked on board and held a knife to Sandy's throat."

"Holy Mother. Is she safe?"

"Yes, yes. Ash nicked her neck to get me to reveal where the wooden box was hidden. I hated to divulge the location but what was I gonna do? Afterwards with the box in his hand, Ash's greed and the strain apparently got to him. He keeled over and fell dead. Probably suffered a massive heart attack. Anyway, the box and letters are safe."

"Must have been a horrible experience for you two."

New thoughts swirled around in Talbot's head. He tried to contain his excitement. "Juan, excuse my shouting," he snapped, "but wake up! I know why the Spanish paid for all four of Columbus' expeditions. And the King need not have known about the forged letters. It explains that we high-minded adults protect children by telling 'em Columbus discovered America even though we know he never set foot on this continent and people were already living here. We've been handing kids a story about a guy living 500 years ago. It's the same cover-up that history puts out to conceal the scandal in the royal court."

"So, tell me. What was really going on?"

In a voice that sounded hoarse, Talbot said slowly, "For a long time I thought the incentive for the King and Queen to support Columbus was their belief he would sail west and reach Marco Polo's Orient. They expected him to bring them back lots of gold, silk, and spices. The monarchs thought they would recoup their expenditures plus realize a handsome profit. As an archaeologist I don't need the vestiges of an ancient civilization in my hands to know that didn't happen."

"Please calm down, *amigo*, and talk more slowly."

"What was Columbus going to barter with? To me, the clincher that the King never financed Columbus out of the goodness of his heart was the rubbish Columbus had to trade with on his first trip under the Spanish flag. There were colored glass beads, pieces of brightly colored cloth, shiny hawks' bells and metal tips. (Men used the metal tips at the ends of strings to close up their clothes.) Such trifles might have appealed to the childlike Indians, but how far could that stuff go in bartering with a sophisticated Oriental potentate? Even your dentist doesn't hand out such worthless junk to his young patients.

"In fact, on all four voyages Columbus never brought along goods he could trade with a high Oriental official. Moreover, King Ferdinand never insisted that Columbus return with gold, silks or spices. No one, as far as I know, ever really demanded where the hell were all the Oriental riches the Admiral had claimed he would bring back. Such things confirm there was another reason the King tried to get rid of Columbus.

"Let me say loud and clear: the Queen died within weeks after Columbus returned from his fourth trip, but the King never broached financing a fifth voyage. Why not? Why didn't the King at least make the gesture? The way I see it, even if Columbus was in poor health, the King should have made the offer, but the King had no more need to keep Columbus away from the Queen, so he had no reason to offer to finance that fifth expedition. Right from the start the King's only goal must have been to keep Columbus away from the Queen during the years she was alive."

Talbot gulped and lowered his voice. "I'm sure there must have been something about the way the Admiral and the Queen acted when they were together that made the King think the pair was overly friendly with each other. Perhaps somebody caught an unguarded look passing between the pair. Or overheard a word softly spoken. Or seen a brushing of the royal bosom or some impertinent fondling of the royal buttocks where no touching of the royal person should ever occur. I'm not saying how they carried on. I don't know. But their behavior must have led the scheming nobles to hatch their plot and think it was plausible."

Talbot took a deep breath before continuing. "There had to be something like that to support everyone's knowledge of a married Spanish woman carrying on with an Italian foreigner. Incredible as it may sound, the forgeries undoubtedly duplicated the Queen's actual love life even though her life was usually curbed by the church and by the circumspect way Spanish society demanded its females conduct themselves. Otherwise, the forgeries would have been laughable and not convinced anyone. I'd bet the ones who penned those vulgar letters and did the art work mysteriously died soon after they finished. Also, the King had the perfect out to refuse financing after the first voyage because Columbus proved the King's experts were correct when they said Columbus would not reach the Orient.

"That tells me the King never expected Columbus to make it to the Orient, so there was no reason to spend royal treasury money on valuable trading goods for Columbus to barter with. The jealous King simply provided finances to get the Admiral away from the Queen. Otherwise, the King could have continued to reject Columbus' ideas, taken the experts' advice and never financed Columbus again. But if the King wanted to get the explorer away, he had to send him out on the uncharted ocean hoping Columbus would get sick and never come back."

There was a moment's stunned silence.

"And get this: I don't believe the letters are forgeries!"

"I already told you the Queen didn't write them. Her authentic handwriting doesn't match that in the letters. This is not the writing of one, but two different people."

"You say these love letters were not written by the Queen. I can go along with that, but they don't have to be forgeries either. Could be, they are copies of the real thing."

"Copies?"

"Copies made by two different scribes. Copying was the business of scribes. The scribes who wrote these letters were probably sworn to the utmost secrecy, even their lives must have been threatened if they so much as let out a peep about any of the secret. I'll bet if I researched, I could find other examples of one of the scribes."

"What did they copy?"

"I would say, either the letters were copied from those in the nobles' plot which probably followed what was actually going on OR...they were copies of authentic love letters of the Queen to Columbus."

"If a romance was really going on, you've uncovered an historical cover-up."

"A cover-up that really works. Not a word of the scandalous behavior of a Spanish woman is mentioned to children. But Columbus is important to America even though he never set foot here and even though Indians lived here long before he was born, so he couldn't be the first to discover America. He is special because he led the European emigration to the New World. His daring and courage in sailing across 2,600 miles of uncharted ocean should be feted by Americans. He is America's roots."

"I hear what you are saying and am overwhelmed."

"Am I being arrogant?" There was gravel in Talbot's voice.

"Not at all, *amigo*. You have become an archaeologist. You add to our knowledge of the past."

"Thank you, and speaking of facts," Talbot continued, "they made Columbus an admiral even though he never commanded a single ship before, let alone a fleet of ships. Think of it, an admiral. That also tells us where the King's head was."

"Piecing things together like that 'til they fit is the work of a true archaeologist. That's what you've become."

"Tantalizing questions remain: Did Queen Isabella actually fall madly in love with Columbus? Or did her loveless marriage to her cousin lead her to have only a great affection for the explorer? Columbus had been a widower for a year before he first met the Queen, so by that time he was ripe for her attention. There have always been rumors circulating of a romantic or sexual relationship between the Queen and Columbus. Just as two and two make four, it all adds up, but history leaves so much unexplained."

"Congratulations. Though a rank beginner, you'll make your mark on archaeology."

Talbot gripped the metal shelf in the booth and pushed the door open wider. Cool air flowed into the small space. Other thoughts crowded into Talbot's mind. He kept some.

Discarded others. "Juan, it took the Admiral's spectacular four voyages to jump start Europe's emigration that eventually flooded our continent. The brave admiral was not like so many of the weak-kneed Europeans who feared the earth was flat or that sea monsters lurked out in the unknown ocean. He was the first to explore that part of the lonely ocean. Probably no original documents of his voyages exist because they were destroyed or lost. Western history leaves us its provocative mysteries. Some of them may never be solved, like who exactly first discovered America and don't tell me the Viking, Leif Ericson."

"Dazzling, *amigo*."

"Let me comment on the cover-up we've been handing little children. It shields them from knowing about a close relationship between Columbus and Queen Isabella that may have prevailed more than 500 years ago. But we need not bring it up to children. We can immortalize Columbus for his courage in sailing over 2,600 miles of uncharted waters and resisting the men who beseeched him to turn back. He brought Europe to the New World. He is America's roots.

"Isn't it old-fashioned to talk about discovering America? Long ago, people were born and living on this continent. Their preliterate ancestors crossed over to Alaska and migrated down. Leif Ericson didn't discover America but he *rediscovered* it for the Vikings. But let's not be too quick to say who discovered America, for we may never know the person who did that or if he/she even had a name."

"Fabulous. You can write exciting, controversial articles

for professional journals about your unusual purchases. Regale the lecture circuit with your thoughts and questions about that period in history. You'll be a sensational speaker/archaeologist! That's what archaeologists do: they study the way things were, fill in some of history's blanks and help us to understand better, even anticipate the future."

"Perhaps there were the plots of both the King and the nobles that involved the Queen's affairs and that led Europe to the New World."

"Perhaps the archaeologist will be in such demand you will need a booking agent. It's all priceless. You'll be a prominent archaeologist."

"Wonderful. Could you give me a rough idea of how much the box and its fake love letters might bring?"

"Are we back to that again?" de Silvo asked with a twinkle in his voice. "Let's wait and see what someone actually pays for them. In the meantime, I'll advance you whatever you need. Incidentally, the Spanish government is anxious to keep this out of the press for at least the next thirty days. The Spaniards will pay almost anything within in reason if you will temporarily delay releasing the letters to the public. It's up to you."

"If they are that eager, how does two thousand dollars plus your commission sound? Is that a reasonable figure? I would like to send that much down to the Paques."

"Sounds like a number the Spanish authorities might go for. I'll see what they say."

"What about the Haitian inspector who wants everything handed over to his republic? I need an official government clearance, don't I?"

"There's Haiti's awful instability to consider; however, that's what you've got me for. I'll work something out." He paused. "Changing the subject, I saw your picture on television. I take it you didn't kill the first mate? Raise your right hand and swear."

"I'm raising it. I swear I've never killed anyone or anything in my whole life. Neither has Sandy. It was those voodoo people."

"Voodoo bastards. Okay, get the box and the original letters up to me as soon as you can."

"I'm going back to our boat right after I hang up. I'll have Sandy fly up with them for you tonight or first thing in the morning before the police confiscate them."

"I look forward to meeting her."

"And, Juan, I have a big favor to ask of you. When Sandy arrives, will you get her into a hospital and have the doctors work on her legs? Those legs give her a lot of pain and failed her on the Miami River. We were lucky to escape my old boss and his henchmen that time because of the way her legs are."

"I'll set it up. No problem."

"Many thanks. I'll repay you soon as I can. You're one helluva guy."

"De nada, amigo mio."

"Easy enough for you Puerto Ricans to say." Talbot smiled again that night. "But I mean it from the bottom of my heart. Thanks a million, Juan. You've been a big help."

"I wish I could reach out and shake the hand of a winner. *Vaya con Dios.*"

"Funny you should say that because all along I had the

feeling He's been by my side."

"*Adios, amigo.*"

Sweat dripping down his face, Talbot hung up the phone and stepped out of the booth.

He jumped back, momentarily startled. Sandy stood in front of him holding a flashlight. The light was shining in his eyes.

"Whew," he said, putting his hand up to shield his eyes from the unexpected glare. "I was just going back to fetch you. What are you doing here?"

"After you left I stayed out on deck to keep away from Ash's body. I saw a police boat approaching with its spotlight focused on our bow. I quickly ducked back into the cabin and lifted the old anchor out of the bag and lowered the bag into Ash's skiff. Then I pushed away."

"Oh, great. I wonder who tipped the police off. By the way, good news. De Silvo believes the letters are worth quite a bit. I'm gonna make it," he grinned.

She screamed with delight and flew into his arms, hugging him tight. "Ooo-o-o, my stomach is doing flip flops. I'm so happy for you. What did de Silvo actually say?"

"He agreed with me. You don't get anything from a Grand Khan by offering to trade worthless glass beads and shiny hawks' bells for gold. It proves a king's jealousy or a queen's love was ultimately responsible for the Europeans emigrating over here. That's my archaeologist's speculation about America's roots.

"Anyway, discovering this continent may be an outmoded concept. The leader of a group for the Spanish or the Vikings is a 're-discoverer' in behalf of that group only.

This continent has been here thousands of years with pre-historic people migrating and re-discovering it all the time. There's nothing new about that."

She turned off her flashlight.

"No time to explain," he said. "You're flying up to New York City right away with the box and the letters. I'll tell you everything later."

"You'll be famous."

Talbot laughed. "At least I'll be able to repay you on that loan you gave me plus lots of interest. In the future I'll do better by you and my sister." He took her hand.

"What's the matter? All of a sudden you look so serious. Did you forget something?" she asked.

"I am serious, and I haven't forgotten a thing." Gazing into her dark eyes, he asked, "Miss Martinez, will you marry me?"

She stood speechless nodding her assent. She reached up with tears in her eyes and kissed him hard on the lips.

"Hey, it's nothing to cry over," he said.

Almost breathless, she sighed. "I can't help it. It's taken so long for you to ask me. You've just filled in another of history's blanks."

Her smile was dazzling as he realized what blank space she was talking about.

Bibliography

Note that many of the publications listed here were released or re-released for the 500th year after 1492.

Adkins, Lesley and Roy. *An Introduction to Archaeology.* Secaucus, N.J.: Chartwell Books, 1989.

Anthony, Michael. *The Golden Quest, The Four Voyages of Christopher Columbus.* London, England: The Macmillan Press, 1992.

Cohen, J.M. *Christopher Columbus, The Four Voyages.* Penguin Books, 1969.

Collis, John Stewart. *Christopher Columbus.* London, England: Sphere Books Ltd., 1989.

Fuson, Robert H. (translator). *The Log of Christopher Columbus.* Shedfield, England: Ashford Press Publishing, 1987.

Henige, David. *In Search of Columbus, the Sources for the first voyage.* The University of Arizona Press, 1991.

Jane, Cecil (translator). *The Journal of Christopher Columbus*, appendix by Skelton, R.A. New York: Bonanza Books, 1960.

Major, R. H. *Christopher Columbus, Four Voyages to the New World*. London, England: Carol Publishing Group, 1992.

Morison, Samuel Eliot. *Admiral of the Ocean Sea, A life of Christopher Columbus*. Little, Brown and Company, Canada Ltd., 1970.

Morison, Samuel Eliot. *Christopher Columbus Mariner*. Penguin Books U.S.A., Inc.

Rienits, Rex and Thea. *The Voyages of Columbus*. New York: Crescent Books, 1989.

*First Voyage to America from the Log of the "Santa Maria,"*Dover Publications, Inc., 1991.